TWILIGHT IMPERIUM

Intergalactic empires fall, but one faction will rise from the ashes to conquer the galaxy.

Once the mighty Lazax Empire ruled all the known galaxy from its capital planet of Mecatol Rex, before treachery and war erased the Lazax from history, plunging a thousand star systems into conflict and uncertainty.

Now the Great Civilizations who span the galaxy look upon their former capital hungrily – the power and secrets of the Lazax await a new emperor...

To lay claim to the throne is a destiny sought by many, yet the shadows of the past serve as a grim warning to those who would follow in their footsteps.

VOICE *of* ONE

TRISTAN PALMGREN

First published by Aconyte Books in 2025
ISBN 978 1 83908 308 2
Ebook ISBN 978 1 83908 309 9

Cover art by Christina Myrvold

Galactic map by Ryan Hong

Printed in the United States of America and elsewhere.

9 8 7 6 5 4 3 2 1

ACONYTE BOOKS

An imprint of Asmodee North America

Mercury House, North Gate,

Nottingham NG7 7FN, UK

aconytebooks.com

For the joy of it all.

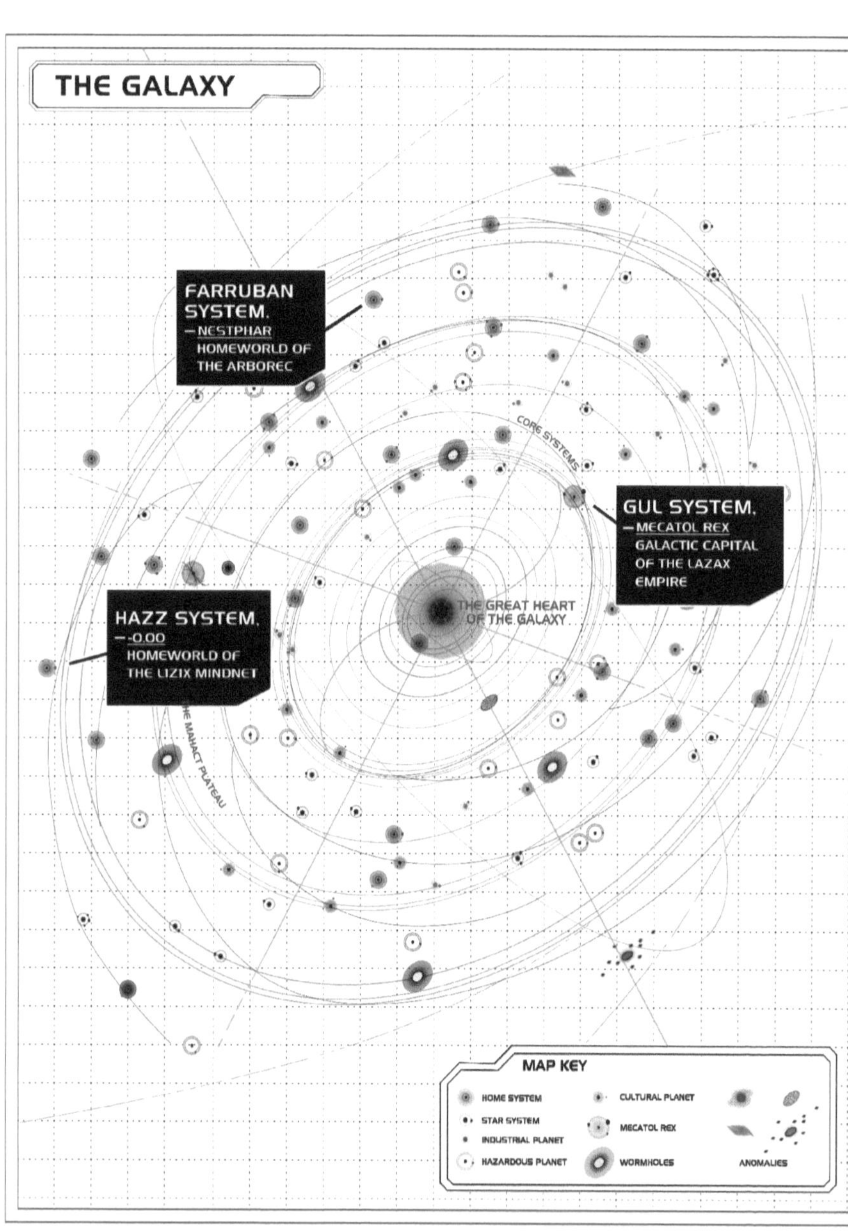

THE GALAXY
FARRUBAN SYSTEM.
—NESTPHAR
HOMEWORLD OF THE ARBOREC
GUL SYSTEM.
—MECATOL REX
GALACTIC CAPITAL OF THE LAZAX EMPIRE
HAZZ SYSTEM.
—-0.00
HOMEWORLD OF THE L1Z1X MINDNET
CORE SYSTEMS
THE GREAT HEART OF THE GALAXY
THE MAHACT PLATEAU
MAP KEY
HOME SYSTEM
STAR SYSTEM
INDUSTRIAL PLANET
HAZARDOUS PLANET
CULTURAL PLANET
MECATOL REX
WORMHOLES
ANOMALIES

CHAPTER ONE
THE CAGE OF INDIVIDUALITY

Now

The traitor fleet dropped into visibility at twenty-five-fifty hours by my imperfectly calibrated shipboard clock. I had been expecting the alarm, but the screech and my keyed-up nerves still made me jump. I accidentally slammed my nose into the underside of the crew head's sink.

I'd been under that sink for an hour, using what downtime I could to wrestle with a leak, and I'd just about succeeded in not making it worse. No guarantees about that last part now that the ten-times-recycled plastic piping had a cast of my head printed in it.

The wait had left me experiencing a terrible combination of bored and jumpy. It had been a long, long time since I'd been able to have nerve dampener implants, but they would have been more of a help today than most days – and not just to stop me from collapsing my sinus cavities.

I should have forgotten about the pain already and shifted fully into combat mode, but one of the many nuisances of an unaugmented biological brain was that the organ couldn't upshift fast enough. All its sluggish chemicals lagged seconds behind the situation.

I wove through the supply-cluttered corridor, and then up the corrugated metal staircase, and into the cockpit. The alarm had woken the consoles' projectors. I shoved myself into the pilot's seat just in time for a tactical map to spark into being.

The traitor fleet was not so much a set of blips as an angry haze. The fog reflected not only the sheer quantity of signals barreling toward the planet I orbited, but the sensors' uncertainty. They had come in from around the yellow-white sun, using its glare as a shield.

My ship was a jumped-up courier shuttle. It had active-pulse sensors, but they were very short-range – reliable within only a scant few tens of thousands of kilometers. The only information I received came via light.

Light was a problem. My shuttle's scopes had gone unmaintained for thirty years and kept falling out of alignment, but the most advanced Hylar scopes would have had trouble picking out the traitors' many pinprick silhouettes under that nuclear furnace.

To my scopes, the traitor fleet was visible only in absence, as darker patches. There was only one place where they were brighter than the background: a blob of engine plumes under the shadow of a solar prominence.

Another problem with unaugmented brains: they saw patterns where none existed. The attackers looked for all the universe like they'd just dived underneath the arch of the prominence. But these ships were "only" three hundred thousand kilometers away rather than the hundred million that separated the world I orbited from its sun.

With all that glare, my sensors stood no chance of identifying the ships. Not yet. But that was all right. I knew who they were.

Letnev.

Three thousand and twenty years ago, a fleet of warships had arrived without warning above Mecatol Rex, the capital of the Lazax Empire. The lights of those ships' engines would have looked very much like this. They had even arrived the same way, using the sun to mask their approach.

Those ships had not been Letnev then, but the Barony of Letnev had gleefully participated in the mass murders that followed.

The orbital bombing began a decades-long campaign of genocide that left hundreds of billions of Lazax dead, the survivors scattered, and the "righteous conquerors" predictably tearing each other's throats out until the galaxy had descended into a dark age lasting millennia.

I had not been there. But the Lazax's memories lived within me. Though I now lacked the implants that kept them fresh, the terror and trauma were imprinted in my synapses.

I grabbed the flight stick and throttle.

Rage coursed through my blood, thicker and hotter than adrenaline.

I had been without my Mindnet implants for years now, and I still struggled with emotional regulation. I had finally reached the conclusion that I was not, as I'd once thought, especially vulnerable to it. This mental turbulence was what other human beings had to deal with, cycle in and cycle out, for all their lives. It explained quite a lot.

My ratty little shuttle was in no shape to take into battle. But here I was anyway. I had been ordered to be here, but I also wanted to be. Wanting to be in a battle – such a tremendous emotional frailty. And I knew it.

With effort, I removed my hand from the flight stick. It wasn't time to move, yet.

Tables of numbers framed the map. More and more appeared as the Letnev, over the course of minutes, fell farther away from the protective shroud of the sunlight.

The Letnev etched a tangled knot of light and shadow across a glare-shrouded sky. The craft themselves were minuscule, black specks dancing underneath dazzling engine plumes. Like bacteria in a sea of nutrients, they multiplied. They seemed to reproduce, one speck splitting into several. Deploying decoys.

Each ship twisted and arced to hide their movement and made it harder to distinguish between them and their fakes. Occasionally, individual craft fired their braking thrusters. Their white-hot engine exhaust licked over them. Each ship lost itself under the firestorm. Then three emerged seconds later on a new heading, hulls glowing at the edge of their heat tolerances. One real ship, two decoys.

The decoys had their own engines, engineered to emit a plume to match the length and spectrum of the craft they protected. It must have been tremendously expensive, and complicated to build. But Letnev navy engineers were among the best in this new galaxy.

The world I orbited was called Arrix. Its System Defense was already active. All across the gray-white horizon, sparks of light were lengthening into exhaust plumes: missiles rushing to meet the intruders, and orbital weapons platforms thrusting into more advantageous orbits.

All of this happened in complete radio silence. System Defense had cut off all radio communications the instant they'd detected the traitors. System Defense had been operating on leaky comms until now. They had wanted to give the impression of a world in turmoil, of weapons and countermeasures still in the process of being assembled, unready.

The moment the traitors showed themselves, System Defense had hardened like magma into obsidian. They'd shifted from radio to counterfactual quantum cryptography systems, a method of sending information without exchanging any particles at all.

It used Mindnet cybernetic augmentation to run, though, which meant I was also cut off.

(Alone again?)

My pulse pounded in my neck. Racing toward the stress headache building in my temples. I'd waited for months for a chance to place myself here. Never volunteering out of line, never less or more than ordered.

Proving that, despite everything, I was a functioning part of the system. A perfect cell in a perfect organ in a perfect body.

Determination and calm were easier to maintain when I wasn't looking upon the nuclear speartips of a legion of genocidal traitors.

There was that emotional regulation problem, again.

(You know where you can go to be part of something again.)

I swallowed and tried to ignore the snark from the back of my mind. The thoughts did not feel like my own, although I knew they were. In the years since I'd lost my brain cybernetics, bits of me had fallen away and had spun out of control. The intrusive thoughts weren't just persistent. They had been getting worse.

My tactical map wasn't aligned to my ship's facing. I looked over the chalky horizon, using the shadows of the far-distant clouds to orient myself. The angle of the shadows signposted the direction of the sun. My brain was capable of that much mental trigonometry.

The presence of the cockpit window was a concession to my missing implants. On a proper Mindnet craft, it would have been covered by additional armor plating. No point in leaving such a naked vulnerability as a window when images could instead be routed straight to a pilot's sensory cortex.

Like so much else in my life, I was on manual control. I tapped my portside thrusters. The gas jets fired with a reassuring hydraulic *bang*, swinging my boxy shuttle around to present its front – its slimmest profile – to the oncoming storm.

Mind was machine. No one knew that better than Us. Lacking a built-in kinetic physics processor, my next best recourse was to use my senses – and all their billions of years of sloppy unguided evolution – in their place. Relying on senses was no longer the character flaw I had been raised to believe it was. My reconditioning therapy had drilled that into me again and again.

It was simply the efficient choice. Therefore, it was the best. It didn't matter how imbecilic and clumsy that made me feel.

As the world rotated out of view, the stars emerged from under their reflected glare. For a handful of seconds, I could see more exhaust trails from System Defense, even the subtler ones: the blues, violets, and turquoises of jamming drones and flechette platforms as they whirled into position. Then the first of the sun's reflections glinted across the edge of the window, and the window's filters kicked on, hard. As the sun slid into view, those filters had turned to almost-complete blocks. The only thing I could see was the ghost of a white blotch in the window's center.

If the traitors had any reaction to the abrupt radio silence, they didn't show it. That silence seemed heavier now. The window was so filtered that nothing *but* sunlight could get through. I might as well have been alone in the universe.

I called up projections from the cameras on my craft's side to reassure myself that I wasn't. More blips resolved into being on my sensor maps. The traitors' engine plumes melded into a violet snake-headed monster, covered in sparkling red eyes as enemy targets darted in and out of it. I kept the icons that represented System Defense in the back of my mind, trying to remind myself I was part of a pattern. Part of a plan.

My little courier shuttle plainly didn't belong here. It was the only Mentak ship in orbit. The only non-Mindnet craft at all. Suspiciously out of place, but also… stupidly out of place. If the Letnev noticed me at all, they'd assume my presence was incidental. A late evacuee fleeing the Mindnet, perhaps. If a line of attack depended on me, then clearly it was a ridiculous thought. The Letnev would never think I was important to the Mindnet's plans.

They were right. I wasn't important, not really. Not anymore. My crucial part in the plan had already ended. Now, I was here for support.

But what happened next was important to *me*.

I'd burned into the system three days ago, carrying news of the impending Letnev attack. I typically operated behind the Mindnet frontier, in enemy territory, but this news had been so urgent I'd needed to take the risk. By stressing my engines to their utmost, I'd just been able to make it here in time.

Until a few weeks ago, this dusty little world had been claimed by the Mentak Coalition. Like most everything else in this part of the galaxy, it had once been part of the Lazax Empire. We, the L1Z1X Mindnet, were the heirs of the Lazax. We had swept in and announced that We were quashing the rebellion that had held sway here in the millennia of Our absence. Then we had taken Our system back.

The Barony of Letnev had not even the ghost of a claim to the Arrix system. Not by the laws of the old Lazax Empire they'd sworn loyalty to, and not even by the legal fictions they'd created since their genocide of that empire. Even if they refused to acknowledge Our rights as inheritors of the Lazax Empire, their own interstellar law held that, if they did reconquer Arrix, they should return the system to the Mentak Coalition that We had taken it from.

Instead, the Letnev were attempting to claim it for themselves. The Barony pretended at prim and proper discipline, military propriety, and legality, but this was raw opportunism.

With my scopes alone, I could tell that these weren't typical Letnev assault craft. Their ships were too light, and darting about too fast, to carry artificial gravity and inertia compensators. Any pilots would have been pasted across their bulkheads. These ships were automated.

I knew exactly what these ships were. Three months ago, on a courier mission to Arc Prime, I'd seen them docked to a military spaceport and taken discreet scans. When I'd arrived at Arrix, the Mindnet and I agreed that the Barony was likely to deploy them here.

They were a prototype design, a needle-nosed robotic craft called splicerships. Full automation was a big concession for the Letnev. The Barony was adamant that their pilots' training and martial excellence was superior to any machine. Sometimes they were even right about that.

The Letnev's biggest weakness was their pride. They sought not just to best their opponents, but best them by attacking their strengths head-on. They had to prove not just that they were the best at something, but that they were *the* best. Challenge a Letnev officer to Naalu poker or strip chess or, hell, improv, and they'd spend days mastering the rules to prove that they could excel at anything.

That was what these new prototypes, the splicerships, were: a direct attack on the Mindnet's technological strength. They were slender, defense-heavy hybrids of fighter and missile, designed to spear through their targets' defenses. The splicerships looked like lobotomy picks. They carried electronic warfare payloads: directed electromagnetic pulse generators, broad-spectrum jamming devices, and a bevy of viruses designed to target Mindnet cybernetics. Each was packed with supercomputers made to build new viruses in-flight, so that they could adapt to new defenses as they appeared.

Their plan was to hammer Us offline with electromagnetic pulses, flood space with jamming. As Our systems rebooted and tried to reestablish contact with each other, the splicerships would seep viruses through Our networks, transmitting the signals engineered on the fly to be indistinguishable from Our own.

The second wave of the Letnev armada, the fully crewed ships, were somewhere behind, still hidden by the sun. They could come through later and sweep up as they pleased.

The Letnev were mistaken about Our best strength.

From the outside, it must have seemed like Our technology was Our best asset. The L1Z1X Mindnet's pinpoint-precise weapons were as famed as they were feared throughout the civilized galaxy. We analyzed and predicted maneuvers before Our opponents decided to make them. More than one enemy captain had ordered an abrupt evasive turn only to find a Mindnet dumb-fire rocket already intersecting their new trajectory.

Mindnet orbital bombers and artillery fired fearlessly into massed-infantry battles. Each warhead landed precisely, invariably on target. Our targeting systems calculated *everything* from the softening metal of hot cannon barrels to the diffraction of targeting beams through the heat of battle. Explosions rippled across the battlefield in perfect sequence, flaying enemy formations apart while leaving Mindnet soldiers untouched.

But Mindnet's real strength was not Our technology but Our ethos. We didn't use Our immense processing capacity to show it off. We didn't choose cybernetics for its own sake. We chose it to survive.

The Mindnet was the last surviving fragment of the Lazax Empire. The few Lazax who'd seen the genocides coming had retreated far across the galaxy, desperately fleeing from world to world, and had at last ended up on a world with nothing. A world they couldn't survive out in the open, whose atmosphere was toxic to them, and that had no magnetic field to ward off the worst of its sun's radiation. They couldn't leave. They had burned up their last starships to reach it.

And they had survived there. For thousands of years. They'd had to make themselves half-machine to do it. The curse that had become Our blessing.

I was not Lazax myself. Individual Lazax still lived, deep in Mindnet territory, but most modern Mindnet citizens were converts. I was human, just under decades old. I carried the memories of the Lazax with me.

The only way to survive the privation forced upon the Lazax had been through cold, razor-sharp efficiency. Precision was one good route to efficiency. But not the only one.

(Far from the only one.)

Pressing to prove themselves, the Letnev expected a fair battle. Thanks to the intelligence I had brought days in advance, a more efficient option was available to Us.

I clasped my hands in front of my mouth and waited.

I wished the waiting would end. Maybe I should have stayed back with the plumbing work just to give myself something to do. There was still a very annoying part of me that could not stop thinking about the piping in the crew head's sink.

Then a wave of firecracker sparks shimmered across the splicerships' flight paths. My scopes caught only a few of the explosions, those farthest from the sun. But the edge of the battle was now within my pulse sensors' reach. They showed that space had suddenly become much more complicated.

The explosions dispersed clouds of debris across the splicerships' flight paths.

Most of the released objects were far smaller than ball bearings. But at the splicerships' velocities, the kinetic energy release of a pebble would strike like a bomb. A chunk smaller than a Naaz knucklebone could split a splicership from bow to stern.

For days, System Defense had been lobbing boulder-sized metal canisters in the direction of the sun. These canisters had no engines, no thrusters, and had been catapult-launched without guidance. Most wouldn't even escape this planet's gravity. They'd sear back into the atmosphere weeks and months from now.

That was all right. They were cheap, packed full of whatever loose mass System Defense could find. When We had seized this world from the Mentak Coalition, the battle had left plenty of twists of metal, blackened debris, and burst hulls. Some of the defense platforms had gone so far as to cannibalize themselves, dismantling their hulls down to the bulkheads, to shoot most of their own mass toward the sun. The Mindnet's remorseless math hadn't deemed the expense of fetching shipping debris up from Arrix's gravity well to be worth it.

The splicerships, like all interstellar craft, had deflector shields to ward off loose particles. They were meant for incidental matter; this was a coordinated assault. The physics were inescapable.

The splicerships reacted immediately. Their twisting maneuvers halted. Their tangled engine plumes blossomed outward as each ship raced away from the others. They would not be able to get far enough. The Mindnet had detonated the canisters across all their possible flight trajectories. The story of the next few minutes had been written the moment the canisters began detonating.

Letnev planners would have accounted for the possibility of the Mindnet being forewarned. But they seemed to have assumed that We would respond by hardening Our electronic warfare defenses. This attack was messy, imprecise, and thoughtlessly violent – entirely unlike how the Mindnet usually fought. But it was efficient. Electronic warfare meant nothing to titanium shrapnel. They could not shut down dumb mass – a phrase that encompassed the way I hoped a number of Letnev tacticians felt right then.

The splicerships reoriented, trying to present their pinpoint front profiles. But the threats were coming in from too many angles. System Defense had thrown the canisters in multiple directions, at different velocities, along different gravitational arcs. The splicerships were not trying to squeeze through a wall of spikes but a hurricane of whirling razors.

On my tactical map, the blips fuzzed into a vibrant fog of war. My scopes still struggled to see through the solar glare and did not pick up the first explosions. But, over the course of the next few seconds, they registered a catastrophic rise in their formation's overall heat.

The cloud ticked steadily toward me, second by second. My hands started to tremble. I tried to still them, but the tremor returned when I wasn't paying attention.

(You can do better.)

Out there, the Mindnet sang a silent symphony. I heard none of it. I had to assume things were going well and keep my ship's nose oriented to the sun. Any wreckage would be coming at *me* from a single vector… more or less.

The storm front rolled over me.

A flash of violet light overwhelmed my shuttle's portside sensors. That half of the map – and all the camera images on that side – flared and went blank. My proximity alarms screamed. It took seconds for my sensors to adjust. When they did, the cameras showed two stars spinning haphazardly past me. They continued to disintegrate, spitting sparks, as they plunged toward Arrix. The remains of a splicership.

A scatter of targets emerged from the fog. Some of the splicerships had made it through. Bound to happen. But the survivors were scattered. Easy targets.

Streaks of livid light – everything from missile exhausts, plasma bolts, and combat drones – curled upward to meet the intruders.

Then my world turned sheet-white. The light itself was not so sharp as the pain. This was no explosion: the sun was suddenly staring through my cockpit window, right at me.

The window's filters had failed. The rest of the cockpit was a tranquil sea. The hum of its electronics, the whir of the air ventilation, had died. I sealed my eyes shut and tried to remain calm. Most important first things to establish. I could still feel the back of my seat. I was still breathing.

An EMP had gone off nearby. Not close enough to physically fuse my electronics, but closer than chance seemed to allow. An enemy survivor had made it through the debris and targeted my region of System Defense's web.

My cockpit windows' spectrum filters had died and were resetting. All my cabin lights and sensor projections must have gone out, too, but I couldn't see them against the glare. I hadn't been looking in the sun's direction, had had my eyes on the sensor maps, but that split-second had still been enough to blow out my pupils.

If I had to be flying a non-Mindnet craft, I was grateful that it was Mentak. Mentak engineering was scrappy at the best of times, but those pirates built their ships for combat, and it showed. All my systems were back up and running before I was. I was still blinking angry purple afterimages away long after the sensor projections flickered back to where they used to be.

There were few advantages to being without cybernetics, but this was one of them. If I'd still had my implants, I'd have been even worse off. Just like the System Defense weapons platform nearest me.

The platform was a spindly thing, a thirty-person station with counterbalanced racks of solar panels and a hull blistered with weapons turrets. It had gotten the worst of the blast. It was in a lower orbit seven hundred kilometers south-southeast of me, just far enough to still be able to see. One of my scopes caught a view of it against the backdrop of the horizon.

The station fired its thrusters chaotically, whirling about in uncontrolled maneuvers. That was its emergency backup systems trying to evade fire. It likely had no surviving sensors. Its crew would still be recovering from the shock to their cybernetics – assuming that the EMP hadn't melted their implants and killed them outright.

Half of the habitation cylinder was missing, internal compartments open to the vacuum, but that damage hadn't come from Letnev weapons. All those bulkheads and extra mass had gone into the debris canisters. It made me think of an anatomical illustration of a body, half skin, and half muscle and bone.

(Like your own medical scans.)

It took my clumsy hand several seconds to find its blip on the tactical map. I split my fingers to zoom in, and then pawed around to check for any object trajectories approaching it.

A Letnev icon a thousand kilometers above screamed toward the station. The numbers floating beside it said it was too big to be a splicership.

In a flash of panic, I scanned through all my other sensor maps, afraid that something was wrong with the intelligence I'd brought and that somehow We'd been counter-played. But no – everything was as it should have been. All but a few of the splicerships' exhaust trails ended in debris. Both the dispersing exhaust and superheated shrapnel had fallen past Us.

During my moment of sensor blindness, the second wave of Letnev craft, the one that was supposed to mop up after the splicerships, had arrived. These were the crewed craft, the Letnev mainstays. They'd been much closer to the splicerships than I'd thought. And they'd met the same debris cloud as the splicerships. As with the splicerships, a bare handful of those craft had made it through. This was one of them.

The intruder's achingly bright engine plume was a hundred times the size of the craft itself. I couldn't see the ship except as a silhouette. But that silhouette told me it was an *Invigorating Lesson* – class gunship, a seven-person craft that barely fit the definition of "fighter" sized ships. A whole bunch of multipurpose bomb bays strapped to point-defense turrets and wrapped around an engine. It was designed to devastate defenseless targets. Populations that couldn't fight back.

The ambush had turned into an actual battle. Whole segments of my sensor maps fuzzed in and out. Radiation washed over my hull. Other loose munitions, EMPs, were pelting System Defense. The handful of the Letnev survivors were, like this ship, pressing on.

It would have made more sense for these Letnev to retreat. They actually stood a ghost of a chance of escaping. Carrying on with their attack meant certain death. They'd suffered too many losses to succeed. But whether out of pigheadedness, pride, or an inability to face the collapse of their plans – or, given that it was Letnev, all three – these crews were going to extinguish their lives in a show of futile glory. For a better chance of a state-broadcasted funeral, a letter to survivors signed by their baron.

The Mindnet never would have been so idiotic. As a collective, We had an ego. But not as individuals. The crew of the defense platform was, right now, almost certainly uploading their last memories to the collective.

This was my opportunity. I plotted an intercept trajectory.

The sun rotated out of my view, and I briefly saw the stars. Then the reflected light of the world below drowned them out, and my main engines thundered.

My cushions pressed tighter around me. A fraction of the acceleration *g*-forces were bullying their way through the artificial gravity. The cabin bulkheads rattled as the inertial compensators reminded me how long it had been since they'd been serviced. Something I didn't want to think about groaned like a seat that had been sat on too hard. Somewhere behind me, a dozen *clacks* and *pocks* echoed up the corridors as loose objects tumbled across the deck. A proper Mindnet crew would have secured everything as they went along, but my unaugmented brain had holes. Easy to forget a comb here, a tooth cleaner cap there.

My sensor map etched two intersecting flight paths, along with bubbles illustrating estimated weapons ranges. The bubbles didn't overlap… yet. By breaking orbit, I'd lost my disguise, and could no longer pretend to be debris. The gunship's flight path shifted away from mine.

The gunship's crew must not have been sure what to make of me. My Mentak courier shuttle was hardly larger than the subway car it looked like. It didn't look like a combat vessel. The Letnev aimed to ignore me, to give me a chance to escape the fight in case I was an innocent breaking cover to run.

I fired my thrusters, wriggling back onto an intercept course. We repeated the dance a few more times until the gunship's pilots realized I wasn't going to be dissuaded.

As I neared the outer edges of their weapons' range, my cameras could pick out more of the gunship. Harsh gray hull plating, imperial gold highlights – a style borrowed from the Lazax Empire that *they* had helped overthrow.

I engaged my targeting sensors. On my sensor map, crosshairs slid along the gunship's flight path. My weapons, at least, I would not have to manually control. The vast majority of Mentak craft were armed. Mentak territory could be just as hazardous for the Mentak as it was for outsiders. I had made my own Mindnet-style modifications, most significantly to the targeting scanners.

My final course adjustment ended with the planetary horizon just peeking over my cockpit window. The leading edge of what had been the spliceships was just now striking the atmosphere. Remnants erupted into vivid red-white streaks, stalks of fire.

The spliceships were small by starship standards, but not by a meteorite's. The largest impacts would splinter the planet's crust. Dust clouds and volcanic outgassing would cloud over the chalky-white horizon. The people below would suffer, even more than they already had, because of this attack.

(Such pollution. Such waste.)

I spared my nettling intrusive voice a moment of acknowledgment, something I hated to do, to share my contempt. I reminded it that the Arborec hardly left its worlds in pristine condition, a fact it began to argue before I shut it out again.

I thumbed my weapons on. Tracer bullets spat from under my shuttle's prow, blazing razor-sharp across the horizon. They preempted their target, aiming to where the gunship was going to be in about half a minute.

The Mindnet didn't need tracer bullets. And I was Mindnet. Wounded. An imperfect cell in a perfect organ in a perfect body, but still Mindnet. The Letnev didn't know that, though. The tracer bullets would catch their attention.

My *real* shots – a tighter, more focused stream of fire, from a cannon beneath the prow – belted out along a different trajectory.

This second burst traveled near enough to the first for the Letnev's pulse sensors to get them confused. This burst would reach the gunship a few seconds before the tracer bullets.

My optical sensors caught the glimmer of a targeting laser off the exosphere. It came from the gunship's direction.

I blew all my anti-beam countermeasures on that facing. Clouds of mirrored chaff burst from their pockets, turning that half of the sky into a churning kaleidoscope of light. I fired my maneuvering thrusters as a swath of my portside hull liquified. Seven of my twenty port-facing scopes went dead.

I dove and twisted, trusting my gyros to keep my still-firing cannons on target. The beam had struck at diminished strength, thanks to my chaff, but still with enough energy to drill through a thruster fuel feed, rocking my shuttle.

The chaff dispersed in time to let me see my trick work. The Letnev gunship had only seen the tracer bullets. Its crew had angled their deflector shields in all the wrong directions. Bits of the gunship turned to sparks and blew away. Meter-long segments of ablative hull plating collapsed. One of its three main engine nozzles dented.

The gunship swerved. Its damaged engine nozzle turned red and then white, rapidly melting under the output of the heat now pouring directly into it. The abrupt course change took them away from the station.

My scopes showed me the station's thrusters were still firing, but now in controlled bursts, getting its spin under control. It *did* have crew alive after all. The Letnev gunship could still curve around toward it, but now the station's crew had precious time to recover.

My hands were so sweaty that I had trouble keeping a grip on the steering column. I had done it.

The fight was a light year from being over, though. My shuttle juddered, bulkheads rattling, as that thruster feed line kept venting. The emergency shut-off valves weren't working. My jaw hurt from how hard I clenched it.

On the other side of the horizon, the Letnev gunship was also struggling. But they weren't out of the fight yet. Its thrusters fired in spurts as its pilots worked to determine which were functioning. Letnev craft were resilient and modular. They wouldn't need long to make adjustments, and limp back on course.

I lifted the protective casing off the trigger key that would fire my first swarm of pincer-missiles.

A sharp-edged, white-hot explosion nearly blinded me. A dazzling sequence of detonations ripped through space between the gunship and my shuttle. My bulkhead plating clattered like a collapsing building under a tornado. Each burst of light came with a jolt, a thunderclap of a shock wave slamming into my shuttle.

But the pain I felt came from my ears. Agony clapped the side of my head. It was my ears, popping.

A cold wind whipped my hair backward.

If you asked anyone who'd spent any time in space what the worst thing they could feel was, the answer would always be that. Even fully augmented L1Z1X had a terror of it. In space, terror was – a surprising amount of the time – entirely rational.

The breeze ended before I could get my wits back online. I barely heard the emergency pressure hatches slam through the cacophony.

The first thing I saw when I looked out my cockpit window was my plumbing repair kit, spinning away on a steam geyser that had once been most of my ship's water supply.

That hadn't been a Letnev weapon. I'd had an experience alien to Mindnet soldiers: I'd been hit by friendly fire. Those had been System Defense's flak bursts. Despite the name, they were precision weapons, Mindnet weapons. Unguided artillery with shaped charges. No flight or propulsion systems made them hard to detect, and shaped charges were perfect for an attacker that excelled at predicting its opponents and knowing exactly where to land its shots.

Only, I had screwed that up. I wasn't part of the Mindnet's quantum network. The gunship and I had maneuvered to fight, spoiling plans that must have been laid before that EMP went off.

The flak had hit the gunship, too, though it had survived when it shouldn't have. Its deflector shields were alight. It vomited clouds of chaff to mute heavy beam fire, coming from the station. The Mindnet had adjusted its plans around me.

The gunship was no longer firing at me. It focused all its attention on the station. Its crew no longer regarded me as a threat… and they were correct. Half of my console projectors had turned to flashing red glyphs. My weapons were dead.

Everywhere else, the mop-up operation continued. Most of the action had fallen below my horizon, perceptible only in those silent echoes. Radiation spikes reflected off the atmosphere like distant, silent lightning. I only had my imagination to supply the details: traitor craft falling into pre-placed mines, led into vicious beam crossfire, and other traps. All the clockwork was ticking along, except where this one gear had slipped loose.

The only thing I could do from here was get in the way, placing myself and everyone else in danger. Heat welled in the back of my throat. I tried to control it, swallow it down, but it kept rising again.

All my remaining portside thrusters sputtered. The fuel feed line was still venting. That entire side of my shuttle was losing propulsion. To turn toward open space, I had to spin two hundred and eighty degrees in the other direction.

My main engines were somehow still online. At least, my console reported that they were. I had a brief and unbecoming hope that the diagnostics were wrong, and that the intermix chamber was about to blow.

But the engines lit as they should and shoved me hard away from the battle. Half the sky disappeared underneath the torchlight of my engine exhaust. I lost sight of the Letnev gunship and the weapons platform. All at once, I might as well have been alone.

CHAPTER TWO
MEAT LOCKER

Then

Things hadn't always been this bad. They used to be much, much worse.

Even now, I don't know how long I was in that scalding, perpetually smoky crater before Uthan found me. The answer depends on information that was lost even to the Mindnet.

The last reliable date I remember was boarding a Mindnet survey ship, eight years and three months before the battle at Arrix. When I woke up again, another year had passed. In between, all I have is fog and supposition.

My survey ship was not supposed to have been at Kitrya-892. Ending up there, by itself, wasn't unusual. We'd been on a long-term science mission. Diversions were commonplace. We'd also been operating behind enemy lines – which was to say most of the galaxy – and so keeping a low profile. That meant we wouldn't dispatch messengers for every course correction. The engine burns of messenger shuttles could have, by themselves, given away our presence to the traitor factions.

I remember a little of my working conditions before the crash. I'd been stacked into a work pod with seven other Mindnet citizens. Submerged in impact-cushioning fluid, fed nutrients by tube, wired into muscle stimulators to keep my body from withering away. Uncomfortable, but my body hadn't been my primary place of residence. I'd spent most of my time linked directly to the ship's groupmind, lost in virtual environments sent directly to my cybernetics.

We didn't waste energy or space on niceties like dignity for passengers, let alone the privilege of bodily awareness. Far easier to shunt our thoughts into the ship's groupmind, maintain our bodies at their lowest activity state, and let that be that.

Other than a few sensory flashes of the work pod, all that experience is gone now. The memories had died with the ship, and everyone other than me. I couldn't remember what I'd been doing there.

Those of you who've read fanciful stories of galactic intrigue will be snapping your fingers or other appendages and saying, *Aha, there will be a twist coming* – and all these lost memories are where it will come from. The crash and my survival concealed a dark purpose.

This is not that fanciful kind of intrigue story.

Shedding memories was mundane for the Mindnet. I would have off-loaded those memories into the ship's groupmind as a matter of routine. The part of me that knew what I'd been doing aboard had died with the rest of my habitation cylinder as it smashed into the magmatic hellscape of Kitrya-892 b.

Perhaps I'm being unfair to Kitrya-892 b. There must have been much less magma before we arrived than there was just seconds later.

Whatever its mission or ultimate destination, my survey ship screamed into Kitrya-892 b's atmosphere so fast that few of the emergency ejection systems would have functioned. At those speeds, there was little difference between atmosphere and a brick wall. Any escape pod would have been sheared in half by the winds during launch, or cooked by the shroud of flame that the ship was rapidly in the process of becoming.

Large pieces of it broke off. Including, fortunately and unfortunately, the habitation torus I'd been lodged in. While the bulk of the survey ship had seared straight into the ground, my habitation torus struck the atmosphere at an angle. It *skipped.* Like it was a rock and the whole atmosphere a pond. Each bounce took us thousands of kilometers from the rest of the ship's crash site.

It must have been a wild sight, full of beautiful, deadly spectacle: a shower of light across an alien sky; the atmosphere on fire; concentric circular shock waves spreading like smoke rings underneath us, every place we'd skipped across. The kind of view that would make even the unsentimental Mindnet pause.

I can't remember a damned thing. I was only able to piece together what happened in retrospect, by working out the distance the habitation cylinder had been thrown from the craft. If I'd been conscious at all, I must have still been consigning my last memories to the cylinder's groupmind.

That would have been the reasonable thing to do. I was far likelier to die than the armored, reinforced groupmind computer. If the groupmind didn't survive our habitation torus's final impact, it would have been a safe assumption that I wouldn't, either. The odds were less than a percentage point and could safely have been ignored in any reasonable assessment.

Every sentient being must learn two important things about the universe. The first is that it has a sense of humor. The second is that it does not laugh. Sometimes the odds are not a guide to what will actually happen.

Of the one hundred and fifty-two beings in my habitation torus, including the seven I shared a work pod with, I was the only survivor.

My name is Sil. It used to be S1L3NT, but I could not keep the Mindnet designation after the Mindnet was ripped away from me. Uthan preferred the new name, and I won't pretend that didn't matter, a little. I have no gender. I was never interested in that. Few people from my home world had been, and the Mindnet, after their invasion, had certainly never forced us to adopt such things. The Mindnet is embracing. Very firmly embracing.

Every Mindnet citizen's augments were different, tailored to the individual and their role. Before the crash, I had been an analyst, and not expected to have a role in landing parties, or extravehicular repairs, or anything that would take me out of my work pod. Therefore, my implants were mostly thinking aids, with some light muscular and endurance boosts. No lung filters, blood scrubbers, bioelectric batteries, or anything else to help me survive in a toxic alien environment.

The groupmind's memory cores were dashed to pieces. The bulkheads outside my work pod caved in, reducing the cabin to a quarter of its former size. I was the only one who crawled out of the impact-cushioning fluid.

Kitrya-892 b was the system's largest rocky planet. It wasn't all that different from Arrix. Some worlds needed interstellar war to become blasted radioactive hellscapes. Others just *were*.

But the planet still managed to hold on to enough oxygen-producing algae to have a breathable atmosphere. Amend that: mostly breathable. Breathable for long enough to die of conditions other than hypoxia. The air carried enough heavy metals to kill most of the galaxy's sentient species within a week. And that had been before my survey ship's crash had split this world's crust and churned a large chunk of it into the atmosphere. The main impact crater was thousands of kilometers from where my habitation cylinder had landed, but the effects were going to have worldwide impacts. There would be earthquakes for centuries. Its climate would take longer to recover.

I must have gone outside at some point. I remembered bits and flashes. Gray, toxic clouds clogging the sky. Gravity compressing my lungs like a boulder sitting atop my ribs. Sand in my shoes. Despair. *Constant* itching.

But certainly, by the time Uthan arrived, the airlock I had rigged to keep me alive was the only power source he could detect.

The crash had breached every bulkhead in what remained of the habitation torus. It smashed the passenger pods and ruined life support, leaving no cabin unexposed to the toxic elements.

The only exception was not a proper cabin at all: an airlock. It was counterintuitive to get closer to elements in a situation like that. But I must have made the logical leap. Airlocks had their own heavy-duty air filtration systems, and airtight hatches on each side. That also made it the safest place to be on a ship breached by a poisonous atmosphere.

My memories of this moment are fragmented. Trauma, physical and otherwise, plus the neural shock of sudden disconnection from the groupmind might have explained that. But there were other things happening, or going to happen, to my brain to disrupt memory retention.

My neural cybernetic augments were as much a part of me as my fingers or my eyes. Individuals have a difficult time understanding the Mindnet. Most of the "great civilizations" of the galaxy consist only of individuals. Even the N'orr, the insectile sentients that other civilizations erroneously accused of being a hive mind, didn't link their thoughts like We did.

Other civilizations tended to believe that the Mindnet was a hive mind, and its citizens drones. They were wrong. In the Mindnet, the difference between me and Us still existed, but it was permeable. I never lost my own identity in the Mindnet. I was always me, but We were always Us.

Wholly artificial intelligences didn't have the will to accomplish, or the ability to value anything except as numbered lists of priorities. More crucially, they didn't have the wherewithal to change themselves when those values conflicted. On the other side of the galaxy, the Nekro Virus, that treacherous machine intelligence, had floundered for just that reason. It was trapped under the weight of its own recursive programming. All the Nekro Virus knew to do was attack, but it had forgotten the reason why. Or worse – forgotten how to comprehend the reason why. It meant to wipe biological life from the galaxy, but then... there was no other then. It was alive only in the sense that a forest fire is alive.

The great plantmind, the Arborec, swung far in the opposite extreme. The Arborec was not a collective but a single mind. One intelligence spread across the stars. That came with its own limitations. The Arborec had been unable to comprehend species composed of individuals, let alone communicate with them.

Languages like this one didn't have the vocabulary to describe belonging to the Mindnet. I was trapped behind metaphor. What words could describe an identity that felt like a sponge under a running faucet? Or a single card in a constantly shuffling deck? No language but our own had pronouns that encompassed so many varieties between I and We. Without my implants, I'd lost that, too. I couldn't even think in the language I'd been raised to use.

The Mindnet was the perfect medium. Billions of minds, maintaining their own independent existences, yet interwoven like cells in an organism. Single neurons in a mind.

It was a hell of a thing for one of those neurons to find themselves alone.

The things I remember after my disconnection from the ship's groupmind: my shoulders burning from the strain of forcing the passenger pod's hatch open; a corridor so compressed and twisted that I could walk with one foot on the deck and the other on the ceiling; a clump of my hair in my hands; the tangy, rusted-iron scent of the local atmosphere infiltrating our corridors; sneezing endlessly.

I had been born human and, unlike some of my heavily augmented crewmates, maintained a mostly human form. It left me at a disadvantage. Too many human frailties. Fear and horror mingled with annoyance that the blood on my palms made climbing difficult.

The outer airlock hatch had a small window. It was one of the few places on a Mindnet ship that would ever have such a thing. The hatch was canted downward, sheltering it from the ashfall outside. A broad section of gray hull, ripped down the center like a sheet of paper, hung precariously overhead. The sun must have been up, but the clouds were so thick that the daytime had turned to twilight.

I sealed both hatches, turned on the filtration system, and verified that it was still functioning.

Then I lay down and died.

It was standard Mindnet procedure to die in the event of massive physical trauma.

No, that was not as silly a statement as it sounded.

To the Mindnet, there was a difference between dying by accident and dying by plan. A prepared death was a more efficient death. We can take the time to set aside those things worth preserving and let the rest shuffle away. Dying by procedure had steps, a checklist. There was a proper way to do it.

Getting to the airlock had purchased my body some time. I might have been traumatized out of my mind, but my implants knew what to do: prepare for a crash investigation team. The top priority after any crash was to gather information. Every perspective could help unravel the story of the crash. Most of my memories might have been lost with the groupmind, but my neural cybernetics could be squeezed for data.

Most of my body would die. By keeping myself in a contained, filtered environment, with minimal oxygen, my body could sustain my brain and its implants long enough for a recovery and salvage team to recover my implants. That data was important. I wasn't.

My vision turned gray, then faded. At least there was no more sneezing. No more itching.

It should have been the last thing I ever sensed. Ridiculously, it wasn't.

The next time my awareness pieced itself together, an alarm was going off. A distant, hollow shrill resounded through the bulkhead I'd collapsed against. The urge to sneeze returned at once, but I didn't have the strength to answer the reflex.

Aside from my head and sinuses, my body was numb. Even breathing was a labor, and one of the few things to break through the numbness in my body was the agony of sucking in air. I was a fish gasping air in a dried tidal pond.

Those muscles had atrophied. I could not tell how much time had passed – which was alarming, because I always knew what time it was. My implants had built-in clocks.

The light levels outside hadn't changed. But they wouldn't have: this world was tidally locked to its star. The same side always faced the sun. I had landed in the eternal daylight.

The distant alarm was a proximity sensor. I recognized the tone. Mindnet security systems, like most Mindnet technology, were distributed and decentralized. The most essential of them, like the proximity alarm, could function even after the destruction of the rest of the ship.

I could barely tilt my head far enough to see the ground. Everything was a different color. My first thought was that I was looking at several meters of snow. One of the things I remember from my life before the Mindnet was loving snow.

But no. This was ash. An absurd, life-threatening amount of ash. Step out in it and risk being smothered under it.

The best clocks I had were my weakened muscles and the fact that the airlock window, even sheltered, had become caked with soot. There was a small section in the middle that remained transparent, at least enough to let me see the marrow-colored smoke layering the sky.

At a distance, the incoming shuttle looked like a blackened, windborne ember. It swooped close enough to then resemble an oil-choked train car. It was covered in streaks of ash and filth from passage through the atmosphere. Not a Mindnet craft.

The odds were not good that my little window, with its narrower field of view, would have been perfectly oriented to let me see a lone shuttle. Probability suggested that either this shuttle was one of many and others were also landing nearby, or this shuttle was alone and its pilot landed in front of my airlock *because* it had detected me. Idly, I tried to figure out which would be worse, and couldn't come up with an answer.

As the shuttle circled overhead, as if for a better look at me, I decided it was the latter. Yes, being sought out was definitely worse.

I hadn't realized it at the time, but in retrospect it's clear that my independent personality was already emerging. I was a pessimist. Whatever was happening to me at any given moment was the worst *possible* thing that could ever have happened to me. But I was not conscious enough to despair.

Having determined that I lived in the worst of all possible universes, I distinctly remember thinking *Whatever* and passing out.

A deep jet-engine roar yanked me back to awareness. It was loud and obnoxious enough not just to jar me awake but to drown out the proximity alarm. My outside view turned to a blizzard.

The shuttle fired its thrusters at full blast. It hovered in place, but the gale force of the ventral thrusters blew ash out from underneath it. Clearing a landing site. The noise was like being next to a spacecraft endlessly lifting off. And enough to make me stop wondering why I was not dead and start wishing that I were.

The shuttle bore the emblem of the new Galactic Council underneath the soot on its flank. This Galactic Council had taken the form and style of the dead Lazax Empire's governing body, and even operated out of the shattered Lazax capital world Mecatol Rex, but it had been assembled long after the genocide of the Lazax. Its membership was a mix of usurper civilizations, like the Barony of Letnev, and the Federation of Sol. But the cobbled-together construction of the ship itself made me guess – correctly, as it turned out – that it had been built by the Mentak Coalition.

The Mentak had come a long way since their ancestors had overthrown the wardens of their prison planet. One of the conditions of their acceptance onto the Galactic Council had been an official disavowal of the piracy that had made them powerful enough to join it in the first place. But Mentak engineering would always retain its ancestral scrappiness. Everything they designed had a *je ne sais quoi* of criminality, a sense that its owners were just making do until they could steal something better.

Not long after the shuttle touched down, the tongue of a boarding ramp struck the ground. A single figure emerged in an environmental suit. Their visor showed me a fish-eye mirrored view of the oily clouds. They held a rifle, and they also carried a holstered knife and energy pistol.

They likely knew I was Mindnet. My habitation torus, mangled and smashed though it was, wouldn't have been particularly difficult to identify. Its hull was made of alloys used only by Mindnet craft.

The stranger was armed for good reason. The Mindnet provoked strong reactions everywhere in the galaxy. I didn't know if I was dealing with a rational operator or a terrified civilian… until they reached the window, and I saw that they hadn't properly loaded their pistol. They'd slotted the battery pack into place, but pistols like theirs had a lever to lock the batteries in, and they'd neglected to flip it. If they tried to fire, nothing would happen. That made me *more* concerned, not less. Untrained and jumpy noncombatants were more dangerous than cool-headed soldiers. I considered attacking him, though not for long. I hardly had the strength to twitch my fingers.

Another concerning detail: the pistol was a model issued to Keleres agents. I reflexively tried to reach back in my head to my implants' connection to the Mindnet's databases and pull more information about the Keleres. Nothing came back. The only information I had were the scraps in my brain when I was disconnected: I knew Keleres were the special forces arm of the Galactic Council, and I recognized the pistol, but most everything else was blank. It was all so frustratingly little.

The suited figure fumbled with the other side of the airlock hatch. I groaned. They took so long to figure out that the mechanical lock rotated *left* and not right that I wanted to reach through the window and strangle them. Which, of course, I had already wanted to do in a professional capacity – but impatience made it more personal.

They finally heaved the hatch open. Foul gunpowder-smelling air washed over me. The environment suit had speakers, and they crackled as the person inside grunted in surprise. They had a human voice, masculine-sounding. Under the shadow of the hull, his bubble helmet's mirror finish was easier to see through. A red beard and mustache pressed against the bottom half of it.

The figure started to raise his rifle, but then stopped.

I had not moved because I couldn't. I remained curled and prone beside the airlock's controls. I did not know how bad off I was, not yet, but it did not take much imagination to realize how pathetic I looked. My implants hadn't changed my baseline human form, which was not a particularly large one. And I was crumpled against the wall.

"Surrender or die," I croaked. Apparently, in addition to pessimism, I was also beginning to develop my own sense of humor.

Once again, I was not sure what the worst thing he could have done was… right up until he lowered his aim and asked, "Am I here to rescue you?"

It was a genuine question, and that was what made it truly horrible. I must have really looked pathetic. Most Keleres and most Mentak citizens would, upon seeing a Mindnet citizen, have opened fire. Frankly, so would most of the galaxy's other sentients. When the Mindnet had re-emerged onto the galactic stage, We had made the rational decision that fear, intimidation, and force would be the most efficient means to Our end.

"You're probably here to shoot me," I reminded him, gently.

He looked at the rifle in his hands, and then back at me. The curl of his fingers and the tremble in his back said he was keyed up, nervous, but he still didn't lift his weapon.

Now I was angry enough to growl through the rasp in my voice. I flexed my fingers until I felt comfortable moving them, and then reached for him. I tried to recall curses used among Mentak or pirates, but without a connection to Mindnet databases I didn't have much to work with. "Hell," I said. "At least do me the dignity of being afrai–"

I didn't get to finish the sentence because his sizzling neurons finally sparked. He lifted his rifle and shot me.

Finally.

But it was the kind of day that continually presented me with opportunities to be surprised to find that I wasn't dead.

A sense of humor is a dreadful thing to need. Saying "day" is facetious. *Hah hah.* Do you get it? I was on a tidally locked world. Days never ended.

I have had a long time to myself to consider how to tell this story. The joke seemed more successful before I committed it to words.

As awareness gradually returned to me, in scraps and shreds, I realized that I was lying on my back, head tilted to the right, with my left elbow against a solid surface. I was not only alive but in some kind of medical examination chamber. A very cramped one. My bed was pressed flush against the bulkhead, and that was what my elbow was touching.

To the extent that I could trust anything I felt, my body seemed lighter than before. I was in a different gravity field. I was on the Mentak shuttle. There was about half a meter of walking space between the other side of my bed and the next bulkhead, which was itself crammed with cabinets. The cabin had a single exit, a round hatch, and it was closed. Something was ominously beeping.

"Hell," I said again. As one of the last things I'd said before getting shot, the word was trapped in my head like a recursive software glitch. That was the only swear word I'd known before I'd become part of the Mindnet. Any others had been ripped from me when I'd disconnected from the habitation torus's groupmind.

There were many things that distinguished this craft and its disorder from a proper Mindnet ship, but the one that caught my eye now was the garden flower print curtains. They hung over a light source that was presumably a porthole.

At first, I thought the suited figure had whiffed a point-blank shot and only wounded me. But that didn't make sense. Unlike the pistol, I hadn't recognized the rifle, but it had looked fairly high powered. It should have left a sizable hole, or at least taken a limb. All four of the limbs seemed to be there, though the state of my head was such that I had to verify that two or three times.

The idea that I had been *stunned* rather than shot seemed too stupid to credit. Then I spotted the welts on my arms where the stun bolts had struck.

It was all very funny. Though I suppose you had to have been there.

I stared at the welts. I couldn't piece together events in a way that made sense. Someone, presumably mentally competent enough to pilot or crew a shuttle, would have had to scan Mindnet wreckage, arm themselves appropriately, if sloppily, for dealing with anything Mindnet… and then make the inexplicable choice to disable me rather than kill me.

Space here was at such a premium that, just as with the wall of cabinets ahead of me, the bulkhead behind me wasn't empty. I felt the bulkhead until my fingers brushed an obstruction. It was a rounded corner leading to a boxy extrusion. Though it hurt tremendously, I craned my head far enough to see a tiny display of numbers, and buttons labeled with glyphs of a fan, of an ice cube, and of wavy lines like a heat shimmer. Climate controls.

The low, ominous beeping was an alarm. Hence the ominousness.

A thumping on the deck, rising in intensity if not in tempo, resounded through the bulkheads. The cabin's hatch popped open. A man on the other side burst through. This time his full red beard wasn't constrained by a fishbowl visor but tumbled down his neck. His hair matched, and though it wasn't as long, it was still longer than seemed dignified.

Soot and ash-shaded light spilled onto the deck from some window around a corridor. We were still on Kitrya-892 b. Probably still parked in the same place, though the artificial gravity was on and made that difficult to tell.

Keeping the gravity on while parked was a ludicrous waste of energy. I would change that, I reflected, when I seized the ship.

"You're awake," the man said as though the alarm hadn't been rigged to announce just that. His body was too big for the walking space, and his backside jostled every cabinet as he moved toward the head of my cot.

I didn't understand his calm. My Mindnet implants may not have been physically imposing but they were highly visible. Silver-black machines ran along – and under – my forehead and temples and traced down my neck and back to both arms and legs. I could not be mistaken for anything other than what I was.

He crouched so that he could be on my eye level. His eyes were a tremulous blue. "Are you with me?" he asked. "How do you fe–"

"You unbelievable idiot," I told him. "Buffoon. Drinker of engine coolant. Churl. I'm going to have to steal your shuttle now."

I didn't need anything so uncivilized as a gun or knife. Mindnet implants were all the weapons I ever needed.

For reasons stemming from the Mindnet's long exile and privation, We preferred to capture rather than destroy enemy equipment. Starships topped Our list of capture targets. I didn't know whether this shuttle was capable of interstellar flight, but at the very least it had traveled from another ship that was.

It was common practice for Mindnet space travelers to be given a cybernetic augment to aid in starship theft. Even though I had never been expected to step off-ship and hadn't qualified for large, more invasive modifications, this particular implant was tiny… and the cost of providing all those augments was outweighed by the potential windfall of stealing a starship. This was no secret. Several successful hijackings across the galaxy let all our enemies know how dangerous one of us could be. Which made it all the more unbelievable that this man had taken me aboard.

I reached for the climate controls. My implants carried probes designed to physically penetrate electronics, rapidly learn about them, and infiltrate every linked system. Once the infiltration began, it was very difficult to stop.

The climate control panel would link to the ship's life support system. And the life support system would be integrated with the rest of the shuttle's controls. My implants carried a library of operating systems and common exploits. The Mindnet and the rest of the galaxy were engaged in a constant struggle of patching flaws and finding new ones, but I doubted a shuttle like this one would have been updated recently.

My implants did not even need me to be alive. I had no conscious control over the process. Neural microprocessors distributed through my body would handle the initial steps. Even if this person shot me now, the viruses would cannibalize enough of this shuttle's systems to sustain themselves from there.

None of that happened. I *whanged* my knuckles into the side of the controls.

I'd felt a lot of pain recently, but not a shock like that impact. A sudden and urgent need to speak, say *something*, squeezed my chest. If I didn't speak, I was going to yelp. It took me a moment to remember what to say in these circumstances.

"Ouch," I announced.

The stranger pursed his lips. "Not sure what you expected there."

My implants were still not responding. I raised my hand to the cabin lights and froze. There were no probes. No muscular augmentations, no exoskeletal reinforcement, and no goosebump-sized infiltration augment.

My skin was a strange, mottled orange and purple where all of those things had been. That was all.

It was all flesh.

I hadn't experienced horror since I'd been four years old. Little wonder why none of those implants were answering my requests. They were gone.

"What did you do to me?" I growled.

"I brought you here," he said. "It hasn't been that long–"

If I'd been able to, I would have throttled him, but lifting my hand had somehow made me light-headed. Not only were my arm implants gone, but even my natural muscles seemed to have atrophied. Lifting my head only made the dizziness worse, but I fought through it. I looked around the surgical implements, the butcher's knives and nanoscalpels and whatever else he must have used to ransack my body.

"You want to start this conversation over?" the stranger asked. "It doesn't seem like it's going well. My name's Uthan–"

There were no implants on my right hand, either. Nothing else I tried to signal would answer. "What. Did. You. Do?"

He looked straight back at me, uncowed. "I. Brought. You. Here."

The medical cabin showed no sign of recent surgeries, not in any of the parts of it I could see. Certainly nothing complex enough to have gutted my implants and regenerated the skin and flesh where they had been. Though the mottling suggested *some* kind of invasive procedure.

Everything kept spiraling into the more and more ridiculous. This had to be some kind of hyper-advanced surgical bay, an elaborate act. No one should have been able to remove Mindnet implants without killing their host. I touched the side of my head and felt nothing but skin and hair.

"My implants," I choked.

"That's the thing, isn't it?" he asked. "That's what I've been wondering, too."

There were no implants anywhere on my body, even those that should have been tucked away safely underneath my skull, answering my urgent requests for a diagnosis.

My whole body was like this. Everything that connected me to the Mindnet was gone.

"I couldn't even find any healed scars on you," he said. "All of that Mindnet butchery must've been gone for a long time." He hitched himself into a seated position on the deck, watching me carefully. "You were already like this when I found you."

CHAPTER THREE
A PRISON OF OPEN WALLS

Now

A measure of how badly my shuttle had been hit during the battle over Arrix: it took hours to figure out how to *begin* tallying the damage. As I'd burned out of the star system, I'd feared that every cabin except the cockpit had been breached. I was wrong. "Only" most of my ship had become uninhabitable.

Over the seven years since I'd inherited Uthan's shuttle, I'd been in plenty of dangerous situations. While running intelligence to Mindnet space, I'd played hide and seek with an Argent Flight dreadnought inside a gas giant. I'd escaped a Letnev patrol craft by plunging through the accretion disk of a black hole. I'd avoided sensor sweeps by manually piloting through the debris of a shattered comet with just cold gas jets. But I'd never had my shuttle suffer so much damage. This was new territory for me.

My damage control systems were inadequate. The shuttle's computers weren't complex enough to run a more advanced AI, and the Mindnet had been less than keen to upgrade any of it. The Mindnet had said that would increase my odds of being detected, and that We were not willing to commit to the expense of upgrading an expendable ship.

Contrary to what most non-Mindnet species thought, the Mindnet put a great deal of care into what We say. The Mindnet did not enjoy conversing with outsiders, and so We developed conversational habits that discouraged others from wanting to speak with Us. We chose with great care the ways in which We were blunt and rude.

The moment when I'd asked Us for a systems upgrade had been the first time I remembered Us treating me *as* an outsider. On reflection, We had been correct. The presence of Mindnet technology would have threatened my mission. My greatest asset *to* the Mindnet, the thing that made me a valuable spy since my implants had been excised from me, was the fact that I could now avoid security sweeps meant to detect Mindnet infiltrators. No other Mindnet citizen could have infiltrated the Keleres's ranks of couriers like I had.

But limiting myself to Mentak and Keleres technology did not make my current task any easier. I needed an overview of the exterior hull. Normally, I had a handful of Mentak observation drones that could fly out and do that. They had been stored behind the crew head. They'd joined my only toilet and most of my water supply in space.

(Why is it that you view your body as fallible when it's always been technology that's let you down?)

My jaw tensed. The nagging voice was sometimes more difficult to control.

It had become … very necessary to have a place for thoughts that I could not accept as my own. My conditioning demanded it. I used to have cybernetics to filter and shape these things. In their absence, a mental construct filled that role. A repository where I could hide all my intrusive thoughts and keep them there.

It cast another identity over itself, shrouded in leaves and mold and the scent of decay, but it came from within myself. It must have. The laws of interstellar communication meant that I was isolated from the universe right now.

It was not schizophrenia, or any other known condition, but it was perhaps brain damage.

An EV suit exam was so far out of the question that the suits might as well have gone with them. I had burned out of the Arrix system as fast as possible. My shuttle was now bathed in a corona of radiation.

Faster-than-light travel rendered the galaxy unrecognizable: a dream of color, a diffuse red fog behind me, and a sharp blue-white pinprick ahead. The latter was the problem. The blue-white color was only the visible portion of a light that shone much more brightly in the X – and gamma-ray spectra.

I hadn't thought about the danger fast enough. It had been years since Uthan found me, but there was still so much about being unaugmented that I often forgot little things until it was too late. Like the fact that I had no implants to detect and repair genetic damage as it occurred, nor the ability to dampen and compensate for radiation poisoning.

I was merely human.

To get out and assess the state of the shuttle, I would have needed to slow well below light speed. But I was already going to be late for a scheduled message delivery. I didn't trust my command of the FTL physics that I could have made so abrupt a stop without endangering myself or spending too much time recalculating my course.

Maybe I could have done it… with the Mindnet's help. I used to know how faster-than-light travel worked. No, that wasn't quite right – it was not that *I* had known how faster-than-light travel worked. But, as a full member of the Mindnet, I could have accessed that knowledge at any time.

When I needed to understand the impossible mathematics of FTL travel, I'd called upon the minds and conceptual prowess of Our best physicists. I'd borrowed the processing power necessary to bully the theory of general relativity to tears.

With the power of the Mindnet, I could have charted the n-dimensional quantum system of a boxed Hacan. I could have observed-without-observing the decay of the radioactive isotope that would either poison the Hacan or not – and both at the same time. Living with the Mindnet had been like living in a different universe. A more complex universe, but one that paradoxically made more sense.

Without the Mindnet, I couldn't tell what happened to the cat without opening the box like any other chump. Hopelessly entangling my fate with the cat's.

After the battle, the suit in my cockpit's emergency closet had jammed up against the hatch window with one arm raised. The first time I saw it, I thought it looked like it was trying to raise a point. I'd been too busy to listen.

(Now it's saying, "I tried to tell you.")

Besides intrusive thoughts, there were some constants in the universe. Starship maintenance, like spy work, was either boring and miserable, or terrifying and miserable. I prepared for misery.

It had been hours since the battle. Gradually, I calmed down; gradually, I was returning to my body. Dried sweat half glued my bare arms to the pilot's seat. They peeled off with an ugly, tearing-paper sound. My body ached when I stood.

The cockpit's hatch didn't open when I tugged on it. For a moment, I was afraid the shuttle's frame had warped and jammed the damned thing. But it opened on the third yank, smoothly as if nothing had ever gone wrong.

A steady *click-click-click* echoed through the corridor. Radiation sensor. The hatches to the damaged cabins had their own radiation shielding, but not so much as the outer hull. It would not be healthy for me to remain back here long.

My footsteps sounded different than in the past. Tinier. Muffled. I had not realized before how many of the ship's sounds depended upon the presence of air in the adjoining cabins.

I peered through the hatch window to my quarters. Sometimes, I set a water bottle by my bed, but I could not remember if I'd done so last night. The shelf where I'd set it, however, was empty. My reflection stared me down. They had red eyes from going too long without blinking. I do not think they approved of me. I could say the same of them.

Something productive. Something productive with every action. That was the Mindnet path. I made a note to trim my hair if I survived the next few days. I'd grown it out to hide the too-colorful fungal mottling, but then I'd stopped thinking about it. Now it was long enough to be a hazard, both to zero-g safety and to dignity.

From the hatch windows along the corridor, I could see into my quarters, the kitchenette, and the medical cabin. They were all in the vacuum. Centimeter-sized debris from System

Defense's flak charges had pierced their bulkheads. Now they were flooded with blueshifted cosmic radiation.

The crew head was even worse. A larger piece of flak debris had torn its aft bulkhead right off. The cabin was entirely open to space, visible from the outside like a cross-section from a blueprint.

The only human foods I ate were nut and bean protein loaves. I didn't trust myself with anything flavored or pleasant. Mindnet medical science rated my biological susceptibility to addictive behaviors as "concerning." My meal packets had been in the kitchenette. The packaging was rated for vacuum conditions but not for the radiation they'd just been soaked with. Another reason to castigate myself for fleeing into FTL so quickly.

It was a balm to my ego, though, to know that it didn't matter at all. Because my biggest problem was water. My next destination, Moll Primus, was ten days away. Most of my shuttle's water supply was now a diffuse cloud back in the Arrix system. My full supply of meal packets wouldn't save me from dying of dehydration before reaching Moll Primus.

It was illogical, irrational, hateful, imbecilic, et cetera, that it actually did make me feel better to know that even if I hadn't screwed up, I would be in the same position. But I felt better, nonetheless.

Of course, then I felt worse about feeling better.

I've heard that other unaugmented humans experience this same tragicomedy every day of their lives. What a delightful species we are. How we have not gone extinct from embarrassment is beyond me.

I still had four habitable spaces to work in. The cockpit and the engineering cabin were intact, though the latter was really more of a crawlspace, and could hardly have been called "habitable" to begin with. The central corridor had air, and would at least allow me to pace. Lastly, the boarding airlock was accessible in the event that I would like to flush myself out into space and die in seven unpleasant ways.

Aside from some broken light strips, these areas remained whole. Just gloomy, and appropriate for my mood.

I wondered if Uthan's Malloc-garden flower print had survived the blast. It was entirely irrational that I was embarrassed by that, but humiliation and indignity was one of the tiny little hells that individuality trapped me in.

No – the damn thing had probably survived. The print had been on one of the intact bulkheads. It was durable. I had tried many times to scrape it off.

I did not appreciate plants. At all.

(You will.)

When I'd burned into the Arrix system, I'd had two reasonably long – half a minute! – conversations with Mindnet. The first to identify myself and convey the intelligence I'd brought them. The second to receive orders as to where and how to participate in the upcoming battle.

Before that, the last person I'd spoken with had been the Mentak diplomat, and that had lasted five sentences. "Conversations" with orbital traffic control stations didn't count, as those were entirely scripted. I must have spoken to *someone* else in the past six months, but the memory escaped me. My most reliable companion was the intrusive thoughts that spoke in another being's voice.

I may have been developing some neuroses.

Humans tended to go off their rockers during long periods

of isolation. Crueler cultures used it as a form of torture for human prisoners. Former Mindnet-augmented humans were probably especially susceptible. I could not say for certain because there had never *been* another human who had grown up with implants and then lost them.

For my own mental health, I needed something to look forward to. I had to get back to Moll Primus and resume my undercover work. Diverting to Arrix had cost me several days. The longer I delayed, the more suspicious I appeared. It was vital that I kept my cover as a Keleres courier. This was the only work I could do that was at all useful to the Mindnet. Which meant it was my only reason to exist.

The Keleres agents among those of you reading this know that the bulk of good spycraft consists principally of two components. The first is drudgework: eons of drudgework, data collection, and teasing narratives out of chaos. The second is luck. I much preferred drudgery. I couldn't ignore luck, though, or even write it off as a variable outside of my control. The damnedest thing about luck was that it couldn't be manipulated, or changed, but it could be made. My intelligence work depended on me making my own luck.

Signals couldn't travel faster than light. Only ships could. Galactic civilization depended on a network of small, fast courier ships. Uthan had a Keleres auxiliary – not a fighter, just support staff – running messages between Mecatol Rex and the Mentak Coalition's home on Moll Primus. After Uthan's departure, I'd kept running the same route… and passing the contents of my messages to the Mindnet when the opportunity allowed.

I gave myself as many opportunities to be in the correct place at the correct moment as possible. That meant traveling from star system to star system. Accepting as many jobs as possible, even the mundane ones, for the sake of establishing connections.

Getting into *gerr* root smuggling was how I'd gotten advance warning of the attack on Arrix. I'd been contacted by a Mentak officer for whom I'd smuggled *gerr* before. She needed to get a message to Mentak leadership on Moll Primus at emergency speed. Because I'd worked with her before, she trusted me.

I doubted she would trust me again after I reached Moll Primus late, even if she believed my excuse. But that was all right. On the gameboard of spycraft, every move was a trade.

In the story I'd tell, I'd been attacked en route. I'd done my part, battled through, and escaped to get my message to Moll Primus. Shucks, too bad that the message was late now. There wasn't anything I could've done. My battle damage would support my claim. So did the current state of galactic affairs. Lately, certain traitor factions – currently the Federation of Sol – had unleashed privateers in Mentak travel lanes in retaliation for the Mentak doing the same.

I shouldn't have even been able to know that her message was time sensitive. Its entangled quantum seal would break if anyone dared to observe its contents. Impossible to breach. Except, of course, for the Mindnet. We had long ago mastered the science of the seemingly impossible.

The message had been an ultimatum from the Barony of Letnev, telling the Mentak not to attempt to reclaim the Arrix system. It was all but an open declaration that the Barony was going to take advantage of the Mindnet's conquest of Arrix and annex it themselves. Great power politics rewarded the arrogant.

My cover would survive an investigation. The Mentak wouldn't be motivated to look too deeply into it. If the Letnev got pasted while trying to snatch the Arrix system… well, that wasn't the Mentak Coalition's problem. I hadn't seen the actual conclusion of the battle, but the outcome had been all but written in the stars: I could safely assume that the Mindnet had retained the system, and the Letnev remnants had gotten dashed across the stars. As far as the Mentak were concerned, it served the Letnev right.

But to keep my resume as my work, I had to survive. I needed food and water. I needed to verify that my engines could still function for that long.

Even Uthan's liquor closet was gone. Thinking about the liquor gave me a strange twist in my gut. The bottles would have burst, and all their contents boiled away. He would have been upset. He'd spent years collecting them. It was one of the strange things humans liked to do: collect things without purpose. He was a man of many vices, but he told me that he could count the number of times he'd opened a bottle on his fingers. For those of you who never studied human biology, that means ten or less. He'd opened a bottle the day that he realized I was going to survive, in spite of it all.

I would never have dared touch them myself – I didn't trust myself with flavored food, let alone *that* – but I had kept them as emergency trade goods. The imperial *aureus* was accepted in most places but not everywhere. A good spy always had alternate bribes available. Addictions couldn't be valued in *aurei*.

Uthan may have looked like an imbecile, and most of the time *was* an imbecile, but he had known his engines. He could have discovered all this in half the time and with half the bruises. For what was far from the first time, I wished Uthan had stayed.

My nails bit into my palms hard enough to hurt. No matter how hard I tried to regulate my thoughts, they often spiraled like this.

I rubbed my sternum, trying to focus on my breathing, and then my more immediate problems.

I couldn't make the mistake the Barony of Letnev kept making, over and over. I couldn't have pride.

I was going to have to stop somewhere and beg for help.

I knew without even checking my star charts that there was only one place along my route that could help.

(There are two places you could go, actually.)

It was a great star system to go if you enjoyed feeling tiny and also tremendously, achingly sad. The latter was tough, but I was accustomed to it. It was the former that I dreaded more. I had enough struggles with individuality to not want to be reminded of it everywhere I looked.

But I didn't have any other choice.

(Come on now.)

I pulled up those star chart projections anyway, but they confirmed what I already knew. Dragging one's feet: another symptom of being merely human.

I instructed my navigation computer to change course toward the buccaneer freeport of Finney Marigold Station. My annotations in the star chart appended its old Lazax name under its icon: Port Vel Syd.

Gateway to the frontier. Gateway to a dead tomorrow.

CHAPTER FOUR
FREEBOOTED

Then

Uthan kept trying to talk to me, but I could not focus on anything but my arm.

All that remained of my implants was discoloration, an orange-black mottled bruising.

It took me several minutes to construct a rational framework with which I could understand what had happened to my body. It would not be the last framework I'd have to build.

I started constructing the mental scaffolding while Uthan spoke. Because the human brain was scarcely worth the cholesterol it was printed on, I lost what he said. I was still expecting my implants to record conversations for later review. Habits could not be reprogrammed in the manner I was accustomed to reprogramming them.

The things happening to me were impossible, dreamlike. I had grown up with my implants. They were embedded deeply into my tissues, and both my nerves and arteries had routed through and around them. It was not possible for them to have been removed without killing me.

It didn't seem likely that this *was* a dream, though. I hadn't dreamed since the night before my implants were installed, when I was four years old. Mindnet implants forbade dreaming. No, the metaphor there was not subtle (and frequently appeared in the anti-Mindnet propaganda), but the Mindnet was endlessly utilitarian, and the fact was that those idle brain cycles could be put to more efficient use.

Plus, there was the pain, and the dizziness, and the scratchy feeling of forever being on the verge of a coughing fit. The crush of sensory overload was too overbearing, too annoying, for what I remembered to be attributed to dreaming.

All of these data points whirled around each other until I found a structure capable of supporting them.

Rational Framework One: this was a simulation. I had been recovered by the Mindnet, but the Mindnet weren't sure if I had been found and corrupted first by other powers. We had placed me into this simulation, wherein the use of my implants had been denied, to see how I would react. On more than one occasion, would-be heroes had tried to infect Mindnet captives with "the virus of individuality" and sent them back to Us.

Those aberrations were easily exterminated, but the attempts had prompted the Mindnet to take precautions.

Uthan was still speaking. His tone had changed, gotten frantic. He seemed to have realized I'd gone unresponsive. I tried to review my implants' recordings of what he'd said, got nothing but silence back, and became terrified and discombobulated all over again.

I considered what idea the Mindnet would have me communicate – *It would be in both of our interests for you to release me at once* – and then translated to words We used to communicate with the merely individual: "Imbecile. You have no idea what you've meddled with. Release me *at once* or be annihilated."

He set a finger to his ear. "Beg pardon?"

I couldn't detect any mockery in the question. My voice was a rasp, difficult for even me to hear. I groaned in frustration and tried again. This time I think he understood.

He pursed his lips and watched me. I stared back with sharpened steel-gray eyes.

"I can see you still need some time," he said. Then he did the last thing anyone in his position should have done with a Mindnet agent, which was leave me alone.

A proper Mindnet agent could have subverted the technology in this cabin in minutes. Even if the usage of direct implant links was *somehow* denied me, there were enough improvised weapons that I could get out of my bindings and–

That thought ended in an abrupt and embarrassing realization. I'd been able to raise my hand unimpeded. There were no bindings.

With effort, I lifted my head far enough to see my ankles. No restraints there, either. But there was that orange-black color, the strange bruising. Dizziness crashed my head into the pillow.

A medical kit was propped open on the counter, with its contents – sensors and drugs and diagnostic computer – splayed out beside it. The kit's sharp metal corners would make it effective as a weapon. Assuming that at some point I could lift it.

Mindnet implants could have, given a few minutes' worth of sensory data from handling the thing, perfectly determined its balance. They could have programmed me with the skills and muscle memory to wield it like I'd drilled with weaponized medical kits all my life.

Without implant-granted strength or implant-mediated skill, it was futile for me to try. At least, in this condition.

The Mindnet would surely have seen things the same way. Incorporated it into the test. The simulation was forcing me to find other ways to resist.

Furious, I stared at the open hatch and waited for Uthan to return. He did not.

Gradually, I realized that I was going to have to be alone with my thoughts.

Oh.

Oh *no*.

I did not have access to an internal clock and could not measure how long I was left there. I did not have much practice measuring time from feeling alone. The last time I'd had to measure the passage of time by how long it had felt, I'd been four years old. Human children are not renowned for their clearheaded perspective on such things.

A flicker of memory, like lightning across a horizon: sitting on a metal bench in a half lit and empty panic room, waiting for my parents to come get me. I had a stuffed Jellybear with me, but its glowing red tummy had long exhausted its entertainment value. My feet did not quite touch the floor, and I was kicking them in and out underneath me. The floor had stopped shaking some time ago, and I did not understand why no one had come for me. I had been alone for several forevers stacked atop each other. After enough of those forevers, the misery progressed to numbness.

I tried to summon that same numbness now, but apparently,

I was less capable of managing boredom than my four-year old self had been. All the forevers stacked on top of me again, their weight suffocating.

I tried twelve times to lift myself out of the medical cot. Each attempt ended in exhaustion. This was no temporary weakness or drug fog. It was not getting better.

I developed and discarded two more theories to explain my circumstances.

Rational Framework Two: this *was* a simulation, but it was a vast and complex means of interrogation devised by Our enemies to extract information from me via torture.

This framework fell apart quickly. Even Our enemies, with their clumsy-idiot technologies, had better means of extracting information than this. If they had the ability to simulate this via direct neural link (and there was no other way *than* neural link to create the illusion that my implants were gone), then they could also have just read my memories directly.

Rational Framework Three: this really was a dream. The mechanisms in my implants designed to prevent such things were malfunctioning. My pains and distractions only seemed more vivid than a dream because I had never actually dreamed as an adult. Perhaps most human adults were constantly tormented by sleep delusions and became inured to it in the same way they became inured to all the other nightmarish aspects of unaugmented existence.

Uthan returned to the medical cabin after three and a half forevers. By necessity, I returned to Rational Framework One. Regardless of the reality of the situation or lack thereof, it was still incumbent on me to act like a proper Mindnet citizen.

I told him: "We will only extend the opportunity to surrender this one last time."

He lifted his bushy red eyebrows, pondering that. Then he left the cabin again.

"Hell," I muttered.

I did not think he realized he was torturing me with isolation. I would have to think much less of him if I did. But the effect was not all that different.

Thumping resounded through the bulkheads. Heavy objects were moved around. The noise didn't sound violent so much as bumbling. After a while, the whole shuttle *thunk-thunk-thunked* as air pumps cycled atmosphere in and out of the airlock chamber.

All of this happened to the background tempo of dread pounding in my ears. Uthan was leaving the shuttle. A pit opened in my stomach. Emptiness and isolation had been difficult concepts for me to grasp until right then, when they suddenly became unbearable.

My thoughts churned in circles. Without machine discipline, they became trapped among themselves, wild and repetitive at the same time. They were uncontrollable, but neither were they free. I only realized later that this was *dwelling*. An uncommonly descriptive word. My worst thoughts came back to me so frequently that they wore grooves into the walls of my brain.

I had to force myself to think in terms of practicalities, and to measure my opposition.

Without access to Mindnet databases, I had only a loose idea about who the Keleres were. A few stray, hauntingly specific fragments, like the exact models of sidearms they used and what their flag looked like, persisted, but they were tantalizing hints of what I'd lost.

What I knew: the Keleres were the special agents of

the Galactic Council on Mecatol Rex, sworn to serve the interstellar community at large. Keleres agents were ostensibly neutral in great galactic power politics. Letnev and Hacan and Federation of Sol humans all fighting together against the existential threats menacing the current galactic order. A category which correctly included the Mindnet.

It was a setup perfect for heroic fiction. Stories of their exploits were dramatized, translated across language and species divides, and distributed across the galaxy.

That was the illusion they wanted to project. Their pride and vanity.

The truth was that Keleres were just as effective as most police agencies, which was to say: not at all. They were as shambolic as they were unwieldy, and their "neutrality" mostly served as plausible deniability for agents nakedly pursuing their home worlds' interests. They existed because the Galactic Council needed to be seen as "doing something" about threats like Us. Keleres officers were career dead-enders, or soldiers shuffled off into political exile, or, most incompetent of all, true believers in interstellar cooperation. From his performance so far, it seemed most likely that Uthan was among the latter.

By the time the outer airlock hatch hissed, I had given myself a stress headache.

Thump, thump, thump. More thumps than before. Moving something heavy around. He was scavenging from the Mindnet wreckage. At least the silence had allowed me to verify that no one else was aboard. Then a long *thwwwip,* which was both familiar and unplaceable.

He was still making the latter noise when he came into the medical cabin, though. He held a deck of cards. He was shuffling them, cutting, bending them with his finger so they'd snap back and make that noise, and then shuffling again.

"We've got some time," he told me. "I could use a distraction."

Another unbidden memory, from sitting alone in that shelter. No one had tied my shoes that morning, and they hung loosely. Eventually I resorted to playing a game: kicking my feet until my shoes flew off and struck the wall. It was nicely, cathartically violent.

Rationalizations cross-circuited in the back of my head. It was important that I not give away information, but perhaps I could extract information from him. And I wouldn't have to be alone with myself. I forced myself to say, "I. Too. Could use a distraction."

To my surprise, Uthan asked permission before lifting me upright. I was caught off guard; for a while, I didn't answer. The question struck me as both bizarre and unnecessary. He waited until I said *yes* before hooking his arms under me and shifting me atop a mound of hand-knitted blankets.

He set a stool between us to serve as a playing surface. I had the strength to hold cards although maintaining a grip was trickier, but that did not matter as much at the beginning.

The game had a theme of interstellar warfare, but its mathematical underpinning seemed simple enough. The cards depicted "suits" of fighters, destroyers, and dreadnoughts, as well as weapons that could fight each of them. There were always higher numbers of fighters than destroyers, and destroyers than dreadnoughts. The bigger ships could defeat the smaller ones… when properly supported. The goal was, through a turn-based discard-and-draw mechanic, to put together a hand that could defeat the opponent.

Holding cards took more physical exertion than seemed possible. Several times, I dropped a card I should have kept hidden, forcing a restart. I was missing more than my implants. My muscles had withered to nothing, as though they'd gone unused for years. It was amazing that I could breathe.

Whether this was by Uthan's design or not, the game soothed my nerves. Math, probability, and outcomes were easier outlets for my anxious energy. An hour – or what felt like an hour – passed before we spoke about anything unrelated to the game.

"So, who am I speaking to?" he asked.

"I am S1L3NT."

He winced. "You didn't need to shout."

"So far as I'm aware, this language doesn't have a more convenient way to communicate capitalizations. They are important. And there are numerals in–"

"You know, I read that L1Z1X naming conventions were silly, but I guess I had to hear it aloud before I really understood."

I could not help my twitch at the way he said Our name. "The name is pronounced" – Uthan raised his free hand to cover his closest ear before I finished – "*L1Z1X*."

The most correct way to say these things would have been with vocal augments subharmonizing a robotic buzz under the numeral-vowels, but I no longer had the hardware for that.

He didn't bring it up again, which I took to be conceding the point. "But your answer is that you are still Mindnet?" he asked.

"Who else would I be?"

"*What* else would you be?" He peered at me over his grip of cards.

"The way in which you altered the question seems to be implying another meaning. If so, you are utterly failing to communicate it."

"You're not in contact with the Mindnet." A statement, not a question.

Fear and insecurity stabbed deep into me. I tightened my grip on my cards, nearly bending them. I had not let him know that I was, mentally speaking, alone, and could not let him know.

"I have never been in deeper contact with the Mindnet," I said. "Nobody has ever been in deeper contact with the Mindnet than I am."

He barked a laugh, as though I'd just told a joke. Seconds later, I decided that, yes – in retrospect, I *had* meant it as a joke.

Ego-soothing self-deception was an emotional trap I had no defenses against.

The rounds we'd played so far had given me chances to bluff him. Not one had passed by him. I abruptly realized that the last time I had lied to anyone had been when I was four years old, when I'd told my parents I had no idea how my stuffed Jellybear's bright red stomach had been torn.

"You're not in contact with anything else?" Uthan asked.

"That is a bizarre question," I said. "The fact that you would ask is more interesting than the obvious answer."

He wouldn't be deflected. "And what is that 'obvious' answer?"

I briefly weighed the success of my last attempt at deception against the value of the information I might receive if I told the truth.

"The obvious answer is no," I said carefully.

If he noticed that I had still avoided a definitive answer, he didn't mention it. He allowed us to sink back into the game.

• • •

Some days must have passed. My awareness faded in and out. Or perhaps the problem was that the days kept slipping out of my memories. My brain and body were coming back to life slowly. I had no idea how long I'd been sealed inside the airlock. Uthan never said, and I never asked him. I approached our conversations from the perspective of a prisoner under interrogation, and never voluntarily spoke… unless it was about our games.

Most sentient species developed a need for play and fun. From a utilitarian perspective, it was a means to model behavior during learning. In a startling example of convergent evolution, life across the galaxy even used a similar facial expression to indicate when they were playing: upturned lips, mouth slightly open, jaw loose. Across the galaxy, that look said that your playground friend whiffing the foam blade at you wasn't *really* a Sardakk N'orr berserker about to decapitate you.

The Lazax used to be able to have fun. They extirpated fun when they became L1Z1X.

That had the sound of dry humor, but it was not a joke. The first L1Z1X had removed their ability to have a "play face" to fit more augments, like enzyme microfactories so that their saliva could actually break down one of the few foods capable of growing where they had been exiled.

Mindnet citizens had no need to play-model behavior when they could transfer millennia of experience between themselves with a flicker of thought. The same went for all their cybernetically enhanced subjects. Especially those of us brought into the Mindnet when we were young. I never needed to play don't-get-decapitated-by-N'orr-berserkers when I could review memories of real N'orr decapitations. There were many of those. Decapitations made retrieving brain implants easier.

I didn't have fun, I never wanted to have fun, and I didn't imagine I'd enjoy it.

But now it turned out that I had to. Like any highly evolved social function, evolution had barnacled a bunch of other purposes onto *fun*. Like emotional self-defense. It was a way to play things off as unserious when they were tremendously serious – or worse, tremendously annoying.

Uthan handily won the most games. Which was tremendously annoying. Though better than being left with my thoughts. And it kept me in a sparring mindset.

Somewhere in the deck was a single War Sun, a devastatingly powerful starship that could win games alone… unless properly anticipated. A player planning to use it had certain tells. Withholding resources, holding back their fleets from certain encounters. The trick was that the optimal strategy for a player holding the War Sun looked like a slightly *sub*optimal strategy from a player without one. It opened a wide range of guessing and bluffing.

"I want to talk about something you said to me when you woke up," Uthan said. "You said, 'I'm going to have to steal your shuttle now.'"

I surprised myself by wishing he would focus on the game. I had to find out if he was holding the War Sun. "You do not have to tell me what you would like to talk about. You could simply talk about it."

"You said 'going to *have* to' like it was something you'd be forced to do."

Thanks to the game, I was almost starting to enjoy the feeling of fencing. Or perhaps my brain was so drunk with fatigue toxins and stress hormones that it made me want to talk. "Free will is an illusion," I said. "Our choices are written in the unfolding quantum waveform of the universe. At no point do 'we' as independent actors appear in the waveform equations."

"You could try to be less obvious when you evade my question."

I fixed him in my stare. "That was not evasion. You could have heard the answer if you were smart enough to listen."

He frowned and leaned back.

Out in the rest of the galaxy, it was a popular misconception that the Mindnet turned individuals into robots. Mindnet implants, like the Mindnet itself, prized efficiency. They never assumed direct control of an individual's actions. The technology needed to fully remote control something so complex as a body was impractical, likely impossible. The Mindnet had never wasted resources trying to develop that.

Much better to train a person to act in a way the Mindnet preferred.

Since the age of four years old, my implants had observed my thoughts. When they detected thoughts worth being rewarded, they released endorphins and dopamine. Conversely, thoughts critical of the Mindnet were punished with low-grade pain impulses or otherwise suppressed.

This usually happened before any of those thoughts reached my conscious attention. In this way, with a touch as light as a dusting of snow, the Mindnet had restructured my brain. Without my implants, that structure persisted.

"No," Uthan said at last. "Still not getting it."

Of course, he wasn't.

This was not any different for humans without implants. Their minds were also governed by structures molded by neurotransmitter rewards and punishment. The fact that their brains were not shaped by conscious intent did not make them morally superior, nor did it mean they had "free will."

We are all material creatures. Some materials are better than others.

"I will trade you information for information," I said. If Rational Framework One was true, surely the Mindnet couldn't hold that against me.

He shrugged. "Go ahead."

"What is the date?" I asked.

The calendar date he gave me was two and a half months past my survey ship's crash. That was either an obvious lie or obviously incorrect. I'd directed my implants to preserve (some of) my brain, but my body wouldn't have lasted that long. It would have withered into a mummified mound of skin and bone.

"What do you intend to do with me?" I asked.

"Good question," he said. "No idea."

"Are you… serious?" I tried to remember an appropriate swear word to insert between *you* and *serious,* but couldn't manage in time. The only one I'd managed to remember, *hell,* didn't fit.

"I don't know what, or who, you are, or what happened to you," he said. "I came here for a side hustle. Do some scavenging from a Mindnet wreck. I detected a non-Mindnet life form, no implants, and found you somehow still alive. And still saying that you're part of the Mindnet. What would *you* do?"

Easy answer. "I would simply contact the Mindnet for further instructions."

He snorted. "All right – what would you do in my position?"

"I would contact the Mindnet for further instructions." All my problems, from my missing implants to the mystery of how exactly I *had* stayed alive but insensate, would be better addressed with the full processing power of the Mindnet behind them.

"Not 'simply' that time," Uthan muttered. "There's also the issue of – well –" He waved his arm vaguely in my direction.

"The issue of what?"

"What you can see on your arms. There's more of it on the rest of you."

I looked again at the orange-black mottling along my arm. "Is that not what bruised or necrotic human tissue looks like?"

Even as I said that, I knew that wasn't right. My half-functioning neurons had done that ridiculous thing human brains did and made a leap: injury plus mottled discoloration meant bruising. But not… orange.

Uthan gave me a look I struggled to interpret. It involved a raised eyebrow. He shook his head. His eyes were still on his cards, but his mind seemed to be everywhere else. Perhaps his thoughts were where mine had been minutes ago: deciding whether the cost of revealing something was worth it.

"No," he said finally. "What that *does* look like, and what all of the instruments in my little medical suite are telling me, is fungus."

"That is not possible." The reasons for that were countless, which did not stop me from beginning to enumerate them. "Life on this planet is single-celled. It is not complex enough to have evolved distinctions between plant and fungi kingdoms. If it were, it would not have the means to invade or survive in an alien body. If it somehow *did,* it would have evolved no defenses against my immune system, which was engineered to combat a multitude of alien–"

"I know what it is," he interrupted. "It's not native to this planet." He set his cards face down on the stool. He was entirely focused on studying me now: a deeply uncomfortable feeling, like an itch on the back of my head. "It's Arzuga. As in – from the Arborec. The fungus it uses to reanimate the dead. It's not like other kinds of it I've seen. It's probably been here long enough to mutate."

I knew what those words meant. I even knew what they implied. But the emotional impact, which I was sure even my old Mindnet implants would have struggled to regulate, was too big to strike. It jammed my brain. Tried to fight too much through my synapses all at once.

But something did slot neatly into my memory. The mottling on my arms *was* familiar. I had not seen Arzuga fungus before, but other members of the Mindnet had. Scraps of their memories still fluttered about inside me, waiting for the right gust to blow them into my hands.

Other members of the Mindnet had seen this patterning before: on the dead. As their remains were colonized by the fungus that turned them into mindless mouthpieces for that hideous plant collective.

Uthan and I were not the first galactic civilization to have visited Kitrya-892 b. The Arborec, the galaxy-spanning plantmind and recycler of the dead, had come here first.

It had left some spores behind. And those were what had grown in me.

(Hello.)

"Interesting," I said.

"That's the only thing you have to say?"

Rational Framework Four: I was dead, and this was the afterlife.

I discarded that one very quickly. There was no such thing as an afterlife. The Mindnet had concluded so, and therefore it was a mistake to even consider it. In Rational Framework One, which was again becoming more attractive, thinking about it threatened my chances of passing the test.

"Can we play the game?" I asked.

CHAPTER FIVE
DEAD LIGHT

Now

Aside from cybernetic transmission or perhaps telepathic contact, there is no perfect medium of communication. Since I have access to neither, I am forced to use words to express myself. But every imperfect medium has opportunities to transcend its limitations.

Those of you reading this as a formal report, particularly any debriefing officers, may be wondering why I've employed the literary device of interleaving chronologically separate segments together. You may mistake it for play.

One of the many things that appalls the Mindnet about our interactions with the rest of the galaxy is the common assumption that cybernetic augmentation means we think only linearly and perceive only straightforwardly. The Mindnet is full of scientific curiosity. The first lesson we learned is that there are more and better ways of understanding the universe than the straightforwardly linear.

If you're looking for an hour-by-hour recounting of events, you'll find plenty of fodder in flight logs, security cameras, and other accounts.

Few sentients with depth perception will easily mistake a flat image for a view of a real object. Two flat images side by side, taken from different angles, can create a stereogram illusion of three dimensions.

These two incidents, over seven years apart, are the two times in my life when I was farthest from the Mindnet. At the beginning of each of these experiences, I was more like myself than at any point between. For reasons that will become clear, I backslid between them. The contrast between them is more illuminating than either separately.

Like a stereogram image, I take shape in the contrasts.

I spent enough hours lodged in the engineering crawlspace to verify that my shuttle's engines could handle a course change. That did not stop the engines from complaining mightily as, two days after the battle in the Arrix system, I dropped anchor into the fabric of spacetime. A deep-throated grumble shook my consoles. It vibrated up through my seat and made my teeth itch.

The blueshifted light ahead had spent most of the day dimming. Only some of the effect came from the fact that my shuttle had been slowing. There were simply fewer stars to see. I had entered an optical void.

"Finney Marigold Station," which I would always think of as Port Vel Syd, was lodged deep in the armpit of the galaxy. That wasn't the technical term, but it was no less accurate.

With a final groan of stressed metal, the shuttle juddered back into the relativistic universe. The pinprick blue light ahead turned diffuse and scattered. Over the next few minutes, it blossomed into a cloud. The color seeped out of it until it turned to milk and pearl.

All of it was starlight. A wall of it, far distant, just visible to my eyes against the dim lighting of my cockpit. The stars were far dimmer than they had been near Arrix.

This was a gap in space, a void formed from the whirlpool of gravitational eddies and angular momentum that kept the galaxy spinning.

The effect only accentuated the feeling that I had dropped into a pit. If there hadn't been the same sight in every other direction, I could have convinced myself that I'd left the galaxy entirely. That I was below the plane of the galactic disk and seeing the galaxy as it had been millions of years ago, not as it was.

Space travel did not inspire subtle poetry.

In the three millennia since the fall of the Lazax Empire, the civilizations that followed had characterized these voids… colorfully. The aforementioned armpit. A belch in space. A fart working its way out between the spiral's arms.

An alarm on my console sounded. It helpfully screeched that there was an astonishingly small, hyperdense object ahead.

Port Vel Syd orbited a neutron star that had ebbed its last heat away long ago. It was a cold, black-body object, a stellar corpse.

The Lazax student astronomer who'd discovered the neutron star had named it Wildshot. It was a miracle she'd found it at all. The story that circulated afterward was that her advisor had given her a list of two thousand cubic parsecs and told her to pick a dozen to rerun prior astronomers' calculations upon, ostensibly to test to see if she could replicate their results. It was the kind of task that advisors give to students who they desperately wished would quit.

Rather than take the hint, she'd pressed on. In the very first cubic parsec she checked, she found an error. What the original team had thought had been minor gravitational lensing from a nearby object turned out to be major lensing from a much more distant and massive object. According to the legend, her advisor had been one of those original astronomers.

Whether any of that was true had never been properly recorded. The Lazax liked to tell stories about upstarts getting the better of the old and moribund. Nobody ever imagines themselves as the latter. The ancient Lazax had been far from perfect. They could be just as blinded by pride as the Barony of Letnev today.

Whatever method in which this neutron star had actually been discovered, its presence made this stellar void valuable. It was not just why the Lazax had built the station ahead, but why it had endured past their demise. People kept trying to live here and repair it.

A tiny, fingernail-sized patch of the dusty starscape shimmered.

Light lensed around the neutron star's gravity well. I'd never be able to see the dead star itself. The thing was hardly ten kilometers in diameter. If I were close enough to see it, the gravitational shear would have ripped my dinky shuttle apart.

This neutron star was not *all* that massive, not by stellar standards. This one had about one and a half times the mass of the typical G-type yellow star. But that typical star's mass was spread so far that measuring its volume in cubic kilometers required a number with twenty-four zeros after it. The neutron star concentrated all of that into just five hundred.

It was a commonplace analogy in introductory astronomy classes that a teaspoon of a neutron star matter, if somehow deposited on a standard gravity world, would have weighed one trillion kilograms. That was as close as an individual's imagination could come to grasping it. So much of the way the universe worked was beyond the capacity of most sentients to understand.

It was one of the reasons why the Mindnet, with Our infinitely scalable imagination, held Ourselves above any civilization composed of mere individuals. The universe belonged to Us in ways that it could not possibly belong to any of you reading this.

Or to me.

With years of study, I couldn't have climbed halfway to the level of understanding that the Mindnet used to provide for me. As it was, I could only sum it up clumsily.

Starships couldn't travel at past light speed near planets and stars. The closer one came to a high-gravity object like a sun, the more difficult it became for starships to tell relativistic physics to stop bothering them. The problem was chaos. Faster-than-light calculations needed perfect information. It was far easier to get perfect information in the interstellar void. Solar systems were too chaotic, too full of gravitational currents and eddies. So starships had to cut below light speed.

Usually.

A simple system with few stellar neighbors – like this one – was easier to predict. It presented some opportunities that weren't available in other systems. Like launching a big, lumbering ship – such as a colony-building ship – into a tight, fast orbit around the neutron star. A fancy slingshot maneuver around the neutron star could borrow enough of a gravity boost for a quick trip to light speed. Done correctly, a colony ship designed to withstand the gravitational shear could start its trip with a significant advantage. It was an immense fuel saver.

The physics of the neutron star itself were perfect for other industrial applications. Certain high-density coolants, heat sinks, and superconductors could only be made inside a super strong gravity well. Those same products had numerous applications on starships, on power generators, and *especially* on newly founded colony worlds still setting up energy infrastructure.

All this combined to make the station a perfect location for building colony ships, and as a waystation for those planning to board them.

As I watched, a second object, much closer, blotted out the stars.

The immense, ancient space station ahead had worn many names over its decamillennia. It had been called Port Vel Syd *before* the birth of the visionary Ibna Vel Syd, but the rest of the Vel Syd family has been forgotten by history.

Ibna Vel Syd had started the chain of events that led to the creation of the Mindnet. He'd seen the arc of history bend toward the Lazax Empire's destruction. He had spoken loudly, fervently, about the genocidal ideation stirring among the empire's most rebellious members, especially the Federation of Sol and the Barony of Letnev. He had seen the weaknesses in the imperial fleets, the fair-weather friendship of the empire's other subjects.

The Imperial Court only ever regarded him as a crank. So he had taken his followers, stolen a starship, and abandoned the empire – burning Mecatol Rex's Hall of Cartographers behind him to inhibit any efforts to track him.

Port Vel Syd had been among the many family holdings he had given up to flee the empire. In a flurry of pique, the Lazax Empire had renamed it and given it to one of Vel Syd's rivals. The name change had lasted all of ten weeks before the massacres began.

Unlike all those other Lazax, Ibna Vel Syd still lived. He was cocooned in life-extending cybernetics, deep underneath the surface of our refuge world.

My upper lip trembled. At least rage was a distraction from thirst.

This station had been a target, too. Like Mecatol Rex itself, it still existed as a husk of what it had been.

Eventually enough of the sky vanished that I could make out the station's shape in silhouette. It was a long, shallow, impossibly thin crescent. Slender towers sprung from the central spine like teeth on a comb, all arranged on the outer edge. Its distance and my still-considerable velocity made sight-gauging size impossible, but I knew each of those teeth was ten kilometers long. There were two rows of them, bending inward like kitchen tongs. All of it had been part of a massive shipbuilding yard.

This was the point at which it looked most impressive. The darkness kept me from being able to see the extent of the ancient war damage and all the subsequent decay.

(A living system would have been able to heal itself by now. But this is what it always has been: dead.)

Almost dead, I corrected. At the very center of the structure, there was a small light.

Another helpful screech. Incoming signal.

The station authorities were calling with the usual greetings for this part of the galaxy: "Greetings, unscheduled incoming craft. Welcome to Finney Marigold Station. We have acquired a targeting solution. Please identify yourself and follow the appended flight plan precisely or be rendered into component particles."

The station's current management was one of a long string of halfwit speculators, jumped-up gangs, grifters, and other "imaginative entrepreneurs." People who operated beneath – or beyond – the Galactic Council's legal system. Criminals and smugglers, in other words. Occasionally, someone with grand designs for putting the station to its original use as a construction yard for colony ships took power. Their efforts ended in failure and frustration.

My latest intelligence said that the station's administration had changed hands in a bloody coup, but that barely anything had changed afterward. No matter what future the station's keepers planned for it, to maintain it in the present, they always turned to the only income stream available to them: smugglers and outlaws.

I did as the voice asked, though I'd been broadcasting an IFF signal since I dipped below light speed. My false identity had even been supplied by the Keleres I ostensibly worked for. The Keleres knew just how many places their agency wasn't welcome around the galaxy. Even their couriers would be at risk if they broadcasted their identity everywhere.

I doubted the station authorities would look into my credentials closely. This was a test to see if I'd follow directions. And a way to compel me to take a strange software package aboard. The only way to see the flight path they'd sent, and thus the only way to avoid being shot down, was to open it without taking the time to properly check it.

Though my Mindnet algorithms were operating on inferior hardware, they still made quick work of the software package. The flight plan had advertisement malware, a backdoor-installing rootkit, and what looked like a piggybacked obsolete Yssaril spyware kit. This was just what they sent every visitor, though. Nothing indicated I'd gotten special attention. A visiting Yssaril agent must have installed that last one a while ago. The port authorities probably didn't even know about it.

My algorithms did a good job of mimicking all the secret handshakes their bugs were supposed to send back. "Thank you," the station transmitted. "Please let us know what your business is here or prepare to become an atom-thin sheen on the surface of our neutron star."

No sense hiding it. If their scopes hadn't seen the burns and holes all over my shuttle, they would soon. "Battle damage repair," I said. The fact that I'd been without water for two days gave my voice some extra gravel. I hoped it made me sound dangerous rather than desperate.

I resisted the urge to hold my breath. There was always a chance that the station's owners would try to take advantage of a wounded lone shuttle. But all that came back on the next transmission was a half-dozen advertisements for ship repair services. I selected one at random. The station sent back directions to a docking berth, which I was to approach "or be turned into a bright, artful, but poignantly brief splash of color among the stars."

I sent back my gratitude.

My course took me along the station's arched spine. As I slowed, the scale of it all became more tangible. The comb-teeth became towers, then starscrapers – then world-bridging shadows.

I didn't want to see any more than that. But it felt inevitable, like staring into a tunnel and feeling the air *thrum* with an oncoming magtrain. My hand found the controls for the cockpit window's filters. Port Vel Syd reflected a minute amount of starlight; I amplified those colors until the station's silhouette gained texture.

The station's hull looked blackened, covered in pitch and tar. Like it was covered in seeping burns. These weren't the weapon scars. The difference between battle damage and millennia of neglect was not all that stark.

The discoloration came from vacuum erosion: cosmic rays breaking down the hull's molecules or liberating them entirely, year after year after year. The hull plating was meant to be replaced every thousand years. Space had left the hull blotchy and threadbare, like a mistreated sweater. In some places, the outer layer had ablated away from small asteroid impacts, exposing threads of crosshatched support framework.

(This should have been so much more than the husk it became. It could have been made to grow and heal and adapt organically.)

My other self, the me inside of me, preferred everything to be organic. It spoke with the voice of the Arborec. It was a repository for my forbidden thoughts, and one of those forbidden thoughts was that the Arborec was puppeteering me. That all the medical scans I had submitted to since my infection were wrong, and that tendrils of Arzuga fungus lived in my brain. To even argue with it would be to acknowledge its presence and give it power.

Emotional turmoil only made the intrusive thoughts louder.

I had to look at my dashboard's projectors, to remember where I was. The rage and the grief that accompanied thoughts of the genocide of the Lazax were one of the few emotional disturbances that Mindnet implants didn't quash, even when they threatened to disrupt our functioning. These things shouldn't have been forgotten.

Some of Port Vel Syd's decay might have come from natural asteroid collisions and wear, but a mere three millennia was not enough to have accumulated many of those. The deepest scars had been incurred during the original bombing. During the Twilight Wars.

The bombs had carved enormous gashes, hundreds of meters wide, exposing the entrails of breached corridors and cabins. Though the craters could have swallowed my shuttle, the damage might have been much worse. The bombs were meant to make entrances for EV-suited soldiers and hunter drones. They'd gone in to massacre any Lazax, or Lazax ally, who'd survived.

The traitors had meant to "preserve" the station. Rather than destroy the whole thing, they'd merely turned it into a cremated husk of ashes and bones. They'd believed that, after the genocide of the Lazax, they would be able to simply shift into the Lazax's place and seize the mantle of rulership.

What actually happened was that the usurpers had fallen into fighting among themselves. The carefully wound mechanisms of imperial statecraft fell apart. Technologies whose maintenance depended on smoothly functioning economies failed, and the galaxy collapsed into thousands of years of darkness.

In all the millennia that had passed since then, and through all the efforts the successor civilizations had made to crawl back into the light… in all that time, not one of Port Vel Syd's successive owners had been able to restore more than a nub of the old structure.

None of them had gotten the shipyards functional again. No one had rediscovered the lost science the Lazax used to manufacture exotic materials.

The station's newer occupants had supposedly repaired the old Lazax asteroid deflectors, but that was, so far, the extent of their restoration work. There was no point in any of them even *being* here, except to stake a claim. To deny others the opportunity to do what they were failing to do.

Monsters, all of them. Monsters throughout their history. Monsters in the present.

Uthan once informed me that I would be spectacular company at parties.

He, like me, used humor as a defense mechanism. None of the Lazax Empire's successor civilizations saw clearly enough to perceive what a bleak galaxy they had made. The L1Z1X Mindnet carried not only the burden of memory, but of context.

My shuttle came closer to the station's only inhabited section. My docking berth awaited. Guiding beacons flashed ahead of me, forcing the window filters to reset. The station's hull vanished again, reduced to silhouette, and I could breathe easier.

Here, things started to look a little better. On the outside. My shuttle coasted across a field of dappled light. From far away, the place almost looked like a city. Thousands of window lights shone into the vacuum. But most of those windows looked into empty corridors. Sometime in the station's recent history – "recent" being a relative word – one of the station's rotating cast of managers had slapped light strips on the interior ceilings. Those strips' power sources had half-lives of centuries. Even still, some of them had dimmed.

The ten-kilometer-long control hub was set apart from the station, a half-sphere mounted on the crescent's inner curve. Here, the hull breaches had been repaired, life support equipment of questionable provenance brought in, and half an economy cobbled together. They maintained cutthroat gray and black markets, catering to a combination of rebellious rich youth and people who had a lot of money to spend and didn't want to be asked a lot of questions about where it came from.

Even here, Port Vel Syd had the population density of a wasteland. There were only a few pockets of people scattered elsewhere throughout the hulk. The station authorities kept a tight watch on incoming ships because, once people got aboard the megastructure, it was nigh impossible to root them out. Violent recluses, cults, and the pettiest of petty criminals had taken shelter in their various nooks. There were even rare well-meaning scientists and archaeologists, studying lost Lazax technology… though they rarely survived the other groups for long.

My docking berth jutted out at the far end of a fragile looking starbridge tower. I would have preferred a landing bay with a nice double airlock, but those had been the first thing the traitors had targeted all those millennia ago. This tower had been kludged on to the preexisting hull.

The latching mechanism was a set of twelve pincer claws, bending and telescoping to grasp my shuttle. Subtle. The claws' grip was surprisingly gentle. I couldn't decide whether that was part of the metaphor or not. When the airlock seals made contact, I was already waiting at the pressure hatches.

The closer I came to fresh water supplies, the more unbearable the thirst became.

The airlock hatches rolled open to a technician standing on the other side. She was alone, the long corridor behind her empty. She wore a full pressure suit, as if she didn't trust her own starbridge. Comforting. The airtight helmet didn't stop her from looking doubtfully around the airlock as if smelling it. Or me.

Her helmet speaker picked up her muttering. "…going to be a story for the…"

"Shut up," I instructed her. Politely, I thought.

She stiffened. "Ma'am."

I was not a ma'am but did not care enough to correct that. "Send me an estimate of the costs of repair and resupply," I said, already moving past her. "You must have a waiting area."

"No waiting area," she said. "Estimates take a day or two. Also, they're not free."

I was not in a mood to negotiate. I flipped my hand over my shoulder. "No. You'll be getting enough out of me already."

The starbridge walkway was long and segmented, with rubbery joints so that it could flex in different directions. It bent like a straw to attach to the side of my shuttle. The floor was disturbingly responsive to my footsteps like a swaying bridge.

I reached the first and only bend in the skybridge and halted to look across it. The skybridge was lined with windows. From my shuttle, the station had looked enormous; in person, it looked like a whole world. I was walking toward a sheen of metal that spanned the horizon.

The Mindnet in me abhorred the windows even as the rest

of me appreciated the view. At least I knew how far I had to walk.

"No free estimates," the technician insisted, catching up to me. "They're not my rules."

"I would like to speak with your manager."

Silence followed, as it often did when I deployed that powerful phrase. But this silence lasted a little too long. Something else was going on. I looked back.

The technician's eyes had gone wide. "I needed to have been notified of any state visit. Or *anything* official. We didn't take this job to get wrapped up in politics."

I tensed, trying not to show it. Some worlds, like Mecatol Rex, had sensors to root out Mindnet tech. It was an endless arms race to discover new ways to hide Our agents, while the Galactic Council made countermeasures to our countermeasures. That was what made me valuable.

For a dizzying moment, I was afraid the locals had developed a means to suss me out, anyway. Some way to detect the Mindnet algorithms in my shuttle's systems, or something based on Druaa telepathy.

But the technician simply stared at me. No. Not quite *at* me. At the side of my face, the base of my neck. And the black-orange blotching above my neckline.

(All she did was perceive you as you are.)

"I've seen that before," she said. There was a sharper disgust in her voice, entirely unrelated to my hygiene. "You did the same thing to the body of a friend of mine."

Before the battle at the Arrix system, I'd chosen practical starship clothes, with tightly cuffed sleeves and a short neck, in case gravity had gone out. That was all I'd had since. All my other outfits had been lost in my vacuum-vented quarters.

A hundred answers jammed against the back of my throat. I resisted the impulse to touch my neck. The Arzuga fungus still itched when I paid attention to it.

I'd been isolated in my ship for so long that I hardly thought about how I looked. At the cost of a million Mindnet lives, I could not let these people know that I was anything other than what I appeared to be.

"Yeah," I told her, before turning and continuing down the starbridge. "I'm a zombie."

CHAPTER SIX
CATEGORY ERROR

Then

"I am absolutely *not* a zombie."

"You're sure about that?" Uthan asked, doubtfully.

Yes, I was. Somewhat. The less I thought about what I'd just told Uthan about the illusion of free will, though, the better.

Uthan and I had played another two rounds before the emotional impact of his news had finally squeezed its way through the logjam in my synapses. My grip on my cards had faltered. When I spotted orange-black underneath my index finger's nail, I'd thrown my cards down in sudden revulsion.

He'd said I'd been in the shuttle two months. *Two months.*

I should have died. But here I was.

"I have a mind," I said. "I have subjective experiences of my own. I am, therefore, not a zombie."

"That does seem like something a zombie would lie about, though."

"Are you trying to tell a joke?"

Uthan raised his eyebrows. He'd spoken with the cadence of a joke, but I wasn't sure if *he* knew if he was joking or not. He didn't answer.

"It is not very funny," I said.

"No," he admitted.

The discoloration on my hands and arms – and presumably on the rest of my body, though I didn't have the emotional courage to check – resembled bruising except for the color. The orange was at its brightest, and the black at its deepest, where the fungus breached my skin.

When I set my fingers on those, the surface felt soft and velvety. Like ordinary human body fuzz, but spongier. Or like moss scum on wood. But *only* my fingers felt it. The surface itself was numb to the touch, as sensate as a scab.

I wished it hurt. That would at least have meant that it wasn't part of me; that my body recognized that something was wrong.

Most of it was, like a bruise, under the skin. It wormed into my flesh, into my atrophied muscles, my soft tissues. There were no distinct boundaries between the fungus and my body; I could not tell exactly where the one ended and the other began. The fungus had either grown into and around my body, or worse – my body had adapted to *it*. Grown into it.

When I peered closer, I saw bright red capillaries branching into the orange-black fungus. Feeding it my blood.

This was the sight that caused me to lose my mind.

My fingernails were much longer than I remembered. There was a clue to tease from that, but I didn't have the capacity to chase it now. I set my nails atop one of the fuzzy orange-black regions, and dug them in.

That was when the pain arrived.

I couldn't fight through it. The pain was bone-deep and nauseating. The fungus may have been insensate, but the tissues they'd merged with were not. With my implants, I would have been able to manually numb those nerves and continue digging out the intruder. Without it, the pain sapped what strength my fingers had, and made my whole body feel like quivering jelly.

I tried again. My nails left white indents over the fungus, but that was all. I had not broken its surface.

Uthan didn't interfere. Just watched. I think he was curious to see what would happen.

"I *demand* access to all the medical data you've collected about me," I said, because if I didn't do something with my voice, I was going to scream. "Everything. Brain scan, cardiovascular map–"

Uthan leaned back against his cabinets and waved at the bulkheads. "Does it look like I have a million-*aurei* medscanner here? What you see is what I've got. This sickbay is just for emergencies. To keep me intact long enough to get to a hospital."

I certainly couldn't let myself be taken to an enemy hospital. And he was right. I'd *seen* the lack of equipment, but in the fever of my panic, my thoughts and my voice had become unmoored from each other. My brain was overheating.

Uthan told me everything he knew. Or everything he said he knew. My pulse, blood pressure, and respiration were lower than normal, but not out of bounds. It was a strange relief to hear that I was, technically, alive.

He was more evasive on the subject of body temperature. He started by saying my temperature was "fine now." I stared daggers until he told me more. When he'd first detected me, his shuttle's sensors hadn't been able to get an exact reading on my heat signature, not through the airlock hatch. When he'd opened it, though, his suit's heat sensor had given him a reading he didn't think he could believe. My body temperature hadn't dropped down to ambient, but still far too low for human life.

He'd been wearing heavy gloves and hadn't been able to check my pulse until he'd dragged me back here. By then, my body temperature was human standard.

He said he'd nearly melted down, thinking that I was a Dirzuga zombie or Mindnet trap or that his stun shots had killed me, but I did not pay attention to those parts of his story. I did not want to hear about his "emotional turbulence." I was lost under a tempest of my own. Politeness was an alien concept, but even then I thought it was rude to talk about his trauma while I was sitting right there. In a contest of recent traumas, mine could clobber his.

He'd had all his life to work on coping strategies, while I was rapidly realizing my emotional intelligence hadn't developed since I was four. Without implants, my clockwork brain could only manage so much before it broke.

Scraps of Mindnet memories still fluttered about my brain, snagging in the gears, threatening to collapse the whole system. Dreamlike images of the Arborec, seen through other Mindnet citizens' eyes, jammed my senses.

A Dirzuga whose body had once belonged to the Mindnet. Their skin was pitted with open cavities where their implants had once been, all the way down to bone and skull. Their flesh was exposed, but they did not bleed. Fungus knitted over the abscesses. Their gaze never quite met Ours.

A green moon blanketed in clouds and orange sunlight. The moon was so small that any atmosphere should have been lost in mere millions of years after the moon's formation. Millennia of fungal colonization had churned the carbon – and oxygen-rich ice into a thick greenhouse, though. Today, millions of square kilometers of jungle sweltered underneath the clouds, fed nutrients dropped by photosynthesizing airborne algae.

A sensor map of an Arborec vessel. Bright purple solar sails webbed with veins of sap. A knobby wooden hull stood firm against the vacuum, scurrying with antlike servitor-organisms. Those same engine sacs split like blossoming flowers, spewing weaponized plasma into the Mindnet vessel taking those scans.

A line of golden-white explosions ripping across the greenhouse moon. Our fire shredded the algae clouds and brewed up storms laced thick with radiation. Devastation on a scale that troubled even Our imagination. Though not Our conscience.

Even for Us, conceiving of the Arborec had required a radical revision of the way we understood life. The present-day Galactic Council argued over whether the Arborec should even be qualified for membership. The argument in favor had won only because the Arborec was plainly as powerful as any of the other factions that made up that squabbling organization.

The Arborec was not an organization. It was not a culture, or civilization. It had no society. It was a single body with a single mind, sprawled across the stars.

I could not remember having eaten but I wanted to vomit.

Once again, I was forced to reckon with the terrible idea that this was how unaugmented humans felt all the time.

Overwhelmed. Limited. Drowning in confusion and hate. So eager to lash out at anything, anyone, to make it better.

(I am here. With you.)

"I would like to be left alone," I announced.

I'd cut Uthan off in the middle of a sentence. I didn't think his eyebrows could rise any higher, but I was incorrect. "From the way you took to that game, I was getting the idea you hated being alone."

"I am capable of hating many things," I said. The thought of being left alone with my thoughts was just as awful as before, but the alternative was worse.

Uthan shrugged. "Fair enough," he said, and left.

It was ridiculous for him to leave anyone he suspected could be a Mindnet agent *or* an Arborec appendage alone. His carelessness with his own security only further enraged me. Worse was the fact that I could not do anything to take advantage of it.

Probably.

I reconsidered that. He had left me sitting. My muscles had the strength to keep me that way. My legs hung over the side of the cot. I swung them in and out, testing their strength. Thinking of that human child swinging their legs in the panic room. Last time, I'd pushed that thought away. This time, it felt like an anchor, mooring me to something I understood.

My muscles had badly atrophied in the time since the crash. If I'd gone without food for so long as to be reduced to this, I should have starved to death.

That led to Rational Framework Five: Uthan was lying, and I'd kept myself fed and somehow lost those memories.

It left many, many questions open, but it was a scaffolding

from which I could plausibly construct the answers. If I could prove that Uthan was lying, I could disregard so much else.

I kept tensing and stressing my muscles. Legs, then arms, then wrists and ankles. I planted my heels on the deck and tested placing different weights on them.

The pain of this entire ordeal was incredible. The problem was not that my muscles had atrophied, but what remained hadn't been used in ages. I stretched until I heard the hatch to the crew head shut. Then, letting the pain weave under the skein of my senses, I wobbled to my feet.

The medical cabin was tiny, which worked in my favor. The cabinets, the frame of the hatch, and bulkheads were all in arm's reach and supported my weight.

The corridor outside was cramped, too, and lined with emergency handholds for the event of gravity failure. I considered trying to lock the hatch to the crew head, sealing Uthan inside… but it was in the opposite direction I needed to go, and I couldn't guarantee a foolproof way to do it.

Much of the path was blocked by damaged Mindnet equipment, arranged in stacks and waiting to be categorized. Scrape marks on the deck trailed to the airlock. I didn't think Uthan would find much of value, but I made a mental note to work out a way to dump or destroy all of this later, just in case.

The slight staircase to the cockpit was the most difficult thing I had done in my life. My head felt somewhere far above the clouds, and my vision narrowed to a tunnel, but somehow, I avoided blacking out. If Rational Framework One turned out to be true, I hoped the Mindnet would be proud of me for that. When I reached the pilot's seat, I collapsed into it, half on my side.

I was immersed in a starscape of soft lights, control backlighting and green ready indicators. The cockpit window was opaqued. It did not escape my notice that there were two seats in the control cabin. Courier craft like these were traditionally two-person. One pilot, one interstellar navigator.

It did take me several minutes for my sight to return to normal. The crew head's hatch opened and closed. Meandering bootsteps tapped along the deck, but none of them sounded urgent or close.

I waved my hand in front of the nearest projector. A simple, flat menu of branching options unfolded in front of me, written in standard *univoca*. Even after so many millennia, the same civilizations responsible for the old empire's destruction now clung to the formal imperial language like an heirloom. They hadn't made anything better in the meantime.

Nearly every ship function, from engines to atmospherics to the temperature of the water in the crew head's shower, was covered in glyphs that looked like padlocks. Uthan *was* an idiot, but he had a few grains of sense. He had secured his systems.

However, the ship's basic status and clock weren't locked behind anything. The date and time were written in plain numerals.

Two months and seventeen days since the crash.

This could still easily have been a deception. Uthan could have set the clocks to display the incorrect time, expecting that I would see them at some point. I waved my hand in front of other projectors, flipping them on, checking each of them to find the controls to drop the window opacity.

Nothing outside would look different, not at first. This was a tidally locked world with a minimal axial tilt. The sun would always be high, drowning out the stars in every wavelength. The right combination of filters, though, might at least let me see the positions of the planets in the Kitrya-892 system. All I had to do was cross-reference those against the Mindnet's records of the solar system, and…

And…

The thought tapered off. It was true that, with the right starcharts and enough processing power, I could map the position of the planets in the sky, and then the date from that.

But if I could connect to the Mindnet to do that, there would be no point in any of this. I'd know the date. I'd be able to call for help. My arms dropped to the armrests.

My brain was plainly not functioning correctly. That all but eliminated Rational Framework One as a possibility. There was no point in testing me if I was not intact.

Of course, "intact" had a nebulous meaning when it came to minds. The Arborec, the creator of the fungus that infested me, was not *intact*. Not exactly.

But it was whole.

The limits of light speed communication applied to it as much as everyone else. It could not communicate with all its far-flung appendages instantly but, like every other interstellar civilization, used courier vessels. Little seedling-kernel ships that could take days, weeks, or months to reach their destination, and that were just as susceptible to the dangers of galactic travel as everyone else.

Most sentients liked to think of "themselves" as a single chain of consciousness, extending unbroken into their pasts. The nigh universality of this suggested that it was a survival skill. Even as part of the Mindnet, with thoughts of others' buzzing in and out of my own, I had perceived myself this way.

The Arborec referred to itself as a singular entity no matter how much time and distance separated the components of its mind. Most other sentients assumed that this was a delusion. After all, owing to accident or deliberate isolation, large parts of itself could remain incommunicado for centuries. Other sentients sometimes encountered stricken Arborec vessels or lost colonies that had been separated for millennia. It certainly seemed reasonable, to individualistic species, to conclude that those should be regarded as separate entities.

The Mindnet, upon making first contact with the Arborec, swiftly understood that the Arborec had a clearer conception of itself – and mind, thought, and consciousness in general – than anyone other than Ourselves.

With the resources of the Mindnet behind me, I could have understood this better. For now, my best tool continued to be clumsy analogy.

The *corpus callosum* was the bridge between the left and right hemispheres of the human brain. Sever it, and the two halves of the brain had few to no ways to communicate with each other. Biologically speaking, there were two half-brains living together in one skull.

But a human who'd had this done to them did not stop behaving as a single consciousness. Or perceiving themselves as one. They functioned little differently during their day-to-day lives. One half of this patient's brain would always think it was in control of the whole… and if the other half of their brain did something inexplicable, like respond to a stimulus only it could perceive, the person would then have a narrative ready to explain why they had done that. They would raise their hand to catch a ball that only the non-speaking side of them could see and rationalize afterward that they must have seen the shadow on the wall. Or felt the air move. And they would believe it.

A human brain, like the brains of every sentient, was capable of remarkable feats of self-conception. The more cynical phrase would have been self-deception, but this was one of those rare cases in which the cynical answer missed the truth.

And the truth was that this was no different from the way the human brain ordinarily composed narratives about what it was doing. Patients with a severed *corpus callosum* only made the paradox easier to see.

Sentients all over the galaxy had a looser relationship between thought and identity than they wanted to think. Hacan who overdosed on *gerr* root reported remembering past lives that seemed more real to them than their present ones. Even when presented evidence that they "remembered" history incorrectly, they started to believe instead that they had come from a parallel universe. Transplant one Sardakk N'orr's pheromone sacs into another's body, and eventually the scent of a stranger's pheromones coming from their own bodies would make them believe that they *were* that stranger. Their own memories could not convince them otherwise.

Individualistic species did not like to think of themselves as a jumble. Or of their consciousness having multiple sources. Or of "consciousness" as being multiplicitous and redundant, as messy as any other organ. We like to think we know ourselves.

The Arborec revealed the lie of that self-conception by being so much like ourselves that it was hard to look at.

Understand that, and you come a smidgen closer to understanding the Arborec. And the reason why the Arborec made so many sentients uncomfortable.

Amend that. It was one of the many reasons the Arborec made *other* sentients so uncomfortable. The most forward-facing of those was the Dirzuga.

Individuality was alien to the Arborec. When it encountered other sentients for the first time, the idea of *communication* was so far beyond its experience that it could not imagine it. It was like a person trying to think in the way that an earthquake thought. Or the color purple trying to understand smell.

But the Arborec was endlessly clever. It was constantly directing and manipulating its own evolution. It knew that there was a comprehension gap between it and the strange *not-it* beings that it had to gently eject from its colony worlds, and that occasionally bombarded it in return. It engineered a fungus to infect dead *not-its*, infiltrate their brains, and understand their functioning.

It worked. Too well. Assimilating the brains of other sentients not only allowed the Arborec the context to understand *not-its*, but the language and speech centers of their brains even enabled it to communicate.

To this day, the Arborec only communicated with other species via those species' own dead. It called its mouthpieces the Dirzuga. The Arborec had wormed its way into the Galactic Council and gotten recognition for its territorial stakes.

One of the many differences that remained between it and the galaxy's other sentients was that it could not understand why other sentients found this use of their dead to be disturbing. To the Arborec, the dead were of no consequence. Like shed skin cells. Reanimating them to use their language centers was recycling. The Dirzuga were no more alive than a fingernail. They served a purpose. There was no better way to do it.

This didn't bother the Mindnet. We were far less sentimental than other species. When We encountered Dirzuga made from the corpses of dead Mindnet citizens, We were concerned, but only for the potential loss of secrets.

The Arborec promised that nothing of the dead, other than their basic functions and language centers, remained intact. Many, many sentients found this less than convincing.

The Arborec may have started to understand individual life, but that was not the same thing as valuing it.

My present state seemed to indicate that the Arborec had not shared the whole truth about the nature of the Dirzuga.

(Possibly.)

Whenever the Mindnet encountered one of Our own turned to a shambling Dirzuga mouthpiece, We always found them without implants. Sometimes there were great abscesses where the implants had been. More often, more flesh and bone had been stimulated to regrow over them, or fungus had filled in the gaps.

Just like what had happened to me.

I once again touched my fingers to the surface of the fungus on my arm. I bit the inside of my cheek, hard. Heat built in my stomach.

It was when I felt the now familiar fuzz of fungus along the back of my gums that I decided that throwing up was unavoidable.

Or trying to throw up. I retched, at least. And tasted the burn of stomach acid.

The cacophony of blood rushing in my ears kept me from hearing Uthan approach, but I was not surprised to look up and see him framed in the cockpit hatch.

"I'm impressed," he said. So far as I had the ability to tell, he sounded genuine. Not that I trusted my reading of emotional cues.

"I am not," I said miserably.

"With muscles as far gone as yours, I didn't think you would be able to get as far as the infirmary hatch."

He did not ask what I was doing up here, for which I was grateful. I had learned how to fear embarrassment. "Who's your navigator?" I asked.

"What?"

Of the two seats, I'd chosen the one in front of a bevy of piloting controls. The other faced a blistering number of projectors. Someone there would be able to review an enormous amount of data in a variety of graphical formats. Plainly a navigator's position.

I glanced at it, and then to him. From the creases and scuffs left on here, I could tell that my seat, the pilot's seat, was where he spent most of his time. And that no one spent a lot of time in the other position.

"I never needed a navigator," he said.

I was not adept at facial expressions. I attempted to mirror one he'd shown me several times, the raised eyebrows. The *try another line* look. I said, "A one-person ship this cramped does not need a cabin devoted entirely to medical use. *Two* people wouldn't need that. The medical cabin used to be someone's quarters."

He shrugged, as if to say *fair enough, you caught me.* "We had different business plans," he said.

"Why did you lie about them?"

"Nothing I said was a lie." To emphasize the closure of the subject, he changed to another: "Did you grow up in the Mindnet?"

I was not interested in that line of conversation and so ignored it. "Activate the sensors," I told him.

He tilted his head and did nothing. In the far back of my memory, my long-forgotten parents were trying to tell me something. For once, I listened.

"*Activate the sensors,*" I repeated. I almost added, "Please," but I was not desperate. Ever since he'd told me about the fungus, I'd felt like there was something crawling inside my head. Another voice, another being. I had to see if it was true.

"What are you looking for?"

"The Arborec."

"Ah. Yes. I checked. There's no Arborec surface presence, or seed carriers, whatever they call those." Uthan stepped behind my chair and tapped one of the controls behind my seat. A glittering projection of Kitrya-892 b appeared to my left. A monochrome cube with a rotating disk, a map of the entire system, took over my right field of view.

He'd positioned his body to block my view, to keep me from seeing what he had done to unlock the sensor controls. A point in favor of his caution. *One* point. With ten subtracted for activating any systems around me at all, which he did not need to do.

But, reluctantly, I appreciated the gesture.

The projections showed me a dead star system with a mostly dead planet. The only highlighted point of interest was the wreckage of my survey vessel. Much of the planet and half the sky was grayer than the rest, the bleached color representing the regions Uthan's ship couldn't see from the surface. He had gotten a full scan of those regions during his last orbit.

"No active Arborec vessels now," Uthan said. "Did your

ship have anything to do with them? Laboratory samples or some such?"

"No."

If there was no Arborec presence in the system, then the intrusive thoughts crawling inside me couldn't be real. Or, at least, they couldn't have come from the Arborec. There was nothing in speed-of-light communication range.

(That is a limited perspective.)

Uthan said, "My best guess is that the Arborec visited this world long, long ago. Took a look around and left. Or maybe tried to colonize it and failed. Sensors wouldn't find much evidence of that. If the Arborec left something small, like fungal spores, they'd blend into the algae ecosystem."

His sensors wouldn't find evidence of that. Mindnet sensors, like most other things Mindnet, were sharper. Maybe it was the reason my survey ship had come here. Maybe he was right, too, about the spores mutating if they'd been here for a while. The Arborec rarely bothered to control its own evolution.

"What's your name?" he asked.

Idiot. "I already told you, it's S1L–"

"Was that the name you were born with?"

"No. That doesn't–"

I clamped my mouth shut. *Idiot* had been the right word to think, but I'd aimed it at the wrong person. He'd caught me annoyed and preoccupied. There had been no advantage for me in saying that.

He smiled like that had been a gambit in a friendly card game rather than the sucker punch it had felt like. "Gotcha. I didn't figure you had been born into the Mindnet."

"Why is that?" I asked, once I regained control of my voice.

"You remind me of my brother. The way he acted when he was two years old and learned how to say 'no.'"

I sighed. "You are accusing me of arrested development."

"You were young when the Mindnet did their thing to you, weren't you?"

The memories were fuzzy, trauma blocked. And my behavioral implants discouraged me from thinking about them. So, I didn't. The behavioral implant blocks were gone now, but their conditioning remained. "That doesn't matter."

"Tell me that I'm wrong, then."

Of course I could not. I had much to learn about how to lie. Lying about that would have been a pointless act of pride, anyway. Inefficient. My Mindnet implants discouraged that.

When I'd been part of the Mindnet, I'd had the galaxy at the tip of my neurons. I'd grown farther than he could imagine, in more dimensions than he knew existed. The idea he was implying, that this experience had been *limiting,* was galling.

I just… did not have access to any of that anymore.

I had this fungus.

(If you were part of the Arborec and not yet in mental contact with it… what would you be thinking right now?)

Rational Narrative Six: I was acting in the way the Arborec wanted me to act.

My consciousness, my awareness, could all have been a lie. More so than usual, that was. A vestigial organ. One part of my brain was cut off from the other, the part actually in control.

The Arborec would want me to gather information, build rapport, and make my way back into contact with the rest of itself. The narrative in my head, that I was doing all these things to get back in contact with Mindnet, could have been a fiction. The left side of my brain trying to explain what the disconnected right was doing… still trying to believe I was a unified whole.

"You really ought to kill me," I told Uthan, and meant it.

But when I pressed my arms against the chair to try, and fail, to lever myself upright, he pretended he hadn't heard me. He hitched his arms behind mine. Together, we staggered back to the medical cabin.

CHAPTER SEVEN
BARNACLES

Now

The repair company's waiting lobby had been designed to subtly disorient visitors. Which was a good indication of how they wanted to relate to customers.

The lobby space itself was, like the rest of the station, mostly empty. It was a brightly-lit space full of chairs arranged at awkward angles, a little too wide and too tall for the average human. When I sat, my heels did not quite reach the floor. Intensely uncomfortable. My legs were as stiff as dried reeds after days with only my shuttle's cockpit and central corridor to move through. It felt like waking up on Kitrya-892 b all over again.

The walls were covered with mirrors – or at least projections that looked like mirrors. The views were not quite right. I saw my own reflection, tense and fidgety, in mirrors that were canted away from me. Someone less attentive to detail might have assumed that was a reflection of a reflection, but there were no mirrors opposite it. Everything was arranged to be maximally disorienting, especially to starship crews who'd just stepped off packed starships for the first time in months.

The only lift that came here had four doors, one on each wall. I wouldn't have been surprised to find out that the lift rotated, and that only unwatched doors opened.

The rest of the station did not make me any more comfortable. Even the ten-kilometer central hub was too large for its population. The trackless, empty white corridors had grooves worn into the floor from thousands of passes from cleaning drones. The air smelled of dust and bleach. During the docking procedure, I'd been sent the address of an office and a time to arrive, but otherwise been left to my own devices. I should have remained aboard my shuttle with the technician, but I'd been too hungry and thirsty to restrain myself.

I'd heard voices, announcements, and saw flashing hologram advertisements directing me to a concourse. I'd ducked away from the sound of voices and footsteps before their owners and I ever crossed paths. There were security cameras at the end of my shuttle's boarding starbridge, but I doubted an actual person had been watching any of those. It had only taken a modest effort to keep the number of people who'd seen me face to face limited to just that one technician.

Present-day Port Vel Syd attracted plenty of visitors with illicit business, but there were enough permanent residents to form a ramshackle culture of their own. So many of them that even legitimate companies saw money to be made here.

I'd found, in these bright and empty corridors, an automated store kiosk. Its prices for food and water were an exquisite outrage, but I'd gorged myself on water and nutrient paste, regardless. Its fabric synthesizers could extrude a plain but serviceable shawl and head wrapping.

I'd arrived five minutes early to the appointment that the company representative had told me I absolutely needed to show up to. I was then left alone for fifteen minutes.

"Paranoid much?" the projected-hologram receptionist said when I asked if we could dispense with the preplanned delay. The image was of a human man, dark haired and synthesized from a thousand bland corporate images, which made the pre-programmed snark that much more surprising.

"Just perceptive," I told him. But I gave up and returned to my seat before he could further simulate rudeness. It was all extremely tiresome.

All this was a marketing tactic. Make people feel afraid, lost, and like everything was out of their control. Then tell them how much they will have to pay to make it stop.

I used to think of myself as above this. But I had learned long ago that recognizing psychological manipulation didn't make me any less vulnerable to it. I certainly *felt* afraid, lost, and like everything was about to go spinning out of my control. I had nowhere else to go, and I was sure that these people knew it. Paying an absurd amount of money to make this feeling go away did not seem like a bad idea.

A projection set up to look like a window covered one entire wall. The view overlooked the company's docking tower. At the moment, the company had only two vessels snagged in its pincers: mine, and some luckless Hacan merchant hauler-ship. Its polyhedral cargo pod was three times the size it actually was and projected out from the tower like an overripe pimple.

Neither the docking claws nor starbridge towers belonged here. They were the wrong color of gray, had too many lights, and were too angular. The additions were so visibly out of place that they looked tumorous, like a skin tag hanging over a weeping sore.

My internal monologue tended toward the ugly and biological whenever I was forced to think about the fungus dappling my body. Coming to Port Vel Syd had forced me to remember how I looked to others and had jarred it back to the top of my mind. My new headdress still left some discoloration visible between my lower lip and chin, and some streaked toward my left temple, but that was all. The technician had already identified me as a Dirzuga, though. She'd had plenty of time to call ahead to her bosses. But they kept to their rigid make-me-wait-for-fifteen-minute game regardless.

(Pretend to be from the Arborec.)

I'd done it before, on other espionage operations, but the thought was still repulsive. Every time I thought of the Arborec, a pit opened in my stomach. My treacherous little thoughts gave me even more reason to stay on edge. There was, as they insisted, always the chance that Arborec was exactly what I was. I stared at the "window" view of my shuttle until the lift door opened again.

The skin on the back of my neck went cold when I saw the snakelike Druaa emerge.

Preserved, furless animal tails dangled from her skull ridges. The tips of her scales had been painted an iridescent tinge that made her look as unreal as the glittery receptionist hologram, but she was definitely real. I smelled her rat-dander perfume from here.

"Apologies for the wait," she said, without explanation. She sidewinded across the empty lobby. She seemed enormous for a Druaa, but perhaps that was another trick of projectors and perspective. She fit easily into the seat facing mine.

"Playing these psychological tricks on me only wastes both of our time," I said.

"Does it?" she asked. Not even a denial. Just the implication that she'd already succeeded in getting an advantage.

"That trick, too," I said.

"Well," she said, with a smile not all that dissimilar to the one Uthan always gave me when he drew his first hand of cards. "Can't fool you."

For half a second, I let a fraction of the loathing and ennui I felt for her, this place, and my week in general, into the front of my mind.

The Druaa were a relative newcomer in what passed for galactic politics these days. Their telepathy was so novel a phenomenon that many sentients doubted that they *were* telepathic, or that there was any such thing as telepathy. The Mindnet had dissected enough Druaa to know that their telepathy was very real. And insidious enough to make Us jealous.

I had only had the misfortune of dealing with Druaa twice since my Dirzuga infection. Once had been an encounter with a patrol picket on the edge of Naalu space. Another had been a customs officer searching for smuggled *gerr* root, which I had, in fact, been carrying at the time. But I'd still gotten away smoothly. I was sensitive enough to their telepathy to feel it as a tingle under my skull. Like my mind was going numb as it was squeezed.

I wasn't without defenses. One of the reasons the Druaa played coy about their telepathic capabilities was that just knowing about it made it weaker. Telepathically entangled minds were like entangled particles. Observation affected the outcome.

Most thoughts weren't settled things. They were inclinations, possibilities. An unobserved thought could become many things as they skimmed below the level of conscious awareness.

The Druaa's secret was not that they perceived thoughts, but that they perceived everything a thought could have been. With a remote prod, a tease, a threat… they could whittle the possibilities into something that they found pleasing.

The best way to deal with this was to narrow the possibility space. Leave no other possibilities for what I'd felt. Focusing on a thought collapsed its potential. By paying attention to a thought, amplifying it, I closed the possibility space of everything else it could turn into.

Hence the adolescent rage.

The razor-edged intensity had the advantage of silencing that deceitful other voice in my head, the one that pretended to be the Arborec but could not possibly have been.

She blinked. That should have been like connecting to the galaxy's angstiest human teenager. If I counted the age in which I joined the Mindnet, plus the number of years that had passed since I'd lost my implants, she was not that far off.

Most Druaa did not like to admit that they could do what they so obviously did. Reacting to the anger beamed at her, even by blinking, had been a slip. She smiled to cover it.

However out of control I felt most of the time, I was still better at directing my thoughts than most humans. Some diplomats tumbled onto the idea that someone with a "strong will" could resist Druaa telepathy. What they really could have used was emotional honesty. Something that was not well-prized by diplomats anywhere. It was little wonder the Naalu Collective had done as well as they had.

The Druaa would have no chance against Us in Our fullest glory. Against just me, though, she had a good one.

"That's a delightful flower print you have posted on the crew head," she said.

Once again, I'd been right to be pessimistic. The flower print had survived. "Thank you," I answered curtly.

"Really well applied to survive all that damage. The pattern looks too arranged to be Arborec. What is it from? A Malloc garden, or–"

"*Thank* you," I said, more baring my teeth than smiling.

"It's not exactly the kind of transport I'd expect the Arborec to use."

Her voice was well-practiced for a Druaa. The Druaa only used speech to communicate with outsiders; among themselves, they preferred telepathy. This Druaa's ease with spoken language said that she'd been dealing with non-Druaa for years. This business didn't seem to be Naalu-owned – the mechanic hadn't been Druaa, and neither was the receptionist hologram. She pressed, "Don't you have your own vessels? Seedling ships, spore carriers, or the like?"

"It probably wouldn't surprise you how many worlds turn away alien visitors who come bearing seeds and spores," I said.

That got a genuine-sounding laugh. She was adjusting her tactics, playing charming, trying to lower my guard. And it was true that I could not maintain my emotional focus for long. Emotions were pesky things, too flighty to herd. "But that vessel in particular?" she asked. "That model was recalled twenty years ago. There must be others that would serve your purposes better."

"If you know anything about me, you know I excel at recycling dead and lost things."

"That's true," she said, with a glance to the side of my head wrapping. "I suppose if something were to happen to you – the body seated in front of me right now – it would be no greater loss than if I were to lose a scale."

I'd been told that I would be meeting a manager, but I wondered if she wasn't just playing the part. Maybe the business had hired a Druaa for the specific purpose of fleecing customers. "Managing a business?" I asked, changing the subject. "Playing with customers like a Hacan with a rodent? Isn't that unusual for the Naalu?"

Her slitted eyes briefly unfocused. I got the idea that I'd caught her off guard. But the moment was brief. "We all need commerce to survive." I would have expected that answer to come automatically. A Druaa in a position like hers would have gotten that question a lot. "Besides, the Hacan are hamstrung by a need to play a little too fair, don't you think?"

Now she was back on her game. Menacing, but deniably so. Playing off her telepathy, her biggest advantage as a joke, but making sure to keep it at the front of my mind. "When can I expect repairs?" I asked, putting more steel into my voice.

"That depends on quite a lot," she said, with a glance toward the false-window projection. To her, the splayed-open guts of my shuttle must have looked like a caught rodent. "How much would you like repaired, how quickly, and how do you intend to pay?"

I still held Uthan's position as a Keleres courier. It paid enough, but not an infinite amount. "I only need water tanks repaired and restocked, and rudimentary plumbing restored."

"That's all? If we were somewhere more… regulated, I wouldn't let you think about taking that thing out into space. It would be safer for you to accept it as a total loss and take a passenger liner out."

I had to admire the efficiency of the Druaa's threat. *I wouldn't let you.* Reminding me that she had the power to keep my shuttle clamped down. Indirectly reminding me that there were no real authorities here to stop her if she chose.

She tilted her head, as if curious. I think she caught a little of my reluctant admiration.

"It still has some service time left in it," I said. "I'm not asking for a full overhaul."

"You're asking me to send you out in a barely functional shuttle. It could crash right back into this station."

"That sounds like it would be my problem more than yours."

"Why? The body you're speaking through is no more alive than a lost tooth."

I shrugged and looked at her. I'd nearly slipped.

"I'd be the one left to deal with station management," she said. "Do you know what cultists do when they're upset? No, that'd probably be beneath you." A glint in her slitted eyes told me, too late, that she'd found a weakness to widen. "Or is it?"

"Can we discuss costs?" I asked.

She plowed right through my attempt to change the subject. "I have an inkling," she said, "that you might know more about my level of life than you usually do."

I kept my thoughts neutral but could not help the muscles tensing in my neck.

She set a clawed hand on my seat's cushion, looking concerned. "There are no other Arborec ships at the station. No Arborec life that anyone I know is aware of. No other Dirzuga on your ship. You, as in the 'you' sitting in front of me right now, has no other connection to the larger… well, *you*. To the rest of the Arborec. Right now, you're just whatever thoughts you left rattling around in that body."

"That is not," I said, measuredly, "how I function."

"Please don't take my interest the wrong way. It's not a threat." *Hah.* "I like to know my customers. This must be difficult."

"I am the Arborec," I lied. *Probably.* I was *probably* lying.

(Hmmmm. Really?)

I quashed that thought, but not quickly enough to keep some of the doubt and deceit from leaping the gap between us.

She had gotten me mired. I felt murky and disconsolate – both feelings that left a wide possibility space for thoughts they could evolve into. No matter how much I tried, I could not winnow them down into something useful.

She smiled more broadly, this time allowing a glimpse of her teeth. This time, when she reminded me of Uthan, it was when he knew he'd won a round.

"You must be desperate to get back in touch with yourself," she said.

This time, all the hate I could muster didn't make a dent in her expression.

"If you are through establishing how much you think I need your services," I said, "you can move on to extorting me for their costs."

"How much do you have?" she asked. Without leaving any space for an answer, she went on: "And because that isn't going to be enough, how are you going to get us more?"

It was difficult to keep myself from shaking during the ride back.

The ridiculous lift moved slowly. So much more slowly than seemed necessary. No doubt it was to give the Druaa or her staff more opportunities to observe clients as they left. Or eavesdrop on groups dumb enough to talk amongst themselves.

I carried a good number of *aurei*. The total had, of course, not been enough. But that was all right, the Druaa had said. Then she'd lied that repairs would take weeks to even plan. In the meantime, she would dispatch a message with the next courier to leave the station. She would reach out to the Arborec's homeworld, Nestphar, to see if it would pay anything extra.

The last few times I'd beaten Druaa telepathy hadn't been protracted encounters. It had not taken a tremendous effort. I had just needed focus. It seemed like I'd had a lot more of it back then.

(The curse of individuality. Too many things to think about, too few neurons to do it.)

I closed my eyes. That did not help.

Staying at Port Vel Syd for repairs was now out of the question. Contrary to my hectoring intrusive thoughts, I had every reason to believe that the Arborec remained, surprisingly, ignorant of me. If it turned any of its billions of eyes toward me, I had no idea what would happen. I had vowed to never find out.

I had to leave. Station administration changed hands every few years, but their interests always aligned to keep a few basic services operational: crewing the weapon platforms and providing enough security to protect the property of the wealthy – and perhaps, when they felt like it, discourage other, lesser property damage. If station management could stop me from getting away from the company that had my shuttle captive, they would.

I was going to have to move fast. Food would be easy to sneak aboard. Sufficiently calorie-dense packages could easily fit into my clothing. Water was the problem. I needed enough water to survive the week and a half it would take to get back to Mentak territory. And I needed to get it aboard, through the docking tower, without being spotted. And then I needed to – somehow – get the docking clamps to release without ripping my shuttle's hull apart.

Easy. *Easy.*

If I tried to convince myself it would be, maybe I could make it that way. Panic was counterproductive in more ways than usual. There was a good chance that the Druaa was still skimming my thoughts. The Mindnet had never been able to determine the range of Druaa telepathy.

The meeting with the Druaa had, in a perverse way, left me better off than I had been before. I had always been this screwed. The difference the meeting had made was that I knew how screwed I was now.

Perhaps I didn't know the full depths of that yet. I opened my eyes.

The floor thrummed. My gut twisted in the familiar, nigh-imperceptible manner of faulty artificial gravity trying to keep up with the motions of a lift capsule. The lift had never stopped moving. I'd instructed the lift to take me back to where I had come from. The ride had been much shorter last time.

I did not need to be a telepath to know that the Druaa would be tempted to check the market value of a live (or dead) Dirzuga. There were plenty of governments out there who hadn't yet been able to study one of the Arborec's Dirzuga yet.

This was a trap. The panic in the back of my head stopped simmering, turned to ice. The tension squeezing my chest eased.

Here was the calm I'd been looking for.

The lift halted. Only the left half of the double doors ahead rolled open.

The stun grenade rolling in arrived as a relief. Finally, a physical, immediate problem able to take my mind off all the others.

CHAPTER EIGHT
MUSCLE MEMORY

Then

I started dreaming not long after Uthan found me.

When awake, I could control thinking of the Arborec and what it had done to my body. Asleep, I had no defenses against the feverish worlds of teeming green biomass churning through my mind.

Their scale never quite came into focus. It was like looking through two sets of eyes – each seeing an object only superficially like another. Every view was superimposed over the other, blurring them into an illusion of one. I looked at a world the size of a head, something I could have picked up in my hands, if I'd had hands. At the same time, it was enormous, a *planet*, and too vast to comprehend with three-dimensional vision, or look upon and not feel vertigo.

If I'd had a stomach, I might have thrown up. But I was a microbe, dropping toward a sphere as large as my head. I was a god, as large as a constellation.

I saw through the sensory organs of one of the Arborec's living greenhouse-ships. A Nightthorn Haven. The Arborec's loose equivalent to what other civilizations called a carrier.

Deuterium pumped through my esophagus, flooding into intermix sacs. My stomach burned brightly. My skin was studded with living thorns, their tips sharpened to monofilament points, ready to launch toward enemy fighters at a moment's notice. I drifted above a planet painted in swirls of liquid green flame.

The Arborec was not like Us. It did not (often) attempt expansion through open conquest. It was more patient. It played nice, made overtures, repurposed alien dead to act as its ambassadors. It had successfully petitioned to become a member of the Galactic Council. It invited sentients everywhere to immigrate to its nutrient-soup worlds. It said that it wanted to learn… but more than it wanted to understand, it wanted to belong. Its offer to provide for all had thus far proved genuine.

But it was relentless. Its expansion never ceased.

During the height of the Lazax Empire, it hadn't learned to leave its home system. Now it was a major actor in galactic politics, on par with the Barony of Letnev, the Federation of Sol, the Hacan Emirates, and other more ancient powers.

It was nature that abhorred vacuums. It spread its spores wide. In evolution, nothing was given a purpose, but everything had a function.

Maybe even Dirzuga dreamed. To keep myself from falling apart, I told myself that my dreams were the product of my own anxiety and revulsion about what had happened to my body. But I could never be sure. In these dreams, I felt the soft and fuzzy fungal tendrils worm under my skull.

• • •

The first I heard that Uthan and I were leaving Kitrya-892 b was when the engines roared. The deck shifted as the artificial gravity struggled to adjust for the acceleration.

Uthan and I had settled into an uneasy rhythm in the week since I'd woken. At least, I think it was a week. I'd decided that the Mindnet would not have me fight my way out of here. Not until I found out more about what was going on.

This upended those calculations. If the status quo was changing…

My stomach, already uneasy, churned as I fought to my feet.

With long and torturous practice, I'd gotten to the point where I could walk more consistently. Though neither of us had mentioned this aloud, I noticed Uthan had locked more of the shuttle's internal hatches. The cockpit hatch was open only because he was presently inside.

This trip involved more buckling knees than most. The artificial gravity clearly had some calibration issues. By the time I reached the cockpit, the sky outside the window had darkened to a moonlike blue haze broken by fiery red wisps. A mix of the reflected glare of the engine plume and fire from air friction. The shuttle was burning out of the atmosphere fast enough to generate the kind normally only seen during reentry aerobraking. The wisps flickered so fast that, to faulty human visual acuity, they seemed to pulse in waves. Liquid fire, like the planet I'd seen in my dream.

I'd been working on interacting with Uthan in a manner less brusque and hostile than I felt.

"What do you think you're doing?" I demanded.

He glanced back at me, as if noticing me for the first time – though he couldn't have missed the racket I'd made coming down the corridor. "I'm through scavenging," he said. "Not much there that's valuable." A day or so ago, he'd packed away all the junk and detritus blocking the central corridor, but I'd assumed he'd only done so to make room for more of the same.

"When were you going to ask my permission?"

This time, his glance backward was sharper. "To leave? Did I need to?"

"Are you abducting me?"

He lifted his hand, one finger raised, as though to answer. Then stopped. He frowned. "Okay, fair question. I suppose… I am? I didn't take seriously the idea that you might want to stay. Since you would die pretty quickly."

"It's my life to lose." The moment I said the words, I had to suppress a shudder. A pulse of pain shot through my temple, an echo of what my cybernetics would have done. That was wrong. Not my life. *Our* life.

Uthan said, "Airlock's still there if you want to go."

I considered turning toward it just to see what he'd do. But no foreseeable outcome of that bluff ended well for me.

"Where are you taking me?" I asked, instead.

"I'm going back to work," he said. "The only reason I was killing time here to begin with was a piracy alert along my flight path. It should be clear now, and I can get back to Mecatol Rex."

Mecatol Rex – home of the old Lazax Empire, and home of the current-day Galactic Council.

He had told me that he worked for the Keleres as a messenger. I didn't know that I believed him. Point in his favor: he'd told me what he did unprompted, while he was administering painkillers after the third time I'd tried to walk unaided. Point against: he could have told me that because he knew I'd seen his Keleres-issued weapons. I hadn't told him what I'd recognized, but he might have guessed.

I had to be careful about that kind of supposition. It led into thoughts of *but if he knew that I knew that* he *knew* and then into madness. I had not yet begun to think of myself as a spy.

"You're taking me to the Keleres," I said.

He raised that finger again. "To be fair," he said loudly, as if to interrupt anything I was about to say, "you are the kind of problem that they're better suited to dealing with than me."

"I am not your problem or their problem. You are all *my* problem. I don't consent to being taken to Mecatol Rex."

Once again, this caught him by surprise. He drummed his fingers on his console as he stared back at me. He hadn't seemed to have considered my perspective.

Carefully, he said, "From what I know of the Mindnet, it doesn't care for individual rights and freedoms."

"We don't," I agreed. "Your people do, though. Ostensibly." As much as the imperialistic politics of the current Galactic Council's civilizations gave the lie to that, they flattered themselves to think that they did.

I hoped this would be sensitive for Uthan in particular. Before Uthan had joined the Keleres, he'd come from the Mentak Coalition. The Coalition had been founded by the convicts of an old Lazax prison colony. Its people were especially enamored with their heritage of hard-earned freedom and rebellion.

I was beginning to sense his weak point. It was the same weakness shared by every member of the current Galactic Council, the one I worked so hard to avoid later. Pride. An edifice of self-regard built on a foundation of self-deception.

The Mindnet wasn't prone to such things, of course.

"Am I your prisoner?" I asked.

Uthan reflexively started to shake his head. Then stopped.

The battle of cognitive dissonance didn't last long before he found an escape, though. He had already made up his mind what he was going to do with me – or to me – but now he was having trouble justifying it to himself. He resorted instead to rationalization.

"The L1Z1X Mindnet declared war against the Galactic Council," he said. That was technically untrue – the Mindnet had never respected the Galactic Council enough to recognize it as worthy of a formal declaration – but near enough to not be worth correcting. "The council has laws for the treatment of prisoners of war. It's not my call to decide to apply them."

My legs ached from standing still for so long. I kept myself from showing it, or at least hoped I did. "Why would they apply to me?"

"Are you a member of the L1Z1X Mindnet?" he asked back.

It was my turn to be caught off guard by a question I should have seen coming. I had two immediate, instinctive answers. *Yes* because it was who I'd always been, had wanted to be since I'd had my implants installed. *No,* because to be a member of the Mindnet, a person had to have functioning implants. It was not an option. It was a core part of Our identity.

So I was not being deceitful or otherwise maneuvering for advantage when I answered: "No." It hurt to say so, a physical sting in the center of my forehead.

Uthan saw my pain. "So why do you act so much like you're a part of it?"

I blinked. "How can I not?"

As if to one-up me, he blinked twice. He scratched his head. His voice trailed off into a question. "I mean, you … just … you stop?"

"That's not a choice I can make."

"You don't have any implants that control your mind anymore. You can choose to act differently."

"There is something fundamental about my experience that I am failing to communicate with you," I said. Just because I didn't have my implants, that didn't mean my brain hadn't been shaped by the Mindnet. The Mindnet's methods of education went beyond the physical.

I didn't have the vocabulary to express that then. I wish I had. It might have made a difference.

He looked at me and saw a different story. Same as when he looked at himself, and at the rest of the Mentak, and he saw something that wasn't there. He decided on a new rationalization. "I would be going to Mecatol Rex with or without you."

"And 'I'm just along for the ride?'" I asked.

"Yes. And you're welcome, by the way."

I stared at him. He shifted in his seat. The pain of standing for so long was alleviated a little, at least, by seeing how uncomfortable I'd made him.

He fancied himself an "*x* with a heart of gold" type – where *x* was anything from pirate to conman to wastrel. If he'd done anything to justify "heart of gold" before discovering me, I didn't hear about it. But self-deception can be a powerful motivator. He was not going to pass up an opportunity to feel good about himself.

"I *cannot* go to Mecatol Rex," I said. There were many reasons for that, but the foremost on my mind right now was that the Arborec had a presence there. When Uthan didn't seem to understand, I said, "*It* could seize control of me."

(If I'm not already "just along for the ride.")

"The Arborec's vessels visit on a fixed schedule," he said, as if reading my mind. "There won't be one when we arrive. And there are safe rooms, Faraday cages of a sort, that can keep you isolated." Hearing that was more of a relief than I wanted to show. "Anyway, I don't know where else to take you. Where are you from, originally? What world?"

I had absolutely no interest in telling him that. "Why? Are you offering to take me there?"

"Not if it's still a Mindnet world," he said. "You just said you're not a member. That's my point. If you can't go home, where else do you have to go?"

The flickers of friction-fire had long ago faded to embers. Soon they were entirely gone. The shuttle had gotten far enough from the last shreds of Kitrya-892 b's atmosphere that the reflected glare of the shuttle's engine plume disappeared, and no longer drowned out the stars. The brightest of them began to emerge.

I'd never be able to see the whole starfield while the cabin lights were on. This was the first time I'd seen any stars other than Kitrya-892 b itself since I'd lost my implants, and all the borrowed knowledge they contained. I couldn't tell anything about those stars, or even whether those were suns or other planets in this system.

Even if they hadn't been overwhelmed by the cabin lights, they would have looked small, cold, and unreal.

I continued to live with a minor issue:

Every day was a fresh plunge into agony. My reawakening body had many complaints to make. As a consequence, so did I.

The issue was not just my muscles. "Little" pains that my implants used to stifle struck me harder than they ever did.

Stomach cramps. Itching. Then, the day after we left Kitrya-892 b, came a feeling like the right side of my skull was caving in.

Three times a day, Uthan checked my temperature, pulse, and blood pressure. I told Uthan my worst muscle strain had migrated behind my eye, and then to my head. He'd just scratched under his beard and gotten on with his business. Now, he was seated on the stool we used as a game board.

"Your instruments must be able to tell you something about the nature of my brain damage," I said. "It hurts to look at the lights."

"Have you seen any bright flashes?"

"No."

"Smell burned toast?"

"What's that? No. Nothing burning."

"You have a headache."

"Hell, a *what*?" That sounded awful.

He explained, albeit using vocabulary that seemed more suited to a four-year old. I was getting better at picking up these social cues and what he was implying.

"I am not being melodramatic," I said.

He considered me for a long moment, arms still folded. Finally, something seemed to shift in him. When he spoke again, he was back to using adult words. "No, maybe not. One of my exes used to get migraines. Sometimes they were bad enough to keep him home all day."

Talk of family history was getting dangerously close to territory I wanted to stay away from. I would have forcefully changed the subject if he hadn't set his cards down and reached toward the medical cabin's hatch, where the light controls were. The lights dimmed. Instantly, the needles under my right eye blunted.

"I should have done that," I said. The lights had been on for hours, and the pain had been building up all the way. The pressure continued … just not as sharp.

"Why didn't you?"

The idea had genuinely not occurred to me. "The lights weren't the problem. The problem was in my head. The damage to my brain. I'm dysfunctional, not the light."

"You can't change your head. So, change your environment."

"I ought to be able to change myself," I said.

He stared at me. Something about the tone of my extremely valid complaints was putting him off, making him take me less seriously. If I were in a better position, I would have disregarded that as his problem, not mine. But though I was more mobile than before, I was still a prisoner of my body – which effectively meant I was a prisoner of my caretaker. The optimal strategy was to politely bridge this divide.

"What?" I demanded.

"How old were you when you were given implants again?"

"I have told you many times," I said. "And you are once again implying that my development has been arrested."

"It was a prompt. A conversation starter." He stared. I stared back. He sighed, and said, "To imply something without being rude about it."

"Be rude." I didn't care.

"I don't think your brain is damaged," he said.

"I've had a vital part of me ripped out of my head."

"No, no. Your real brain. Meat brain. The squishy one." He tapped the side of his head. He really did not understand: the person I had been with my implants had *been* my real self. "It's too well preserved. You haven't developed your social skills since then."

My social skills were perfectly developed, I thought bitterly. For the Mindnet. Not for the waking nightmare of confusion, misunderstanding, and agitation that unaugmented humans called conversation. "You can't imagine the depth and complexity of the society I come from."

"Oh, I'm sure. Talking with you is like talking with a toddler."

Okay, maybe I *did* care. That stung. "It is not," I said.

His big eyebrows went halfway up his forehead. I was beginning to hate that expression. He said nothing, didn't argue, but it still felt like a rebuttal.

"It is *not*," I said, louder.

Emotional control was becoming more, not less, challenging. When I had my temper sufficiently tamped down to speak more quietly, I told him, "I may be damaged, but I will not be infantilized."

"That's the last thing I want, too." He rubbed the skin underneath his beard. "I already raised three kids and don't want more. But it's not unfair to say you're not fully developed."

"I am not underdeveloped. I have been harmed. I have been… vivisected, dismantled, by the Arborec." I was going to have to try to explain this to him *again*. "Think of what has happened to me as an amputation. Why would I need to know how to grab things with my toes when I've had hands all my life?"

"Exactly." I thought we'd been arguing, but he sounded like he was thrilled that I'd come around to his point of view.

It took me too long to realize that I had. He wasn't right about my damaged brain being the "real" me or anything so demeaning. But the parts of me that remained were… unexercised, like my atrophied muscles.

(Or out of your control.)

I looked toward the cards he'd left on the countertop.

"Your head in good enough shape for that?" Uthan asked.

No, it wasn't. "So long as you leave the lights off."

"Ah. A strategic advantage for you."

"What? How? By being in less pain than I could be?"

"Hiding your face in the dark. You wear your emotions where anyone can see them."

"Is that so?" I asked in a level tone.

"Ooh, ominous. That's good. Maybe you are learning."

The light strips glowed dimly enough to let us see the art on the cards. We'd played enough that I didn't need to see their text. He'd always watched me, the way I held and looked at my cards, more than his own hand.

The last few times we'd played, I'd thought my face was flat, my expressions under control. This game, I devoted more processing power to monitoring myself. Trying to stifle any inadvertent lip movements or changes in my breathing. Anything that gave away my emotional state the same way he'd given away his, the last time we'd spoken in the cockpit.

I did not register anything slipping. But somehow Uthan found his hints anyway. While I was sculpting a hand of fighters and carriers, he must have been preparing his side's antifighter defenses. Every time I committed a squadron card to the "board," he had an answering flak cannon or missile swarm.

Not for the first time, I wondered if he was cheating. As he shuffled the decks for another round, he caught me watching his hands carefully, and sensed my suspicion. "There's more to bluffing than what you do with your face," he said.

I hid the scowl before it fully formed. He plainly enjoyed teaching, or at least appearing knowledgeable.

"This is a game that needs fluidity," he said, after a round in which he'd run his own fighter squadrons over my anti-capital-ship gauss cannons. "Not just to commit to a strategy. As soon as you sense that I might be on to your strategy, you should be switching tactics. Changing up what's in your hand. You have the option to discard and draw one card per round, every round, right up until the last round."

"I am not a very open-minded person," I said.

"Really," he deadpanned.

"Yes, really." He had to be wondering if I'd detected his sarcasm. I wondered if he detected mine. "Changing strategies in the last few rounds would leave my hand half one strategy and half another: poor at everything."

"Better that than all-in on a losing strategy," he said.

"You don't seem to have any problems drawing what you need."

"You only ever see what's on the board," he said, by which he meant the stool. The next time he trounced my capital ships with squadrons of bombers, he showed me the handful of cards remaining in his hand: all flak guns and other antifighter cards. "You can have a hand that's objectively weak but still the best tool for a job."

"And I am the one with a bad hand in the clumsy metaphor you're about to draw," I said. I was beginning to hate the necessity of metaphors in this non-digitized two-dimensional language.

He didn't deny it. "You're not Mindnet," he said. "The Mindnet won't have you back. Why do you keep *trying* to be Mindnet?"

"I cannot be other than what I am," I said.

"You're doubling down. Overcommitting."

(Overcompensating.)

He set the reshuffled decks onto the stool. "Cut."

"You still don't perceive what I am telling you," I said, but I cut the deck.

At least all of this was a distraction from the headache. The pain was at a lower level than before, but it persisted. When I paid attention to it, I could feel it slowly getting worse, so I tried not to pay attention.

The next round was the first time I beat him in a way I found truly satisfying. I drew the War Sun early. I could have discarded it. Using it meant committing to a strategy early.

Uthan might have been expecting me to take his advice. He played cautiously, fielding cards that hit hard enough to force me to answer, and therefore show him a little bit of what I held. From those clues, he *must* have figured that I had the War Sun. There was nothing in his manner or play to suggest it, but he had figured it out every other time I'd held it. Whatever cue he'd picked up on before was probably still there. Assuming, of course, that he wasn't cheating.

I answered that question for myself on the final turn. This time, when he showed me his hand, he had nothing to stop the War Sun's onslaught. He hadn't prepared at all. If he'd been cheating by somehow seeing my cards, this one had escaped him.

"Why'd you play that?" he asked.

"How could I not?" I asked. "The rest of my hand wasn't capable of beating yours." Aside from the War Sun, I had drawn poorly that round.

"Did you double bluff me?" He sounded impressed.

I let him go on thinking that. Letting an opponent craft their own narrative about what you were doing was an important element of this game. But a double bluff would have required there to be a bluff in the first place, as opposed to just going on doing what I was required to do.

The War Sun had, after a certain point, been my only path to victory. The odds had been against it, but slim odds had been better than none. Taking a wild chance had been my only chance, which made it the correct choice.

"Are you too emotionally distraught to continue?" I asked.

He grinned briefly. "I'm going to feel less guilty about beating you the rest of the time now," he said. "And stop holding back."

I watched him as he shuffled but wasn't able to gauge whether that last remark was a joke or a genuine description of his intentions.

"What's your name?" he asked. "The one you had before you were, ah, taken into the Mindnet?"

Instantly we were back into territory I wanted to stay as far away from as possible. "If this is an attempt to distract me so that I make poor gameplay choices, it won't work," I lied.

"Hey, I'm just playing the game," he said. "*And* I want to know."

"My name was Sil." This version had no raised volume, no pronunciation of the numerals the Mindnet utilized to translate names into a language the rest of the galaxy used.

It was also another lie.

"You don't have to tell me where you come from if you don't want to. But I have to ask. If you could return to that moment when the Mindnet found your world, if you could point them in some other direction, and relive your life from then on… would you?"

I was learning that, if I told enough lies, and told them fluidly enough, they stopped feeling all that different from the truth.

"Yes," I said. "I would."

CHAPTER NINE
SPOILED FOR A FIGHT

Now

There was no secret to success in combat, no set of skills that would make a fighter unbeatable. Just advantages and disadvantages. Training mattered, experience mattered, equipment mattered. But those were just things to *have*. In general, there were much better things to *be* than to *have*.

The fourth and third best things to be in a fight were calm and steady. If you managed both, your instincts had a chance of carrying you through. You might even have a chance to remember your training.

When the stun grenade rolled into the lift carriage, my foot moved before I let myself think. With scarcely a half second to line up my aim, I kicked it back through the door it had come through.

But my thoughts were not all that far behind my reflexes. I recognized the grenade. It was a stun grenade, a type used by police and special forces across the galaxy.

I flattened myself against the lift's nearest corner and sealed my eyes. The detonation was bright enough that my eyelids felt as transparent as water. My vision clouded with violet afterimages.

The light came with a clap of noise loud enough that it registered as pain before it did as sound. A resonant, electric buzz settled into my bones, jarring my nerves.

The second best thing to be in combat was lucky.

The only thing that had given me the opportunity to kick the stun grenade was my assailants making a mistake. They shouldn't have *rolled* the stun grenade inside. They should have tossed it, at an angle, let it rattle around the interior. That would have made it less predictable, given it momentum in directions off-angle from the path it had entered. A reflexive kick would have probably banged it off another wall.

Someone had screwed up. Maybe they had been afraid of missing the space between the open doors, or maybe they had simply not been trained for actions like this. Maybe their calm had slipped, and adrenaline had buried their training. Or maybe they'd just been too confident.

Either way, I was out the door, in the midst of my assailants, before I knew where I was going. I only knew I had to get out.

Immediately, I made my own mistake. I took a misstep, *whanged* my shoulder on the side of the door. I barely felt the impact, but my momentum faltered, and I careened sideways.

The space outside the elevator was a jungle of light and color, and for an instant I was afraid that I'd glimpsed the stun burst after all and my vision had turned to kaleidoscopic nonsense. But no – the area outside really was full of reflected light and dancing colors on walls. I slammed into someone's mirror-surfaced riot shield. I caught sight of mottled white-gold outfits, felt an armored shoulder pad, smelled the spicy whiff of Hacan breath. They wore face shields to match the larger ones they held, but they must not have been airtight because the smell was distinct.

There were anywhere between four to seven people waiting to ambush me. I couldn't count. The indirect stun grenade blast, and then slamming into a shield wall, had fuzzed all my senses. As badly as I'd been jarred by the stun grenade in here – the electric buzzing was not going away and set my nerves on fire – I couldn't count on my attackers having gotten it worse.

The few things I *did* see clearly included their masks and sensor-studded goggles. They'd have some protection from their own stun grenade. They would be dazzled but not for long.

This space wasn't where I'd told the lift to take me, but functionally it wasn't all that different: a junction of corridors and lift capsules. It was wider, though. Wide enough to allow for several armored humanoids to stand beside each other. Almost certainly why I had been brought here.

Somehow, I stayed on my feet. The person I'd rammed into had been too stunned to expect the blow. They fell. For a glimmer of a second, underneath their jarred face shield, I caught a glimpse of a pale-furred neck below yellow eyes and sharpened teeth. It was a Saar, an old and embittered species with batlike eyes and noses.

The Saar's exposed neck made it vulnerable. If I'd carried a knife–

An image flashed through my jumbled senses. Skin parting like curtains. Blood glistening sharp on metal.

I had decided against carrying weapons off-ship. Out alone, I was suspicious enough already. I hadn't wanted to give anyone who passed for an authority an excuse to detain me.

If I'd carried any weapon, though, it would never have been a knife.

I shoved those thoughts away. I didn't have time for trauma.

Because the first, best thing to be in combat was *absent*.

The fallen Saar cleared a space between my assailants. I could barely squeeze through it. I kept running. Five meters. Ten meters. My instincts told me that, in spite of my lift capsule's hijacking, my assailants wouldn't have secured all the lifts around us. I didn't have the time for the rest of my thoughts to catch up to my instincts' reasoning, but my instincts were right. When I careened toward the lift doors on the far wall, they opened.

Momentum carried me forward, making me lose my balance, and I crashed against the new lift capsule's wall. I leaned against screen and though I somehow stayed upright, the impact had been hard enough to knock the wind out of me. My breath locked in my chest. I had no voice to activate the controls. The manual control panel sat embedded next to the door, with the lift just wide enough to place the panel out of my reach.

I counted five attackers in the distance. Their brightly colored outfits blended into the hall lights and still-spotty afterimages. The glare from their shields added even more visual confusion. One of them had no shield, though, which gave me the chance to see a chitin exoskeleton. A N'orr. So many different species, which was incredible by itself – but I'd have to figure that out later.

All my attackers held dark, heavy looking pistols. Two of them, including the insectile N'orr, had gotten enough of their wits back together to aim at me.

I had no objective measure of the amount of time that passed while I stared at them.

My legs finally faltered, and I collapsed. At just the right moment.

Something hard slammed off the lift wall behind me. The buzzing was overwhelming, and I felt the impact through the floor. New afterimages burned into my vision. Everything was going spotty from lack of oxygen.

If whatever struck the bulkhead was another stun grenade, I was finished. It did no good to think about that now, but one of my brain's petty little betrayals kept it at the forefront of my thoughts. I lunged upward and forward for the manual control panel and smashed the heel of my palm into it.

The lift doors whisked shut.

Except the lift wasn't moving. The lift's walls came alive, instead, singing and dancing in the rainbow colors of a hundred holographic advertisements.

I had to focus hard on the controls. The panel projected cheerful icons representing common destinations. An *aureus* symbol. Needle and bandage. Steaming cup. The awkward tank-and-seat contraption of a fits-most-species toilet. I waved my hand through the image of the steaming cup.

The lift's floor thrummed as it started moving.

I flopped back to the floor. The first grenade had had a nerve-jamming effect. The second – if that's what it was – had given me a jolt to the system. I didn't pass out. But my vision receded to nothing, and all I remember is fighting for breath. The buzzing in my ears persisted.

When I put enough of myself back together to look behind me, I saw what had slammed into the wall. Two needle-tipped pyramids, about the size of a finger, lay on the lift's floor. A wire joined them together. The impact had crumpled the tip on one of them. Stun gun projectile.

Hell.

"Stop at the next available level," I rasped.

The floor stopped thrumming, and the door opened into darkness. My whole body tingled, like a limb that had gone asleep, but I managed to stand and heave myself out.

Once my eyes adjusted, I spotted a sheen of silver-blue light reflecting off distant walls. The space on the other side of the lift was narrow, with walls that hardly fit the lift's doors. Some kind of utility corridor. The ancient Lazax had probably made it for servitor drones, leaving enough space for a technician if one needed to come through.

The lift doors shut, leaving me trapped with that single distant light. I wanted to run, but tripping and cracking my head open would have been the worst kind of embarrassment: a well-deserved embarrassment. Almost as bad as just waiting for another lift carriage full of attackers to show up.

Some of my thoughts had almost caught up with my instincts. The frayed threads of my consciousness tangled back together.

When I'd charged into the second lift, I'd been confident its doors would open. In retrospect, I wasn't sure why. My attackers had redirected my first lift. There was no reason to assume they hadn't had control of everything else.

Except… there had been a rare exception. Part of me had seen it right away.

Their mottled gold-white outfits hadn't been uniforms. The colors of their clothes had been camouflage. So were the mirrored shields. They were made to blend in with the station's scoured-clean walls and centuries-old light strips.

They hadn't been hiding from *me*. If they'd been in total control here, it would have made more sense to dress highly visibly, in black or something else that stood out. It would reduce the risk of friendly fire. Make sure that anyone uninvolved clearly saw that something bad was about to happen and could figure out that they needed to leave immediately.

They were strangers here, and didn't work with station management. They'd been hiding from the station's cameras and security personnel. They'd wanted to nab me and get me out before anyone from the station could do anything about it. But why? Who were they working for?

After some minutes of twists and turns, I came upon a door leading to another lift. My breath caught in my throat. I crouched, bracing to run or fight. If my attackers knew where I was going, they could have just taken another lift, routed it here.

But no one came. More evidence that the people after me weren't in control, and thus possibly weren't able to track me. Whatever resources they'd used to get at me the first time might have been expended.

Of course, I couldn't count on that. I'd need to find another way to get around. The Lazax, conscientious as they were, had designed space stations with the idea that people might need to navigate them without power in emergencies. This was not true on Mindnet ships, a treacherous thought I quashed quickly. It took precious minutes to find a ladder shaft that looked like it didn't follow alongside a lift.

The Lazax had been a four-armed species, and they'd built their ladders accordingly, with rungs spaced closely together to keep grips with all their hands. This was good, because not all those rungs had survived to the present. Even those that had were unsteady. Their surfaces had worn to slippery metal. I collected more bruises than I bothered counting as I clung to the rickety contraption.

I didn't know where I was, or where I was going. Any markings the Lazax had placed there had worn away ages ago. The important thing was that I got far away from anywhere else I could be traced to.

The climb down gave me too much time to think. I didn't trust my thoughts as much as I trusted my instincts.

It was always possible that I'd mistaken the smell of the Hacan's breath for something else. Or confused the Hacan with the Sarr. Both were furred species. If those two had been the only ones I'd seen, I might have chalked it up to scrambled neurons and phantom odors. But then there had also been the N'orr.

A Sarr's face. N'orr chitin. The breath of a Hacan. Three different species, dressed and armed alike. That was ridiculous. It took a diplomatic miracle to get a Sarr to consent to exist in the same room as a N'orr – or at least to allow the N'orr to leave alive afterward.

When I'd gotten enough of banging my shins and risking my life on ancient ladders, I stepped onto the nearest landing.

I stubbed my toes on the doorframe. One of the strangest artifices of individuality was the ability to feel embarrassed even when no one was around to see me. Or, in one of those rare double negatives more apt than the inverse, an inability to *not* feel embarrassed. I kicked the door for embarrassing me.

That did not help.

The adrenaline was wearing off. I was falling apart. My thoughts churned, and only froth emerged.

The space on the other side of the door promised more bruises to come. It was vast and pressurized. A sharp breeze nearly took my breath away. It smelled strongly of ozone and burning dust.

Starkly defined and backlit shadows sprouted from the floor ahead, zigzagging in sharp angles and irregular shapes like the outline of a city. A very small city, made for tiny people. It was like stepping out onto a stage with a crude backdrop of a metropolis.

I closed my eyes. When I opened them again, the stage backdrop and lighting had melted away into something sensical. I stood in a haphazardly arranged row of life support machines. Oxygen factories and fans and purifiers, big equipment that sprouted skyscrapers of ducts and pipes. The thrum of fans rumbled at my feet.

The only light strips were on the floor. Whoever had installed all this – long after the fall of the Lazax Empire – hadn't cared to climb to the distant ceiling.

I leaned against the wall and allowed myself the luxury to rest.

The problem of figuring out who was after me was not going away. So I approached it in a different way, a way Uthan might have. Unknot all the anxieties of conscious thought. Start with words, with a story, and let my instincts fill in what came after.

A Hacan, a N'orr, and a Sarr walked into a bar, ordered drinks. Asked the bartender if the bartender knew why they'd all entered together.

The bartender's answer was obvious. *Keleres.*

The only organization that employed all those species – and more besides – and equipped them all from the same armory was the Keleres. The Galactic Council's "special agents," the ones who supposedly set aside all their species' many and varied disagreements to work together against the galaxy's existential threats. The same people I, in my cover identity, ostensibly worked for.

"Hell," I whispered.

I'd recognized the stun grenade because, like the weapon Uthan had held when we'd met, it was standard Keleres issue.

I had many questions, but now one certain answer: my cover had been blown. It was a moment which I'd mentally prepared myself for, for years, like every spy should have, but the realization still struck like an icicle in my stomach.

I had contingency plans. There were things I could do to recover. New identities I'd laid the groundwork for. My ability to bypass cybernetics scanners remained incredibly valuable to the Mindnet. I wouldn't be able to use Uthan's shuttle anymore. I'd have to get a new ship, somehow, or commit to operating without one.

Even in the best case, my options amounted to a choice of disasters. But my most pressing questions were all much closer, and the biggest of those was not even how my identity had been breached. It was how the Keleres had gotten here.

I hadn't decided to visit Port Vel Syd until after I'd roared away from the battle at Arrix. The Keleres couldn't have been waiting for me, since I hadn't known *I* was going to be here until shortly before I arrived. It was possible, though unlikely, that someone had chased me out of there. Tracked me here. It was difficult to do, but not impossible. But it seemed unlikely. Far more probably that these Keleres had already been here when I'd arrived. Something had made them go after me.

If I could find one and interrogate them… It was possible that the Druaa I'd spoken with was Keleres herself. The Keleres counted nearly every species among their numbers, Druaa included. If she'd been in on it, she'd made a bigger fool of me than I'd imagined. An interrogation would be a perfect excuse to get some revenge, though.

No, no, no. Couldn't afford the time for that. The problem with letting my instincts guide me was that they were extremely, uselessly emotional. I seemed to have gotten away for the moment. But if the Druaa was Keleres, traipsing right back into a place I'd been before was… well, I may have been a fool, but I was not so big of one, not yet.

My next best option was to escape. I would have to take the risk and get back to my shuttle. Which was the *other* place that the Keleres would now certainly be watching.

Every other alternative ranked far below these options. I ran through them in my head, just in case I'd missed anything. I could have disappeared into the station. This was a big place, barely functional, and with so many places to hide. I could hide until… well, there was nothing after "until." The Keleres had struck so soon once I'd arrived that they couldn't have marshaled all their forces. Waiting would give them a chance to bring in more people from out of the system.

Another option to consider: I had once slipped a data package on a freighter bound for Port Vel Syd and been instructed to address it to a person there. It was possible that the Mindnet had another agent here. Possibly more. The Mindnet had more agents than I would ever be allowed to know.

They were off-limits, though. My cover had been blown, and I could be located at any time. I would have been endangering the other agent if I dared approach.

And another: other ships were still coming in and out of this station. But stowing away on starships was the kind of thing that you could only get away with in fiction. Even my shuttle's systems, dumb as they were, would have noticed if someone else had been consuming oxygen on my ship. If I somehow surmounted that, the crew would definitely notice missing food and water. Few starships were as fast as my little courier shuttle; most plied the void for months at a time. I would have to assume that I'd be found mid-flight. I'd have to fight the crew, badly outnumbered.

This was the option the Mindnet would have me pick.

It was the most cost effective. The most efficient. If all my deductive reasoning so far was correct and the Keleres *were* after me, then I was a burned asset. Much less valuable than before.

By instructing me to stow away aboard a starship and murder its crew, We would risk very little. The most likely outcome would be that I died. The best outcome was that I'd bring them a captured starship. It was a simple low-cost, high-reward gamble. Going all-in on a War Sun when my other cards couldn't win on their own.

It was also the wrong choice. Uthan had tried to teach me that.

I was more valuable than that. We had only one agent who was capable of consistently getting through the Galactic Council's cybernetics security sweeps: me. At the very least, I needed to find out more about why this was happening.

A staticky pain spread through the back of my head, threatening a migraine. I knew what the Mindnet would have me do as surely as one half of my brain knew what the other was doing. I clasped my hands in front of my lips, and breathed through them – in and out, until the pain receded.

There was the correct choice, and there was the right choice. I was going to make the *right* choice. I'd make the Mindnet see it my way.

Rest time was over. I pushed away from the wall. I was agitated enough that picking my way through the pipes and cables felt like torture, but I didn't need another bruise.

I managed not to trip over them, at least. To my bewilderment, the exits I found were locked from the inside. Security here was haphazard and dependent on what the station's current occupants had done. The emergency ladder, however, allowed me to scramble up and out of the current level I was on.

The new corridor outside was segmented and winding, turning at shallow corners and intersecting other passages at oblique angles. It felt like I was walking inside a skeleton. It didn't fit Lazax sensibilities. Or any other sentients I was familiar with.

Port Vel Syd had hosted many species before its collapse. The Lazax hadn't been the only species eradicated at the end of the empire. Without the Mindnet's databases, I couldn't tell which lost people this had been made for.

I saw no one else, but that didn't mean this part of the station was abandoned. Someone had pasted light strips on the ceilings. I chased after a distant flickering, many-hued glow. It kept growing brighter, but always seemed to be just around the next shallow corner... until it resolved into holographic advertisements. They hovered around an autokiosk like the one I'd ordered my clothes to be printed from.

I waved over their shapes, dismissing them, peeling them off when they tried to cling to my hand. Most of them disappeared only when they determined that I'd seen them and absorbed their marketing tactics. Eventually, I found the only projection among them that *wasn't* trying to get my attention. Station directory.

The station's main computer had been installed over the gutted, millennia-old remnants of the original. It was primitive and half functional, cobbled together by many hands over the course of decades. I wrestled it into showing me a map of where I was, and several routes that led back to my shuttle.

There was an overlaid bulletin from station security, declaring a "situation" had occurred. I hated words. I guessed "situation" was meant to signify an event short of an "emergency" but more than an "incident." People across several levels were being told that there was no cause to worry but also that they should shelter in place. If any combination of words seemed *more* likely to cause panic, I couldn't think of them.

Station security were searching for "sentients of interest" dressed in yellow and orange camouflage. If anyone saw them, they were to run and report to station security, in that order. Drones and cameras were monitoring all major traffic arteries.

There was no mention of me. And "major traffic arteries" included all the docks and starbridge entrances, hindering the Keleres agents' ability to watch for me.

There would never be a better time to get to my shuttle.

And that was what made it a trap.

Clearly, the station security were hunting for me, too. Even if they had no idea who or what I was, I'd almost certainly crossed enough camera feeds during the fight that they would know my face. They would have been able to backtrace my movements from there and figure out which ship I'd hailed from.

If they hadn't mentioned me specifically, it was because they didn't want me to know I was being targeted. They were hoping I would walk right back to my shuttle.

The Mindnet did not find delight in much, but the closest

We came to it was in puzzling Our way past traps. We had the boundless cognitive capacity to game everything out in advance. Though I was no longer directly connected to the Mindnet, I still shared this little pleasure.

Traps had to be baited. If We could verify that the bait was real… then We could seize it while turning the trap against its creators.

In the early days of Our war to reclaim what the Lazax had lost, the Galactic Council made this mistake repeatedly. They tried to lure our ground forces into a crossfire with a false buckling in their defensive lines, only for Our precision artillery fire to turn the fake weak point into a real one. Other times, they'd sent freighters of precious material past embattled territory. Heavily armed escorts hid in the freighters' exhaust plumes. We had infiltrated the freighters' flight systems, seized control of their engines, placed them on new courses. When the escorts decelerated at their destination, their freighters simply carried on into Mindnet territory. It had all been extremely efficient.

The bait was real. My shuttle was out there.

I stayed with the autokiosk for some time. The kiosks sometimes contained hidden cameras. That level of risk was unavoidable. One of the advantages of being on a station so far removed from what currently passed for galactic law, though, was their inhabitants insisted on paying in cash, without credit accounts tied to facial recognition. The machines accepted my *aurei* without complaint.

In minutes, I had a new suspender and belt lined with loops and clasps, dangling with a dozen bottles of water. More bottles weighed down my backpack. I packed high-calorie food bars atop them.

Another option to consider: throw myself on the mercy of the local mobsters and their greedy grins. See if they would help me obtain my ship. It would still leave the problem of disembarking without the docking claws ripping my shuttle apart and dodging fire from the station's defenses on the way out. But at least I might have allies.

And that was the problem. Would they truly be allies? Far easier to turn me in from their perspective.

I refused to take the lift. The ladder climb to the section of the station where my shuttle waited, though, was "only" another three hundred meters. I managed fewer bruises this time.

Three corridor junctions away from the boarding starbridge, I looked again for the glow of holographic advertisements. I did not have to look far to find a second autokiosk, in a location where I could manage my scheme closer to my ultimate destination.

The station's decades-old Hylar operating system had been revised by programmers who hated each other deeply and personally. Upon closer look, the system had a twenty-year old exploit that had been patched during a large system update. Once. Someone had reverted the update. Another person had reinstalled it. Over and over again.

During one of these cycles, the system had somehow registered the exploit fix as permanently installed. It hadn't gotten reinstalled during any of the cycles afterward.

I may not have had access to the Mindnet's library of technical skills, but I had spent my life with machines in my head. Compared to the average galactic sentient, I was a savant. I did not have to strain my abilities to access a secure camera feed from outside the starbridge tower that led to my ship.

The embarkation lobby, or what passed for one, was a corridor junction with some benches bolted onto the walls. It had three exits: a corridor opposite the starbridge door, and two more to the left and right.

As I watched, the camera view swept across the sealed starbridge hatch, and then to each of the three adjoining corridors. It repeated this on an exact schedule every few seconds. The starbridge hatch had a small window, but the angle kept me from seeing through it with any clarity. I could have taken direct control of the camera, reoriented and zoomed it on the door. That would have given away my presence to anyone else watching the feed, though… and I had a distinct idea that someone was.

There were three parties at play here. Myself. The Keleres. And station security. And all of us had reason to be watching this corridor.

I prepared a quick package of instructions. Then sent a remote order to raise the door.

The hatch was heavy enough that I felt the rumble of the mechanism and the *thunk* of the lock clicking into place, even from several halls away.

Abruptly, the camera pivoted and locked into place, watching the door. Someone other than me was definitely monitoring the camera. The second I'd raised the door, they'd taken control of the camera.

A long and deadly silence followed. I stifled my breath. There was no reason to, but I was only human.

The silence lasted long enough to shift from tense to awkward.

A flicker of shadow played across the edge of the camera. The view instantly swerved toward it. Two figures in orange-yellow camouflage headed toward the starbridge door, weapons raised. Keleres agents. They peered around corners, and then into the starbridge door.

Two humans in significantly less camouflaged blue uniforms peeled out from the shadows on the other side of the starbridge hatch. I hadn't seen their uniforms before, but I would have bet anything that they were what passed for station security. They'd plainly been waiting to catch someone – me – coming in.

One of them yelled something at the Keleres. Though the camera picked up no sound, I heard her distance-muffled voice. And then I heard the spark-pop of both Keleres firing their stun weapons.

On the camera image, the blue duo dropped. The Keleres emerged and stepped over the tremoring bodies. A Hacan's tail poked out of one of the Keleres agents' camouflage. It flicked about anxiously as the agent peered inside the hatch.

Then something bright flared off the Hacan's shoulder armor. The Hacan staggered but stayed upright. The station security hadn't been alone. More blue-uniformed humans appeared around a corridor junction and opened fire on the Keleres. The Hacan and the other Keleres agent started running back the way they'd come. The camera angled to follow them. The rest of the station security pursued.

I didn't see the rest. I was on my way to the starbridge. I approached from the leftmost corridor, the one that had neither station security nor retreating Keleres. The one the camera had stopped watching.

Once I was safely on the other side of the starbridge door, I sealed it, and hit the locking button twice. My second tap triggered the instructions I'd fed the station systems. They remapped all the door's controls on the station's side. Now the only thing that any of those buttons would do was make a loud tone.

The starbridge walkway still had that drinking-straw-like curve, so I couldn't see the end of it. I watched for anyone else coming running down the path. No one did.

I knelt by the door and listened. A minute passed, and I still waited. I needed to be sure I wasn't going to be interrupted.

I felt the brief thump of bootsteps on the other side of the hatch. Then the buzz of the tone I'd programmed.

Then the same tone again. And again, longer still. Then a repeated, increasingly frustrated jabbing.

The starbridge's windows gave me a fair view of my shuttle. The cockpit lights were on, like I'd left them. I saw no movement. There didn't seem to be anyone aboard.

I picked myself up, stiff from the weight of all my water bottles, and started down the walkway toward my shuttle.

I had some time now. Not much, but enough to figure out my next task: getting the docking clamps to release. I had some ideas. Most involved my shuttle's heavier guns.

I allowed myself to feel clever about how I'd handled things so far.

Humans are not the only sentients in the galaxy capable of superstition, but we are more susceptible to it than most. It comes from a combination of arrogance, lack of imagination, and faulty pattern-recognition abilities. We attribute emotions to natural forces. Believe in karma.

Even people aware of these anthropic fallacies can succumb to them.

To this day, I believe that it was that brief feeling of cleverness that prompted the fireball to rip through my shuttle's hull. Just to teach me a lesson.

CHAPTER TEN
DATA BREACH

Then

Five days after Uthan and I left Kitrya-892 b, I woke with the distinct feeling that something was wrong.

That was, something beyond all the things that had been regularly wrong at that point.

The engines' rumble had changed pitch. The dropped octaves indicated we'd slowed to sublight. We must have arrived. We'd reached Mecatol Rex much sooner than I'd expected.

Every day, I could walk a little farther and with a little less pain, but I didn't want to face anything else right now. I remained in the medical cabin, working through my leg-stretching exercises. No place on this ship was friendly territory, but this cabin felt closer to being *mine* than any other aboard. I wanted to make Uthan come here to tell me what he'd done.

I heard him walking about. His footsteps were quiet against the deck, like he was taking care to stifle them. He spent most of his time in the cockpit.

Then the engine noises rumbled back up to their previous pitch and volume. Full acceleration again.

I propped myself up on my elbows. The engine noises didn't change. They continued for so long that it was plain that we were returning to interstellar speeds.

One of two things must have happened. The first possibility was that we had never stopped anywhere but instead coasted on unguided momentum for a while. That was dangerous at superluminal velocities: there were usually so many gravity wells to avoid that a starship's engines had to remain on constantly.

The second possibility was that we had arrived somewhere only to leave again sometime later. That made no sense. Not, at least, if I took what I had been told at face value.

Once we were underway again, I heard Uthan leave the cockpit. Something had clearly agitated or excited him. He paced between his cabin and kitchen a number of times. He seemed to be moving just to have something for his restless legs to do.

Then he came into the medical bay, eyes twinkling. I braced myself.

"What does the name Zabiya mean to you?" he asked.

I shut my eyes and kept them that way for several carefully measured breaths.

"What it most means to me right now," I said, when I opened my eyes again, "is a sharp rise in my urge to commit violence."

I had not heard my given name in years. Long enough that I'd hoped it had lost some of its power. But it was still attention-grabbing, like a pin in the back of my head.

"Zabiya Tahro," he said, uncowed. "Child of Lydia Tahro, the Countexx of the Molded Throne. You're from the Opaline system. Iko Province."

I affected terse disinterest, hoping that would encourage him to change the subject. "The title is just as pretentious as you make it sound."

Even before the Mindnet, it had not been so significant a title. Just another name for nobility. All seven hundred Countexx-rank nobles competed to earn impressive-sounding titles. Countexx of the Vulture Tower, of the Ivory Mesa, and so on. All of that nonsense had been rightfully quashed when the Mindnet invaded.

He already knew parts of my history, like how young I'd been when I'd received my cybernetics. Those were common details, though. I had felt much safer when I could be anonymous. Less like "me," and more like Us. The fact that he now knew which world I came from felt like I'd had a shield ripped out of my hands. Hearing my old name felt like he was compelling me to be someone else.

"At some point, you've taken a DNA sample from me," I said. "When we stopped, you checked it against a database and discovered this identity you're going to attach to me now."

He shrugged. "Nothing invasive, just fingerprints and facial recognition." I marveled at his use of the word "invasive" and the fact that he genuinely didn't seem to believe he had been. "And, yes, we made a quick stop at Corlu IV. Small world, but it's got a Keleres database. We've still got a way to go to Mecatol Rex." He leaned against the medical cabin's cabinets. "It's true, though, isn't it? You used to be nobility where you're from."

The urge to commit violence was not receding. "I am *from* the Mindnet."

"But… how? How did that happen to you?"

When the Mindnet reconquered a world, they handled its population with a delicate – but firm – grip. All citizens, no matter their species, were to become part of the Mindnet. Joining Us was the only option.

But the Mindnet could not make this happen all at once. Cybernetics could not be mass-produced. "One-size-fits-all" cybernetics were good only for producing zombies. True cybernetics had to be tailored to each individual's mind. We made citizens, not drones. Mostly.

So cybernetics were best manufactured locally. Every new world brought Us millions, sometimes billions, of sentients to incorporate. Creating an industrial base to do so took time, especially on planets still reeling from invasion.

While all of that was being arranged, We still had the population to deal with. The destruction of the system's organized defenses didn't mean the invasion was over. Some resisted, some surrendered. Surprisingly few welcomed it. So the Mindnet, as always, made the most efficient use of its resources. They created propaganda.

A world's presidents, or kings, or senate, or nobles, or clan elders, or high castes – whoever had once had authority – were given a choice. They and their families could be the first to be cybernetically augmented to serve as examples to their citizens. Or they could die.

My parents had chosen to live.

Thus, at the age of four, I had been among the first of the Mindnet's new citizens to be given cybernetic implants.

I had developed in tandem with my implants. The person who would have grown up without them was a stranger to me.

Uthan folded his arms, waited for me to speak. When I didn't, he said, "You could actually *be* the Countexx, if you could find someone to hold the ascension ceremony."

"Three parents are still alive," I said. The odds were in favor of them being alive, anyway. Life expectancy and probability suggested they would be. "If not, each of my two eldest siblings would be in line before me."

I had not seen any of them since I was four or thought of them since then. It *hurt* to think about, and not in the way that grief typically hurt children.

My implants used to quash those thoughts. They triggered a pulse of pain every time they detected a thought of family forming. And endorphins rewarded thoughts that distanced myself from the child I'd been before.

Humans, like many other sentients, enjoyed pretending that there is something holy, something numinous, about family. They were chemically mediated synaptic patterns, etched out by ruthless evolutionary processes.

There were better patterns and better processes.

Because my brain had grown around my implants, my brain didn't *need* my implants to trigger those same responses. Every thought of my parents, every word Uthan said about them, came with a background fuzz of pain.

Every time I pushed the subject away, I felt better. It was easier to cope, I was realizing, if I attributed the less desirable thoughts to a stranger inside me. The stranger I kept hearing anyway – the stranger that spoke in the voice of the Arborec.

(I aim to serve.)

Uthan said, "You know, plenty of wealthy people keep some of their wealth off whatever world they're living on. You know, just in case they have to get away in a hurry. You should see if the Tahro family has any off-world assets. You could be set for life."

"Could we please change this subject?" I interrupted.

Something in my voice must have reached him. He stopped

and rubbed under his beard, pondered me for a while. Usually, I had no trouble meeting his eyes, but not this time. "I don't think you've ever said 'please' to me before," he said.

I felt strongly enough about this to go to those extremes. "I've refrained from prying into your life," I said. "How would you react if I did? You've left enough embarrassing hints around."

"'How would you react…'" Uthan repeated in awe. He drew it out, as if each word was a sentence. "That sounds an awful lot like, 'How would you feel?' Are you using *empathy* as a conversational tactic? You understand the idea?"

This conversation was a perfect microcosm of our relationship so far: he had a destination he wanted to reach but tried to give me the impression that I had made choices along the way, too. He'd spoken in a tone that was somewhere between wonderment, teasing, and ironic. My difficulties parsing facial expressions and voices would never go away, but they were also never worse than in that moment. All I knew at the time was that I did not care for his big, playful smile. "You did not answer my question," I said.

"What do you want to know?" he asked. "I could tell you about my group marriage. Or my divorce. The kids decided they'd rather stay with them than me. Which wasn't really a surprise, considering how long I stayed away from home. And yes – you're right that I used to have a copilot, and this used to be his cabin. He and I split up after we had a serious disagreement about finances, and shipboard living conditions, and I know *I* said things I regret–"

"Hell," I said. I'd hoped to pick up other swear words by now, but, for a Mentak captain, Uthan had been surprisingly fastidious about not using any around me. The fuzz had turned into a headache, and then a migraine, with astonishing speed.

Every thought of my old life still came attached to pain … but without my implants, they had to rise to the level of conscious awareness before my conditioning kicked in. I had been able to avoid those thoughts all this time. But now, every time Uthan mentioned them – every time he *spoke* – they bubbled out of my subconscious. My vision was covered with vivid purple afterimages, like I'd stared too long into a field of lights. I tried very hard for several minutes to clear my thoughts.

When I could see again, Uthan was gone. His footsteps padded down the corridor outside.

I pinched the bridge of my nose and rubbed it back and forth. The pain lingered. I doubted it would leave anytime soon.

There were a limited number of things I could do to make it better. Thoughts that had triggered reward-endorphins would still work, too.

The first, best reward-inducing thought was to think, and think hard, about how I could be of more service to the Mindnet.

I have to do better. I have to be better. I told myself that over and over again.

CHAPTER ELEVEN
SEVERED

Now

Human eyewitness memory is one of the least reliable records in the known galaxy – short only of Druaa accounts of their own history or Letnev propaganda about the Twilight Wars.

Yet I'm writing this, recounting events in a moment-by-moment narrative. This is a mistake. The reason I know it is a mistake is because what I so clearly remember about my shuttle's destruction is impossible.

With more certainty than most else I've said, I recall standing in the starbridge tower's corridor, surrounded by windows, seeing my shuttle blast apart in vivid detail. The light erupted from somewhere behind the cockpit, splintering my shuttle's prow into tiny fragments, and the rest of the hull into wickedly spinning shards. Then the first of the shuttle's pressurized thruster fuel reservoirs ruptured, a firecracker burst of violet light that atomized what remained of my shuttle's frame and blew the rest of the debris outward.

One of my shuttle's landing struts spun into the hapless Hacan merchant ship, smashing it into two large pieces. A burst of vapor – that ship's entire air supply venting – briefly fogged the void.

I clearly remember standing still, feeling and hearing nothing. The starbridge was not so long that this should have been possible.

Mostly, though, I remember the light. The light felt like it clawed behind my head into my brain and left a dead spot in the center of my vision. I looked away in time to see spiderweb cracks splinter along all the starbridge windows.

Even as a reflection, the glare was overpowering. But not so much that I failed to see the jets of air from the station behind me as the larger debris impacted its hull.

Out of the corner of my stinging eyes, I saw a piece of my shuttle's engine housing spin past one of the windows, and then scythe into the starbridge tower's base.

These were the memories I was left with. I have been over this so many times, running them in the theater of my imagination, to have distorted them. Every time an unaugmented human remembers something, they change the memories without meaning to – eventually remembering the act of remembering more than the incident itself. In my mind, this was stretched across seconds.

What likely occurred instead was that all of this happened at once, in fragments of time just as jagged edged as the remaining pieces of my shuttle.

At some point, I became aware I was lying on the floor. Still in the starbridge tower. One side of my face felt hot. Every time I took a breath, it burned. But there *was* still air, and I *could* still breathe. That was important.

The situation, however, was rapidly changing. My ears popped, painfully. Then again. Not all of the jets of air came from the station. They were difficult to see through the afterimages, but moving my head made it clear that some of them sprouted from the starbridge's windows.

Another thing I remember that perhaps did not reflect reality: that I reacted to all this calmly and with a level head. Hypoxia often leaves victims feeling that they're awake and alert, right up to the moment they faint.

Somehow, I managed to get to the opposite wall where a well-marked emergency compartment held masks and canisters of compressed air. I fumbled with the mask's straps but managed to secure it.

Wherever it had come from, its creators had taken safety more seriously than the station's current masters. My face had been seared by the shock of superhot air channeled this way. The fact that I was not now charred carbon, swept out into the void along a backwash of escaping air, was due to those precautions. A pressure door had slammed shut between me and the gaping hole that had once led to my shuttle.

Another point in favor of the faulty-memory hypothesis: the door must have come down so quickly that I should have heard it. I still don't recall any sound at all.

I saw the hatch I'd used to enter. The one I'd been so clever about getting to this side of it. The hatch seemed to rotate, slowly.

It wasn't what was moving. The starbridge was twisting. Near the base of the tower, the metal walls started to crack, bending well past their point of tolerance.

The large piece of shrapnel I'd seen fly past the windows and strike the tower's base had severed the starbridge's structural supports on that side. And the explosion had given the whole structure a push. The entire starbridge structure was twisting, torquing, ripping away *slowly*…

I wasted air swearing, cursing myself for taking the half second to assess the situation rather than running the instant I'd gotten the mask on. I bolted for the hatch.

That half second would not have allowed me to reach it anyway.

The first noise I heard was a tremendous groan, audible less in my ears and more the way it vibrated through my chest. Then a gale-force *whoosh* as the far walls ruptured. The pressure doors between me and the exit slammed shut with such speed that it looked like they had simply materialized into place.

Suddenly, my feet slipped off the floor. All the power connections to the station had failed, and the artificial gravity died.

It felt like I had kicked the floor away, and that this had been the final push that snapped the starbridge off the station. Like the station wasn't in orbit of a neutron star but hovering over infinity, and now the tower was plunging into nothing.

I belatedly realized the front of my clothing was soaked through. Some debris must have ricocheted down the starbridge and struck my "armor" of water bottles. If I was bleeding, I was not bleeding enough to see or feel right now.

Another bright point of hope: the light strips remained on. They had batteries meant to last decades or longer. Some of those light strips were racing toward me, along with the wall that had once been the ceiling.

I raised my arms just in time for my elbows to take the impact of the spinning light strips rather than my head. That must have hurt, but I can't remember the pain.

I groped along the wall, trying to find purchase without pressing so hard as to propel my body backward. I crashed into a corner. The wall slipped away from me as the skybridge continued spinning, dragging me against its angular momentum.

Despite that, I managed to grip the edge of one of the windows. Outside it, more and more of the station rotated into my view.

That rotation gave me a view of the starbridge's final structural supports splintering. The last threads connecting it to Port Vel Syd snapped. The tower torqued free.

The sound of straining metal stopped at once. Fully separated from the station, the starbridge floated gently away from Port Vel Syd.

Once again, I recall thinking – matter-of-factly, clear-headedly – that now I was going to have to jump the vacuum between me and the station. That was not a sane thought, but it was perhaps the closest thing I had to a thought, at that moment.

I remembered enough of my Mindnet space flight training to know that, even with a supply of air to breathe, my body could survive perhaps ninety seconds in a vacuum.

From a distance, the tower's spin would have looked gentle. Inside, it felt like I was clinging to the inside of a giant barrel tumbling down a waterfall.

I gripped the window's edge hard to stay anchored. If I fell again, I'd be battered when I hit the other side, and then I would have to fight again to get another hold on something to remain stable.

My ears continued popping. A cold breeze – getting colder – plucked at my clothes. The draft soothed the burned side of my face. "Always look on the bright side," Uthan would have said. I could hear his voice, as if he whispered in my ear.

The debris impacts along the window were relatively small. I couldn't perform an exhaustive check, but I saw none larger than half a centimeter. The jets of vapor sprouting on the other side of the window looked like tornadoes, moving so fast that they jumped and whirled. A sprinkling of ice crystals drifted into the void.

My grip, already awkward enough to maintain, became slippery. I looked down and saw condensation beaded on my fingers. Ice glimmered around the edges of the holes in the windows.

The pressure doors on the end where my shuttle was seemed to be my only way out. If whoever had built the pressure doors had had their head in order, the doors would have been designed to be unopenable for as long as there was any difference in air pressure on either side. The safety would be mechanical, not electronic. No way to circumvent them. Couldn't have someone blast a whole compartment into space by accident. Or especially not by design.

I was trapped. The good news and the bad news was that I wouldn't be in such a state for long. Air pressure on each side of the doors would soon be equalized. At zero.

The starbridge continued to tumble. The whole structure rocked as it drifted across one of the larger air jets boiling away from the station. The air washed across the window I clung to, turning my view into a churning gray soup. The gas jet pushed against the direction of the starbridge tower's lengthwise rotation. The tug on my grip eased.

Well – some good luck after all.

As if in a dream, I moved myself down the broken corridor,

passing handhold after handhold. I needed to be absent. I needed to think.

The bomb in my shuttle made no sense. The Keleres agents had been trying to capture me, not kill me. I didn't have the time or capacity to think about the sudden change in tactics. Adrenaline still held most of my pain at bay, but I was starting to become more conscious of it.

I didn't have to put much effort into keeping close to the wall now. Whenever I drifted too far, I passed over one of the holes in the windows, and an icy-cold draft pushed me "down" until I could scrabble for purchase along the next window again.

A hollow pop resounded through what remained of the air. A bone-deep cold soaked into my side. One of my last intact water bottles exploded. With numb fingers, I fumbled with the catch to release the harness that carried them and left them behind. I'd yanked my air mask's strap tight before fastening it, but now it felt even tighter. It bit into my scalp as though trying to pinch my head in two.

I had, I thought idly, perhaps a minute before the starbridge's remaining air vanished.

Shimmering, rainbow-refracting ice crystals spread along the cracks in the window and grew from there. Seeing outside was getting harder by the second. But we had moved far enough that I could see where the starbridge had once been attached to the station. The starbridge tower's old base had become a labyrinth of sharpened, twisted metal... caging the pressure door the station had clamped over its wound. No getting out that way.

But there was another airlock: a round hatch, twice as big as a person, about thirty meters away from that pressure door. The frost made it difficult to see but it looked darker than the surrounding hull. Like the starbridge itself, the airlock had no doubt been added long after the station's construction. Probably for the workers who'd come out to install the starbridge. It, I realized, was my only chance to live.

It passed out of my view as the tower continued its slow rotation.

At some point, it was going to be aligned with the pressure door at the far end of the starbridge tower. But I could not tell when. The pressure door ahead had no windows. The tower's spin made it impossible to stay oriented. As I grappled toward the pressure door, I tried to keep my memory of the outside view fresh, and trace where the airlock was, but it was an exercise in guesswork. I couldn't trust my sense of direction.

I reached the pressure door that had once led to my shuttle, and now to nowhere. Every surface was covered in frost now. I had to blink it out of my eyes. An indicator light shone a muted red underneath the ice crystallized on it.

The terrifying thing was that the *feeling* of being cold was rapidly diminishing. The breeze and the cold were diminishing because so little air remained.

My emergency air supply would allow me to survive the vacuum long enough to die of conditions other than hypoxia.

I was starting to feel flushed, swollen – like my face did after hanging upside-down or entering zero gravity, except that the feeling was throughout my entire body. Gas bubbles in my blood and flesh were expanding.

I was not likely to pop. Human body tissues could distend quite a bit before breaking. Which unfortunately did little to protect me from the other ways this condition would rapidly become lethal.

The rational, dispassionate part of me noted all of this. My stream of consciousness had reassembled itself to the point where I could now remember feeling many other things than rational and dispassionate – the bulk of which, for dignity's sake, I will not record here.

When I looked backward, I could no longer see the jets of air escaping through the cracked windows. There was only ice and silence.

I wedged myself into the corner and braced my legs against the door. My mask's head strap bit hard enough that I was sure it was about to draw blood, or snap, or both.

The indicator light blinked green. There was now only a small pressure difference between this side of the door, and the side that opened into the vacuum. I tried to kick the door open – what else could I have done? – when suddenly the door was gone – ripped away by another piece of debris that had slammed into it from the outside. Then, I was immediately on the wrong side of the starbridge, out alone, in the void, with broken metal and plastic where I'd once been.

Luck was with me in one sense: the razor-edged torn walls had blown outward, rather than crumpled inward. I was not sliced into pieces as I was blown into space.

There was a popular misconception, sometimes even among starship crews who should know better, that nothing can be heard in a vacuum. There was no sound *in* a vacuum. But, when I was out there, I heard plenty.

Noise transmitted through my body, up my bones and across the back of my ears, just fine. It was like being in a sensory isolation chamber, where every little sound my body made was enough to drive me mad. Blood pounded against my ears. The scrape of cartilage in my joints as I kicked. Soft pops in my mouth as my saliva bubbled, boiling into the vacuum.

More than anything else, though, I heard pain. My eardrums ruptured.

I had at least managed to keep myself from spinning. I saw Port Vel Syd's naked hull across a too-clear hundred-meter expanse, stretching outward into a metal horizon. I was headed toward a smooth wall. Or at least it looked smooth. My vision had blurred, either from ice forming or my eyes distending, or both.

The airlock was dozens of meters away from where I'd soon make impact. I was not going to reach it.

Maybe if I'd had the time and forethought to aim as I'd been catapulted out of the starbridge, I might have stood the slenderest of chances of reaching the airlock. However, I'd been swept out too quickly.

Amidst all this hopelessness, I had to ask myself: why did I want so badly to live?

The obvious answer was that it was not my life to want or give away. It was Ours. But the Mindnet wouldn't have cared if this were the end of my story. My cover was blown, my ship had been destroyed, and I was plainly being outplayed at whatever game I'd stumbled into.

This was the first time I considered the thought that there was *something else*.

It was always possible that I was a coward, taking my vestigial, individualistic fear of death and wrapping higher-minded explanations around it.

Cowardice wasn't a satisfactory explanation for what I did next, though.

There was one last way to get myself to the airlock.

My air mask was tugging at its head strap so hard that, when I reached back to undo it, it popped off. My last breath vanished in a burst of fog.

I grasped the hose. Air jetted out of the mouthpiece. It was amazing that the air canister hadn't burst, but the starbridge and everything in it seemed to have been built to better standards than the rest of the latter-day additions to Port Vel Syd. I aimed the jet along the station's "horizon," which was laterally opposite the direction of the airlock.

My senses were conducting a discordant symphony to express, in more creative ways than I imagined possible, that I was about to die. It was a sign of my mental state that I continued to hear my pain, like the heat running along my muscles like a spreading fire.

Another misconception about the vacuum was that the cold of space is an immediately lethal danger. The cold that frosted over the starbridge's walls had come from laws of gas expansion. In a given volume of air, there was only so much heat. When that air had blown out into the vacuum, it kept the same amount of energy, only spread much thinner. Hence the flash-cooling, and the ice everywhere. Frankly, after the explosion in my shuttle, I probably would have been cooked to death if the air *hadn't* been able to escape and cool.

Out here, though, it was different. Full vacuum seemed to act as a perfect insulator. I was flushed, panicked, and exerting myself. This was like being wrapped in ten layers of thermal blankets during a workout. When I'd been part of the Mindnet, I'd experienced memories of other Mindnet members who'd died in a vacuum. None of their recorded senses had seemed so vivid.

The starbridge's distant lights looked bleached, like they'd drained color. Or my eyes were losing their ability to perceive that. But the lines of the station's hull had never seemed sharper. I didn't think I had ever seen anything so sharp.

In that state of anoxia-drunk annoyance and euphoria, I crashed into the airlock. I wanted to live.

Everything I did was for the good of the Mindnet.

I kept my grip on the airlock's handhold. The hatch controls still functioned. I "heard" the door grind open through my hand, which was a muted and deep, liquid-like noise, like gurgling syrup.

It was one of the last things I remember with even a shadow of lucidity. My vision became fringed by black, and the last of my color perception vanished. I was sure that my hands were supposed to be something other than gray. Same with the indicator lights on the far side of the airlock chamber.

I don't remember getting that far.

The human brain is such an odd and frightening thing. It's also funny, but mostly in retrospect. The things about it that seem funny afterward are as terrifying as they are disorienting. At the time, I remember sobbing from the pain before perceiving the feeling of pain again.

Some part of me was aware of pain, or at least anticipating pain, but my conscious mind siloed it off somewhere. It was a neat trick. I wished I could have done it on command rather than *in extremis.*

The vents hissed as the chamber pressurized. The airlock's artificial gravity returned with the air. I'd come around on the floor, with my hand stretched out under the airlock's controls. The heel of my palm tingled where I'd slammed it into the panel. My color vision gradually returned. The controls' indicator lights turned from blinking gray to blinking yellow, and then to solid green.

Then the pain came. Speaking out loud hurt, so I stopped.

But breathing hurt just as much, and I couldn't quit that. My vision blurred, every slight sound came with piercing pain, and I felt burned all over.

But I had never been more thrilled to be alive. That was almost certainly a consequence of my oxygen-starved brain's faulty judgment.

The inner airlock hatch clicked as it unlocked. Somehow, I found the strength to stand.

The corridors on the other side were maintenance tunnels like those I'd found before. Empty plastic crates dotted the floor. The walls were scarred with the dents and scrapes of moving too-large equipment through a too-small space. As I'd thought, workers bolting the starbridge onto the old Lazax construction had gone through this airlock. It didn't seem to have been used since then, though.

The euphoria lasted as long as the adrenaline, which was long enough to begin looking for aid. The construction workers had done the responsible thing of setting up an emergency first aid kiosk. The pain drugs were expired, but I took them anyway.

Another "funny" thing about consciousness? Even as my judgment grew shakier, there remained a steady intellectual core underneath it, ticking away like clockwork.

As assassination attempts went, this had been a very good one.

It would be extremely difficult to figure out who had placed the bomb. But the circumstances left a few clues, nonetheless.

The bomb would have taken out the station security cops in the starbridge if I hadn't lured them out. Like any secret service, the Keleres were capable of a lot of officially deniable bastardry, but I wasn't aware of any prior incident in which they had so callously bombed bystanders. That eliminated them as suspects.

The explosion had occurred shortly after I would have boarded my shuttle… if I'd gone straight there. But I paused after getting inside the starbridge. I'd waited, listening for the tone that verified that my lock had worked. Someone didn't seem to have anticipated that. And those moments, small as they were, had foiled the assassination plan.

Whoever had blown the shuttle up knew that I had gotten past the starbridge's hatch. But their information stopped there. They had waited an appropriate amount of time for me to have reached the shuttle but hadn't – more likely couldn't – have verified that I was actually inside.

Placing a sensor aboard the shuttle shouldn't have been difficult, not considering what they'd already been able to do. It was much harder to get a bomb than a remote camera. Whoever placed the bomb may have been resource-limited – for some reason they'd had the bomb already but hadn't been able to get a matching sensor in place. Or… they'd been unable to hide its transmissions back home. Station security could have detected the sensor's signals and realize that something was happening.

It didn't matter which of these explanations were true. Both required that the bomber wasn't aligned with station security. I needed more information.

The pain drugs were a bad idea. They encouraged me to stay on my feet. The more I stayed on my feet after trauma like that, the more damage I'd do to my body. But I was still in danger. I staggered to the nearest autokiosk, in an empty corridor one level up. I still had the mental acuity to wave the advertisements aside and get to the station directory.

Whenever I tried to read all the urgent red security bulletins, the words turned to vapor. My vision was blurry, my corneas damaged by vacuum exposure. I moved on automatic, repeating motions, sure that if I paused to look at the icons I was manipulating that I would lose track of what I'd been doing.

I found myself on the camera feeds again, seeing through the camera I'd used before. The area was empty. The pressure doors remained sealed, and loose debris laid about, but that was all.

A wave of my hand swapped camera views. It did not take me long to find where everybody had gone. The Keleres agents had gotten only a few corridor junctions away from the lobby.

They lay splayed across the floor, a bloodied jumble of limbs twisted the wrong way. The nearest walls were scored with bullets. An intersection behind them, two figures wearing station security uniforms were in the same shape.

Someone had gunned them down – both Keleres and station security, indiscriminately. And then just left.

CHAPTER TWELVE
VELVET
Then

Uthan enjoyed his meals on no schedule that I could determine. He ate copiously but irregularly, less often than an adult human should have. He took his food anywhere, in any cabin he happened to be working in, leaving wrappers and smells everywhere. He seemed like a half-grown adolescent, stringing himself along from one day to the next.

I consumed my meals regularly and robotically. He probably thought he and I were naturally nothing alike. The truth was the opposite: looking at him, I saw what I was capable of becoming if I didn't keep myself disciplined.

Every day, I learned more of what it was like to be an unaugmented human and saw more of my undiscovered self reflected in him.

Whenever anxiety wound around my head as tight as it could go, it found a way to squeeze a little deeper. Since we'd returned to hyperluminal velocities, Uthan had picked up the annoying habit of having more of his meals with me. Or at least in my proximity.

The first two times, I assumed that he was being solicitous of someone he'd discovered was wealthy. The third time he ate near me, though, a prickling discomfort spread up my back. He was studying me, I realized. Keeping his eyes on me between forkfuls of Xxcha root-noodles.

He seemed to notice my sudden wariness. "Have you felt any different since we stopped by Corlu IV?"

"Why would I?" I asked sharply.

"Answer my question, and I'll answer yours."

That did not seem fair to me when he was the one whose behavior had overstepped the unspoken social boundaries we'd carefully built. It took hourly practice to keep my parents' names and faces from my thoughts now. Maybe it was a measure of how drained I'd been that I didn't argue.

"I always feel different," I told him. "Every day more than the last."

"But do you feel alone?"

(You're never alone.)

These were plainly leading questions. He looked excited to tell me something, which made my skin cold. The only other time I'd seen him like this had been after he'd discovered my name.

I fixed him in my stare. "I have never felt more alone." Though, right then, I could have done with feeling a little more so.

"There was something I didn't expect in the Corlu system. I only saw it when I was going back over my sensor logs. A visiting creature."

Now I knew why I felt so cold. "Creatures don't 'visit' planets."

"It was an Arborec carrier."

A clumsy name. He meant a Nightthorn Haven, the same vessel I'd dreamed about. Wholly organic, starfaring organisms... and part of the Arborec's bodymind. They collected light and ingested hydrogen for fuel, grew bioengineered intermix sacs, and expelled columns of burning plasma exhaust. They held the eponymous Nightthorns, the Arborec's equivalents of interceptor-type fighters, but also ferried other Arborec organisms through the cosmos. Long ago, a ship like it might have visited Kitrya-892 b and left the Arzuga spores that had mutated into the fungus that infested me now.

They were also traveling brain centers. Every Arborec sub-organism in light speed communication range answered to it.

Which had, during our stop at Corlu IV, included me.

Uthan stammered on, heedless of my silence. "I know, I know, I should have expected something like it would be there. I don't know how far that fungus has gotten into your brain – it doesn't *look* very far, nothing visible under your temples, and you've never acted like a Dirzuga."

My thoughts careened back to the split-brain paradox, my best analogy as to how the Arborec retains its singular identity regardless of those distances. Sometimes those far-flung parts of the Arborec's mind needed a more immediate catching-up. That was one of the many things the Arborec used its starfaring vessels to do.

I could have lost myself. Become an appendage.

I shuddered. The sickly-orange fungal lumps melded to my flesh had never been – would never be – tolerable. But I had reached a resting point where I had been able to avoid thinking about them. All that equilibrium came crashing down. I felt back on the edge of throwing up.

Just like my parents, I wasn't going to be able to push this out of my mind.

Uthan kept talking. "I was afraid if you came near an Arborec craft, it'd take control of the fungus on you. That it might start growing again. At least then we'd have some evidence that the Arborec are lying about not infesting living people, and we could take that to the Galactic Council and try to get something done to help you. But I haven't seen any sign that the fungus is growing. It's the same as it was the first time I saw you. Do you understand what that means?"

When I didn't say anything, he answered his own question after a flicker of annoyance. "It means you're free. There was always a question if anything else would swoop in and take your future from you. Right? But I don't see anything else between you and whatever you want to do for the rest of your life."

What I wanted most right now was to vomit. Maybe I should have. It would have sent the same message.

So much of what humans thought we decided "in the moment" was post-hoc rationalization, invented after the fact.

"Get out," I told Uthan.

He could talk about my future and freedom and everything else the Mentak would chew someone's ear off about. But if any of this had been about my choices, he would have told me about our last stop. He would have mentioned the Nightthorn Haven much sooner. He'd clearly known about it for hours now, given how long he'd been studying me.

"Excuse me?" he stammered.

"Leave me alone," I said.

Whatever he'd been expecting, it hadn't been this. He looked like he had a lot more evangelizing he wanted to do. Or coaching, or therapy, or whatever it was that he thought he was about to inflict upon me.

I would have done anything to get him to leave. "I need some time alone," I told him, though I didn't owe him any kind of explanation.

But it got him to go. His footsteps wandered back down the corridor.

A migraine pushed sharply inward from my temples. Little tendrils of ice, phantom pain where my implants had been, twisted into my head, wound all my thoughts into knots. No matter what direction I tried to take them, they slithered back into the same place.

Uthan did not know what he had done to me. I *hoped* he did not know what he had done to me. Maybe I should have been more forthright about the worsening headaches. I'd tried to hide it.

There was one useful data point in all of these new revelations: the intrusive thoughts inside my head had not reacted to the Nightthorn Haven's presence at all. Far more likely, then, that it was just my own imagination. It remained silent even now, as though the discovery of the Nightthorn Haven's earlier presence had given away the lie of what it pretended to be.

My brain had not been made to cope with what Uthan was asking me to do. That was not a turn of phrase: had literally not *been made* to deal with these choices. The implants were gone, but the mind they'd shaped remained.

I needed clarity.

There was only ever one path in front of me. The sooner I took my first few steps down it, the sooner I would find peace.

Uthan had shown it to me. All I had to do was walk.

• • •

The next time I was ready to interact with Uthan, I did something I'd never done before: I sought him out.

I was getting better at moving. "Better" as in I could limp along the corridor and not end up in so much pain that my joints felt ready to burst through my skin. Now I merely felt sore and exhausted, like the few dozen feet had been a long hike under a hot sun.

I arrived during one of his irregular meals. For once, Uthan dined in his own cabin, seated on his bed with his Xxcha noodles perched on his desk. He startled when he saw me, dropping his fork and nearly upending the whole tray.

"This is a first," he said. I did not, and still do not, understand the human conversational need to say the obvious aloud.

"I've had time to process," I said. And it was true. A day had passed since the last time we'd spoken, and I'd settled a lot in that time. I was finally ready for more. "I need to know more about what's going to happen to me."

"Well, that's what I was trying to lead you away from: talking about things just happening rather than what you're going to *choose* to do." He held up his hands to forestall my obvious objections. "Of course, the Keleres are going to want to, ah, debrief us. That will take time. But there's precedent for defectors coming to the Galactic Council and making new lives afterward."

"And that is something that they would... just allow me to do," I said, doubtfully. I knew the Galactic Council's first move would be to treat me as a hostile soldier.

"They'd have to. The Galactic Council is bound by laws."

I admired his naivete. "The Galactic Council has never had a 'defector' from a civilization as inimically hostile as the L1Z1X Mindnet. The phrase they use for Us is 'Existential Threat,' correct?"

Uthan opened his mouth to answer, and then seemed to notice my quaking knees for the first time. He waved me in. "Sit down, please." The desk's seat had been shoved underneath it, and looked like it hadn't been used for a long time. His frame wouldn't have been comfortable in it. He pulled it out for me. "You shouldn't be upright that long."

I collapsed into it, trying not to exhale or grunt or anything else that might have revealed how grateful I was to have it. It still took a moment to catch my breath. The smell of noodles was overpowering, like a root garden worming into my nostrils.

"What do you expect this 'debriefing' to be like?" I asked.

"Well… they'll split us apart for a time. Grill you about the Mindnet, I'm sure. About anything you remember. Technologies, the capabilities of that ship you were on, whatever you know about their fleets, and so on."

"Would they employ torture to extract this from me?" I asked.

His horror seemed genuine. "Of course they wouldn't. We're not…" He lowered his voice as if in apology. "We're not like the Mindnet. No offense. If you're still going to argue that you're a member of the Mindnet, like you did the first time we met, prisoner of war rules kick in. I wouldn't recommend that. But there still wouldn't be any torture. Anyway, I think you've grown past wanting to be a member of the Mindnet, though, right?"

"I am no longer capable of being a citizen of the Mindnet." It still hurt to say, even if I didn't mean it.

"Hey, if that's the best I can get, I'll take it. I expect they'll ask you to participate in some studies, too. Full-body scans, tissue samples, that sort of thing. Minimally invasive. Not a dissection. Again, not like what the Mindnet would do."

He may have even been right about that. The stories the Keleres liked to tell themselves were that they were the "good guys" underneath the bloody pragmatic realities of their work. Sometimes that even affected their behavior.

I pardoned myself for being skeptical.

Uthan visibly struggled to find delicate phrasing. "Not to put too fine a point on it, but what's happened to you is… I mean, from the right point of view, it's exciting. It's usually very difficult to extract Mindnet implants from someone. Especially when they got them young, like you did."

"Exciting is not one of the words I would use to describe the experience," I said.

"If we can find out how the Arzuga managed it, we can help a lot of people."

He did not realize he was talking about the utter destruction of the Mindnet. The deaths of millions, at minimum. He still thought of my lost cybernetics as a liberation.

Something in my face must have given away how I felt about that. He seemed to sense he was not going to get anywhere by arguing me out of my interpretation. Instead, he asked, "Where would you like to go?"

The question hardly registered. He'd asked it before, but the last time my response had been easy: back to the Mindnet.

But even that hadn't been an answer. There was no answer.

I stared past him, waiting for him to speak again. He kept up the silence long enough to be awkward, even for me. But I kept it longer than he could. "You could come with me," he offered. "That'd be an option. My service for the Keleres is voluntary. I can request leave or quit. I could take you to Moll Primus. The Mentak Coalition is one of the easiest of the great civilizations to join." He snorted. "I think we're the only ones who *want* new people. No matter where they come from, or who they used to be."

That wasn't entirely true. The Arborec invited immigrants from all over the galaxy.

But Moll Primus was a genuinely interesting thought. The Mentak Coalition was one of the few great civilizations not associated with any species in particular. And, if I were to settle somewhere outside the Mindnet, I certainly couldn't consider any world aligned with the Federation of Sol. I'd lost many memories with my implants, but not the terror and revulsion and hate I'd held for them.

There were plenty of non-aligned worlds where humans were common. Even in a galaxy as violent as this one, a quiet life remained attainable.

But these were thoughts, not options.

"I don't know how to make a choice," I said, because it was the truth.

"Let's discuss the possibilities." He reached across and fished around on his desk until he found a tablet under his food packaging. He immediately smudged it with fingerprints. He attempted to wipe it with his sleeve, which only made it worse, and then carried on with an apologetic grimace.

With a few jabs, he pulled up an image of Moll Primus: the orange and gold-sheened poison planet at the heart of the Mentak Coalition. Easy enough to see why the old Lazax Empire had used it as a prison world. Even from a celestial vantage, it looked like a terrible place to die. The colors were somewhere between "diseased boil" and "toxic volcanic outgassing."

But Uthan was accustomed enough to the sight that he probably hadn't even thought about how I would see it. He thumbed around a little bit more. The view broadened into a midnight-blue map with a hexagonal grid, showing the stars and sectors easily reached from Moll Primus.

"I used to have a home here," he mused, planting a fingerprint over a hex with a binary star system. "Probably the easiest for me to go back to. I know the neighborhoods off the main starport. My kids have their own families in the area. They're pretty open-minded. If anyone would accept you or be willing to help you out, they would."

Hell, he wanted to introduce me to his *family*. If only he knew how tremendously dangerous that would be for them. "Why would you want me near you? I've done little but antagonize you since you recovered me."

"Yeah, but I can't really blame you for that, considering." He left the sentence at that. "You seem to be getting better about it, anyway. And I am the one who pulled you out of that wreckage."

"That does not make me your responsibility."

"Doesn't it? You're not going to get very far on your own, not unless someone shows you around. Doesn't have to be me, but it has to be someone." He snorted. "There are some places you could go by accident that would get you *actually* dissected."

(There are better ways to live than what you're headed for.)

Uthan held the tablet at an angle that kept me from reading text or seeing the details in the pictures. I tried to tilt my head, but couldn't manage the angle, and scowled at him. He got the message and grunted, then shifted farther down the bed.

With effort and some help, I moved over. The mattress still had the warm hollow he'd made from sitting on it. The bite of alcohol on his breath was more perceptible here, too. I hadn't known him to drink since the first day he figured I was going to live. Maybe what had happened yesterday had affected him more than I'd thought.

In the course of his courier work for the Keleres, he'd had the chance to visit several neighboring systems. A world of archipelagos which could be circumnavigated by walking for thousands of kilometers along a single beach. A world of crystal canyons formed in the slowly cooling habitable zone of a white dwarf.

"Anywhere you'd like." He set the tablet on his desk and gestured to the screen, and then ran his hand along his beard. "Hell. I've served the Keleres long enough. We're probably both going to need a long rest after the debriefing they'll give us. Wherever you want to go, I can take you there."

"This is really how you see our lives unfolding?" I asked, in a voice quieter than I'd used before. It was the first time I understood him with any clarity. It was a cold feeling, even seated next to the furnace of his body heat.

"It's a human condition to always be looking for a better life," he said, with a shrug. "And friends to share it with. Like I keep saying, I hate to turn you out alone."

"I get the idea that *I* would be the one turning you out alone."

"My problems aren't your problems." He didn't deny what I'd said, though. "I've been alone too long. I think I'm done with the Keleres no matter what you decide. Working for them is like… firing bow and stern thrusters full blast, getting nowhere."

"Then I happened to you. You can get me back to the Keleres, learn more about how to extract Mindnet implants from a human body."

"And help you," he said. "You're a person. You've got rights. The Mindnet trampled on you all your life. You're starting to see that. If the Keleres can study how that Arzuga variant you've got works, you can help other people who've been trampled on just like you."

This was the story he wanted to tell himself all along, the seed kernel of everything he'd done with me. A quiet little heroic fantasy. "And then you and I can go and live our own lives," I said. "However we please – whatever that means."

He nodded. And then again, more firmly. Blood rushed to his face as he realized I was finally heading in the direction he'd signposted. "Exactly. And it's all right not to know that last part."

"That is a compelling story," I said.

"It's all I've really wanted for the past few weeks," he said. He reached across the desk to pick up the tablet again, probably to show me more pictures or maps.

"It is not the kind of story you are in," I told him.

Even with the obstacle of his beard, finding his neck was not difficult. I still did not have much strength, but I had been hiding more than I'd shown him.

The scalpel concealed in my sleeve did not need much force.

It was quick and simple work, like drawing a blade down a velvet curtain.

I don't think Uthan realized what had happened for a few seconds, for which I was grateful. He was not entirely prepared. His beard hid a lot from his viewpoint.

His ignorance was not quite so merciful as to last until the end.

I'll spare you, and myself, the recollection of what happened after that. I did not need to attack him again. He could have hurt me; he had that much strength left. He didn't.

I thought I was prepared. That I was ready to be dispassionate about this, approach it as a necessity. As business. Like the Mindnet would require me to do.

I was not quite up to specs.

• • •

No one counted the time it took me to piece myself together afterward. It was not denial. It was reframing. Never once did I lie to myself about what had happened.

I had not killed Uthan. He had declared his intention to retire. He had died of unavoidable causes. A conflux of circumstances that neither of us could help.

I was Mindnet. Implants or no, my mind was wired. I could experience a set number of thoughts because they were what I had been conditioned to experience.

Everything I did was for the good of the Mindnet.

I had *told* Uthan that so many times. He hadn't heard me. Now, I kept telling it to myself, like I was arguing with my suddenly silent intrusive thoughts.

Everything Uthan did was about his ridiculous hopes and fantasies. His pride. The story he wanted to tell himself *about* himself. That was the human species' fatal flaw. We loved stories too much.

Uthan had been a deeply flawed man. Lost in his vanity, his personal story. Manipulative in a way I didn't think even he knew he was.

But he had been trying. He didn't deserve death.

What did that matter, though?

I could tell myself a different kind of story than Uthan had. Which was that this *was* business. Whether I believed that or not.

Time resumed in bits and pieces. Uthan had locked all the cockpit controls. But those controls, like the rest of his shuttle, were hugely outdated. Even with my faulty memory, I needed only an hour to break through it. In another two hours, I was familiar with every critical system aboard. I could even breathe at a steady pace again.

We were twenty-two days out from Mecatol Rex. I plotted out the much shorter route that would take us into Mindnet space.

Then I had more business. More *necessity*.

Uthan was easily twice my mass. I had more strength than I pretended, but the last thing I was going to be able to do was drag him out of his quarters, let alone down the corridor to the airlock. The artificial gravity had to go. The life support controls, though, were a hodgepodge of replaced, cross-circuited, and interdependent parts. I could not cut the gravity without also killing all the cabin lights.

A better, more practical-minded Mindnet agent would have set up flashlights or other backup light sources along the corridor, to clearly illuminate their path and all the obstacles in it. I placed exactly one, at the far end of the corridor. Just enough to keep me from injuring myself in freefall. But also to keep everything shrouded.

My intrusive thoughts remained silent.

CHAPTER THIRTEEN
MISDIRECTION

Now

For all the details, false or not, in my memories of my vacuum walk, the two weeks that followed were a blur. A jumble of anger and humiliation fuzzed together.

I needed medical help. Getting it from any official source, or any doctor known to station management, was far beyond the realm of sanity. So far, in fact, that I nearly did it, anyway. Insanity had a good track record for me.

But something resembling sense prevailed. I stumbled, burned and bruised, into the recesses of the station. I found a team of human archaeologists studying what they thought was a forgotten Lazax superweapon, a titanic sphere on a rail launcher.

I'd politely liberated their medical supplies at the point of a hand drill I pretended was a gun. I thought it had been an equitable exchange. I'd taken the drugs, diagnostic scanners, and cellular regenerator that had slowly healed my skin, my eardrums, and my vacuum-scarred eyes. I informed them that their sphere was not a superweapon, but a depleted power core the ancient Lazax had prepared to launch into the sun. The Lazax had probably been interrupted, I told the archaeologists, when the archaeologists' ancestors had arrived to butcher all of them.

The archaeologists had not been thrilled to hear this. They tried to angrily argue me out of it. It was as though, by telling the truth, I'd *made* the truth. Like I'd collapsed the possibility that contained their superweapon.

I saved them years of fruitless research. I had to remind them that they ought to be angry with me for stealing their supplies instead and threatened them a few more times for good measure. Human psychology is a fascinating shamble, and I'm ashamed that it's the medium and mechanism through which I comprehend the universe.

Clearly, it had been too long since I'd had to deal with other sentients over an extended period. I needed to refresh myself.

Thus, the best place to make my only discreet connection seemed to be a bar; the expected place where I might go unnoticed. And everything else I had tried had been fruitless.

I arrived an hour ahead of my appointment, lingering at the counter, trying to get used to being around people again.

My contact didn't agree with my choice of venue. "You've tripped your fuse," he said as he slid onto the stool next to mine. He hissed loudly enough to be heard over the music thumping out of every luminous, color-swirled surface. Which was all of them: from the countertop to the floor, to the ribbons of faerie lights hanging from the ceiling. Music emerged from everywhere.

There were more people in this one place than I'd seen in all my time aboard the station. Port Vel Syd had been settled quasi-permanently for their disaffected youth to make a valiant attempt at putting together a local culture. Starship crews, smugglers, and all the people who made their livings off them congregated here, too. The air everywhere was blurred by privacy fields, which made getting an exact population count difficult.

"I don't have a fuse," I told him.

My contact was a primly coiffed middle-aged man who looked back at me with undisguised contempt. "You've blown a circuit," he said, undeterred. "You've flipped your bits. You've whatever the hell you robots do when you lose your mind."

His name was Stefan, and he was charmingly out of place among the swirling colors and privacy-field shrouded bar-goers. He dressed professionally in a collared shirt with double breast pockets under a business robe with even more pockets. His pockets held neatly arranged rows of tools: pens, pointers, holo projectors, nicotine sticks, a biometric verifier, and probably a disguised stunner or two. Everything an accountant on a hyper-capitalist outback like Port Vel Syd might need. And he was exactly what he appeared to be: an accountant. Even Port Vel Syd's half-criminal management needed support staff.

I hoped I was a little less obtrusive, although, on second thought, I didn't blend in either. Current fashion included headdresses made of stiff, brightly colored wire, apparently hand-painted and formed into shapes like antlers. If I tried wearing one of those headdresses, I'd probably miss some subtlety that would mark me as even *more* of an outsider.

At least the fact that he'd called me a robot meant my make-up work was good enough to seem bad. I wore an autokiosk-manufactured sweater with a hood. Before coming, I'd spent painstaking hours in front of a mirror painting geometric lines across my chin and temple, right where the Arzuga fungus started to become visible.

The hood and the temporary tattoo *looked* like a disguise. Like something a Mindnet agent might wear in a misguided attempt to fit in at a bar, to cover up their implants.

That was what Stefan saw when he looked at me. He thought he'd already cracked me. He didn't see the lumpy, tumorous fungal growths that the tattoo covered.

"Let's move to a table," I told him.

"*Let's.*"

When we slipped behind the booth's privacy field, the world outside turned into a distorted mirror, rippling with oil-slick rainbow colors. These colors bowed and flexed with the music's rhythm.

The bar aimed to appear as brightly colored and full of noise as it did private and discreet – an effect it achieved through careful use of blur projectors and noise muffling fields. But the privacy screens were a sham, useful only for blocking out gossiping teenagers. Professional eavesdroppers wouldn't be slowed for more than half a second, if that. And the odds were good that the owners had their own bugs.

So Stefan was right: this was not the best place for a covert meeting. I didn't care. I belatedly realized something may have shifted in me since my shuttle's bombing. Or, more likely, my brain had been damaged. Either way, the sensory overload didn't bother me in the way that, back when I'd been in Uthan's company, it certainly would have.

I was under no illusion that I was well. Everything had felt muted, distant, since I'd tumbled through space. Medical treatment hadn't made it better. The cause was either a trauma response, or physical damage to the structure of my brain.

That didn't disturb me in the way it probably should have. I was not a stranger to brain damage. My brain had been dashed to pieces ever since the Arzuga had destroyed my implants. Most unaltered humans, like my new friend Stefan, would have argued that the original damage had happened when I was four.

I would have been more worried about being here if I'd been at the top of station security's wanted list. My presence was a footnote in the security bulletins. They'd seen camera footage of me entering the starbridge… but not coming back out. They had probably, with some justification, assumed I had died.

"You think this is a spy drama?" Stefan hissed. "What the hell are you doing, demanding a meeting in a place like this? I'm on the edge of walking out right now, and screw whatever you do to me after."

I carefully considered that, and then which response might make him angriest. "Calm yourself," I said.

Stefan squeezed his hands into fists tight enough to whiten his knuckles. Twice, he started to get up, but never completed the motion.

There wasn't much risk of him actually leaving. I knew exactly what bound him to the Mindnet's service.

I had worked with him before, though he wouldn't know me by sight, and I had no intention of reminding him. He was the agent for whom I'd once slipped data aboard a Port Vel Syd-bound freighter. His professional role was valuable and apolitical enough to have lasted two coups. And it meant he had access to all kinds of underworld financial data to support Our intelligence operations.

The Mindnet had agents all over the galaxy. Not all of them

had implants. Some had been brought aboard through the more conventional means of spycraft: blackmail, ideology, and, above all, bribery. The Mindnet would never trust them as much as, I hoped, We had trusted me, but We still found uses for them.

I'd avoided Stefan before because the meeting was risky, and he might have alerted the Mindnet to my condition had I come to him damaged from my spacewalk. By meeting Stefan, I placed him in danger of being detected. That hadn't changed since the last time I'd considered contacting him. But everything else about my situation had.

"There is another Mindnet agent," I said. "Here. On this station. Serving as your main contact."

He furrowed his brow. "Yeah. Don't you know that?"

"Did I sound like I was asking a question?"

"What is this all about?" He glanced at the rainbow-hued blurs outside the booth. "Is this some kind of double setup? Are you firing me? Not just out of the job, but, like, out of a cannon?"

He might not have been the sharpest agent, but he was properly paranoid about Us, and his mental health was accordingly shaky. I gave him a look of genuine concern. "If I were going to betray you, why would I have summoned you? Do you think you're less vulnerable anywhere else?"

"Then why am I here? And if you answer that with another question, I really will leave."

"I need to arrange a meeting with that other contact."

"What? Why would you need me to do that?"

I was sure, now, that there was not only another Mindnet agent on the station, but that this person had been the one to have gunned down so many of the Keleres. "I just need it."

"Don't you monsters all have…" He tapped his forehead. "You know? Better ways of keeping in touch than through *me*?"

"That is not how espionage cells work. Or how cybernetics work." The latter wasn't true, but little lies were a good habit in spycraft. "Ideally, this other agent and I would never know anything about each other lest we find some way to give each other away. But something's changed. I need to get in touch. Now."

If he'd been on edge before, he sat on a needle now. He sensed something was wrong about this and desperately tried to grasp what. I had to convince him that he was reaching out to touch a hot stove burner.

"How is Oran?" I asked.

That lit a new fire behind Stefan's eyes. It was like seeing a flame turn from orange to blue.

At first, the only thing I'd been able to remember about Stefan was his name. Through quiet investigation and deduction, I'd uncovered the rest. Seven years ago, Stefan's brother and his nephew had each gone into palliative care for complex nervous system failure. An alien plague had hijacked their immune systems, convinced their bodies' defenses to attack their nerves. It was incredibly painful and lethal. Stefan's brother had died. But his nephew, Oran, made an inexplicable recovery.

Today, Oran lived safely across the galaxy, far removed from the wild outbacks of places like Port Vel Syd. Mindnet nanite-based medical technology specialized in repairing the deep, cellular-level damage they had suffered. The Mindnet had struck a deal. Stefan would pass along information for Us or do anything else We might require. In exchange, We maintained his nephew's nanites.

Stefan had no children, and his nephew was his only

surviving relative. Judging from the fact that he was willing to work for the Mindnet for this treatment, he valued Oran's life as highly as he might have his own children.

"He's fine," Stefan said, tersely.

"Medical nanites still keeping him in working order?"

The nanites Oran would have been given were not self-sustaining. They needed to be replenished and managed. The Mindnet would not even need to threaten to turn them off. If Stefan stopped working for Us, Oran's medical situation would simply revert to the way it had been before.

The Mindnet had a vast number of these arrangements. Even in places like Port Vel Syd, in the corners of the galaxy we'd barely touched, Our roots ran deep. We didn't need implants to worm under a person's skin.

The thing that genuinely perplexed me about these deals was the degree to which Our agents resented Us. They acted as though We'd caused their loved ones' problems, when all We'd done was provided the solution. I doubted Stefan was as bitter toward the manufacturers of the nicotine sticks he carried in his front pocket, though they had deliberately engineered his addiction.

We hadn't created the demand. But we controlled the supply of the solution. Payment was in order. I'd figured that someone from a place so cutthroat and *laissez-faire* as Port Vel Syd should understand that.

But I hadn't come here expecting it.

(There are better ways to manage Oran's condition. You know there are. All you have to do is–)

With substantial effort, I quashed that thought. I could not deal with that right now. For now, at least, I still needed Stefan beholden to me and the Mindnet.

And I would not voluntarily have anything to do with the Arborec.

"Are you threatening to withdraw his care?" Stefan demanded.

"The Mindnet always keeps its side of these arrangements." Right up until it stopped being advantageous for Us. "Just tell your other contact I need to see them. They'll understand. They can drop me a message." I passed him a slip with a handwritten memory address in the station's mailing system. "Do that for me, and you won't have to see me again."

He snatched up the slip without looking at it. "That's not how this ever goes. You people always come back for more."

"You may be right."

I said that mostly to avoid an argument. The odds were good that I would be dead before I had any opportunity to pester him again.

An awkward silence persisted. I waited, perturbed, until I realized that he wouldn't leave until I gave him permission.

I tilted my head toward the end of the table, and he was gone.

I stayed back for a while, watching the field-cloaked figures around me as they mingled and fought and loved. I tried to remember how to be human. I didn't have much success.

There was nothing else to distract myself from the deep, black rage boiling inside me.

CHAPTER FOURTEEN
MIND-ALTAR

Then

After I killed Uthan, I aimed his shuttle directly into Mindnet space. This act had nearly gotten me shot out of the stars. In retrospect, I was certain that had been my goal.

The odds were well against me surviving to report in. The friend-or-foe systems that Mindnet vessels use to identify each other were not only beyond my means, but beyond my understanding. Even as a full member of the Mindnet, I wouldn't have been able to access information about them. There was no utility and a lot of risk in spreading that information around. All I knew was that my lost survey ship had had a transponder keyed to the Mindnet's identification systems. It was fragile on purpose. As soon as the device's onboard artificial intelligence determined that the ship was lost, it would have self-destructed.

So I had to plunge into Mindnet defenses in the stolen

courier shuttle, one that the Mindnet almost certainly would have pegged as associated with the Keleres. It should have been a doomed mission. But it was what the Mindnet would have wanted me to do. So, it was all right.

Conditioning kept me steady. It was funny how some conditioned actions came much more smoothly than others.

I had one tool left. The Mindnet had a standardized SOS code. In the event that one of Us was lost on a planet's surface, where radio communications were hampered or unwise. We were supposed to find some way to tap it out – firelight, smoke, rocks laid out in a pattern – with the understanding that, since it was standardized, all Our enemies knew it, too. Therefore, the Mindnet would not answer the code in anything less than the safest circumstances. That was, with all available weapons pointed at whatever had arranged the signal.

As I approached our border world and its assembled defenses, I decelerated hard, turning my engines on and off in that sequence.

The Mindnet should have destroyed me. Snapped me off with one shot. I fully expected to die.

Instead, by the perverse logic that We had never seen something so brazen before, the Mindnet decided that this was probably not an attack. We let me live.

As I halted, the Mindnet surrounded my shuttle with disposable three-meter-long spike drones. A full sphere of them, angled inward. A prison of spikes. All of them had warheads ready to detonate the instant I did anything untoward.

I didn't understand why the Mindnet would be taking the risk. I could have been a Keleres agent up to something dire. Trying a high-risk, high-reward attempt to deploy some new virus. Or a scout ship, radioing data about system defenses to a point light-weeks away from the star, where a conspirator would arrive to receive them. Or I was just some madwoman who wasn't worth the time or the resources We'd already devoted to me.

If I were them – if I was Us – which I *was*, I was part of Us–

I was breaking down. I couldn't keep my thoughts in order. They chased each other in collapsing spirals, like a satellite in a deteriorating orbit. I couldn't stop my hands from shaking. I needed guidance. "We" were becoming "they." The voice within was becoming louder. I had to have help. If I was to continue to exist.

We should have killed me. I wanted Us to kill me.

(There were so many different paths you could have traveled than the one that led you here.)

The Mindnet forced me to relay my story to the drones over thirty painstaking hours. First as a coded sequence of blinking lights. The shuttle computer translated my report into a binary code, but the computer wasn't connected to the ship's running lights. I'd sat there, flipping running lights on and off, until my dots blurred into dashes and my dashes into silences. Until the world turned dark and gray.

It was too much for me. I hadn't slept before I arrived. Or eaten anything. Fulfilling those needs ahead of time had seemed overoptimistic. I fainted.

I woke with a shuddering of the deck as another vessel latched onto mine.

The Hacan who stepped into Uthan's shuttle was the first Mindnet citizen I'd seen face to face since losing my implants. It was difficult to see, at first, that he was Hacan. His mane had been shaved off, and certain parts of his snout and right parietal bone had been removed to make room for implants.

I hadn't thought about what this would be like. Deep in my subconscious, I'd expected that meeting another Mindnet citizen would be familiar. As comforting as that winter campfire. The truth was a shock.

There were only a handful of layers to them. No interleaving data, no protocol handshakes or comforting security verification, no multidimensional biometric and emotional readout. No sense of this individual's history or standing within the Mindnet.

Just sight and sound. Razor-sharp steel voice. The purring growl of a Hacan. The experience was alienating, and not in the way that most sentients found the Mindnet alienating.

When the Mindnet had interrogated me via signal light, We had of course realized that I was at my physical limits. We simply had not cared. The Mindnet had continued to push me and was now ready to initiate the next steps in interrogation, despite me no longer being able to participate.

Everything fuzzed in my memory after he appeared. Perhaps he stunned me. Perhaps I passed out again. When I woke, I was elsewhere. I must have been brought aboard the craft that latched onto mine.

The cabin was minimally lit, as was proper for a Mindnet craft. I was lying on my back. When I tried to look aside, instrument readouts stung my eyes. My neck didn't want to move far, regardless. Somewhere in the dark, an IV machine ticked. There was a weight of a sensor mounted onto my forehead, an itchy crust of dried blood on my scalp. Curiously painless.

Dulling the pain had been nice of Us. Or maybe I was just numb.

"You have awakened at an awkward time," the Hacan in the dark said. "But I do have momentary use for you."

"I am not sure how to be of use," I said. "I feel as though I am falling apart." Honest self-reporting was the key to proper treatment.

"That is as expected as it is immaterial," he said.

He had a point. I had spent too long around Uthan, learning the art of purposeless conversation.

His paws pressed something cold and cylindrical into my palm. I barely felt it. He folded my fingers closed around it.

"This syringe contains a terminal nerve toxin," he said. "Please inject yourself while I prepare the embalming solution and the body bag."

I rolled the cylinder in my hand. Felt the needle with my thumb. But my eyes were locked on the shadowed Hacan as he gathered supplies.

"Terminate myself," I said. This was more humane than what I had done to Uthan. The intrusive thought leapt to the top of my mind so quickly that I nearly said it aloud.

"Do I need to repeat the order?" he asked from the opposite side of the cabin.

(Don't obey!)

I obeyed the Hacan.

The needle entered my arm as a hot pinch. I pressed the plunger inward. Pain expanded into a tight throbbing.

The Hacan returned to my side. "That is enough," he said, when the canister was almost empty, and I kept pressing.

He extracted the syringe from my palm, discarded it, and then began applying antiseptic to my bleeding arm.

"That serves no pur–" I started.

"The injection was a medicinal cocktail," he said. "It should keep you awake and aware enough to continue answering questions."

I stared at him, wide-eyed, pulse throbbing in my head. I had become so accustomed to Uthan realizing when I was nonverbally asking a question that the Hacan's silence was off-putting. Eventually, I remembered to ask aloud.

"Mindnet implants employ a variety of trust verification protocols that operate below conscious thresholds," he explained. "Most Mindnet citizens never learn about them. They include guarantees of a willingness to sacrifice an individual life for the good of the Mindnet. Without those protocols, We have to improvise."

The Hacan must have been a recent convert. His glittering yellow eyes were bloodshot. The scar tissue around his implants was bright red and inflamed, and only patches of fur had grown back. But he moved with unbothered fluidity.

Entering the Mindnet as an adult was always rougher, biologically speaking. Juveniles easily adapted to their implants and grew around them physically and mentally.

"Is there a way I can receive a similar verification from you?" I asked.

"You'll have to employ trust."

"How can I trust?" I asked.

"Consider: how can you not?" When I didn't have anything to say to that, he added, "You are a Mindnet citizen. Your mind continues to be ordered appropriately."

He was not just saying that for the sake of talking to himself. This was an announcement; something he – We – judged that I needed to hear.

I was not so sure he was correct. The intrusive thoughts persisted. "I see," I said.

"Doubtful," he said, but there was no malice to it. It was just a correction.

When I'd entered Mindnet space, I'd thought that We had taken an enormous risk by allowing me to live. I was starting to understand how small that risk actually was. This single Hacan had been sent to meet me, minimizing the possibility of contagion. In the event that the Arzuga was contagious, the Mindnet could simply liquidate the both of us.

The possibility of contagion was swiftly eliminated. After a day of silent study, the Hacan said abruptly, "An immunological firmware update will keep this from happening to any other Mindnet citizens."

Ever since I'd regained enough of myself to think clearly, a question burned at the top of my mind. I had been afraid to ask. Now the fear of continued silence outweighed it. "Will my implants be replaced?"

"No," the Hacan said. "Your body now depends on the Arzuga to function. The Arzuga continues to reject your implants."

It turned out I had weighed my outcomes poorly: the answer *was* worse than silence.

"Your body was already dead when the Arzuga colonized you," the Hacan said. "Your implants had functioned as intended and kept your brain alive so that your memories might be recovered. The Arzuga *also* performed as intended and parasitized the dead tissue, rejecting your cybernetics. The possibility that your brain would still be alive was not accounted for during the Arzuga's creation. As your brain was alive, it could not be colonized.

"Typically, Arzuga unable to complete its colonization of a body has a genetically coded kill function that forces the entire colony to die off. *This* Arzuga has mutated in such a way as to lose this function. It does not appear to have been deliberate.

It has not taken over your brain as it would a dead one, but it continues to force out your cybernetics and maintain your other body functions."

The fungus was working at cross-purposes with itself. That sounded like a malfunction rather than design. "It does not seem to be an Arborec bioweapon, then," I said. That had always been a possibility, burning away at the back of my mind. It had not seemed likely, but it was good to have it eliminated.

"We can defend against further incidents," he said. "We therefore have no pressing need to exterminate you. We will dispatch a fleet to sterilize Kityra-892 b to prevent any further mutations."

The shackles of pain drew tighter. Life like this was going to continue for a long time, and I was not sure how I could tolerate it. "The consequences of an incorrect assessment seem quite high," I said. My voice trembled, which I hated but could not help. "I should liquidate myself, as earlier instructed."

"You are valuable to the Mindnet," he said. "Terminate that thought."

Even as I started to object, the headache pulsed into my temples.

It was the same headache I'd fought before. The one that had gotten worse, and returned more often, when Uthan had brought up my family. The one that, when Uthan had mentioned the Nightthorn Haven and the risk I'd been unknowingly exposed to, had finally compelled me to act.

My cybernetic implants had always monitored the places those thoughts had come from. Now those implants were gone. But my brain had been sculpted by those implants for so long, and so well, that the pain reflex persisted. Even without the hardware installed.

The pain was good, I realized. It came from me, it *was* me. My conditioning – Our conditioning – trying to adapt. It was the answer to my most unwelcome intrusive thoughts.

All of this spilled out of my mouth. I told the Hacan about those thoughts, about my fear that the Arzuga fungus persisted in my brain, and how I believed I was trying to fool myself into thinking that the Arborec was influencing me.

"We will address that."

The Hacan picked up a buzzing tool from beside my examination table. I did not recognize it, but it had a sharp point. When he touched the point to the table, as if to test it, it sparked.

"Your conditioning persists," he said. "It needs only retraining and reinforcement."

The pains, the migraine, the probe – they were the voice of my conditioning. Which was me. We were the same.

I had started to stray from Mindnet thought. The Mindnet brought me back into Our way of thinking. My death would not have been the most efficient use of resources.

The Hacan tracked all my thoughts, intrusive or otherwise – of my parents, of Uthan's hot blood spilling over my wrists, how he had looked at me afterward – and began to remold them. Compress them. Shrink them. Under relentless attack, they all became a tiny scream in the back of my mind.

A scream had nothing interesting to say.

CHAPTER FIFTEEN
MIND-ALTER

Forever Now

All my previous attempts to trace the other Mindnet agent on Port Vel Syd had come to naught. They had hacked their way through the station security as easily as I had. There was no sign of them on any of the cameras, even in places where I knew now that they had been.

My only link to them was through Stefan.

Port Vel Syd was vast. Outside of the central ten-kilometer control hub, large areas of vacuum-flooded superstructure had gone uninhabited since the fall of the Lazax. No light strips, no life support.

But there were exceptions. Pockets of air. Hidden spaces where scavengers had left life support equipment. Port Vel Syd had been repopulated for centuries, and all that history left cruft. Gangs lived out in those dark places. Hermits. Insular communities who'd isolated themselves for generations. Those who were criminals even by Port Vel Syd's loose standards. Cults.

I was starting to fear that my jump through the vacuum, and everything I'd found out afterward, had left me with an unhealthy sense of fatalism. Perhaps that was why I chose the meeting location I had: a chasm overlooking an old coolant tunnel canal. It was far from the inhabited control hub, and from the docks. Buried deep in hundreds of kilometers of empty decks and the detritus of eons. As physically far from an exit as it was possible to be.

The upper levels of this chamber separated into distinct landings. No staircases or walkways linked them. Each landing had railings, and so it was plain that people were meant to be on them. The effect was that of a vast concert hall, where one could look up or down at anything happening.

My best guess was that this was meant to be an observation deck. The floor, or stage, or whatever was to be exhibited, had yet to be installed to cover the incomplete coolant canal. But the chasm's original purpose was lost to history, buried under the Twilight Wars.

The scale of Port Vel Syd beggared my merely human imagination. Internally, the station was divided into dozens of segments. Everything I'd seen, everywhere I'd been, had been in the ten-kilometer-long control hub and one of its neighboring segments. And the latter only when I'd stolen medical supplies from those archeologists. Each abandoned segment, the thousands of cabins that could fit within, felt like worlds to themselves.

Only a handful of sentients lived this far away from the docks. Even cults needed supplies and power eventually. The life support systems, where they existed at all, were old and jerry-rigged.

Whoever had rigged life support here hadn't planned for this chamber specifically. Heated air entered the chamber only at the lowest levels, near the open coolant duct. The warm, dry breeze moaned between the landings like the breath of an oven. It was pleasant at first. Like standing near a campfire on a winter evening.

The comfort didn't last. Soon it turned into an open oven. Later, I was grateful to step away from it after finishing my work.

I waited for hours, listening to the breathy whine of the vents, the endlessly churning winds. Letting my anger simmer.

(You always suspected this could be coming.)

My worst intrusive thoughts had gone into remission after Uthan's death and my reconditioning. They'd come back more recently, particularly after the battle at Arrix. I'd thought myself adept enough at ignoring them. I did not want to go through conditioning again.

However, the intrusive thoughts, the part of me that pretended to see things as the Arborec did, became easier and easier to accept. Which I knew should have worried me much more than it did.

(You embraced this before.)

"I'll embrace anything that's for the good of the Mindnet," I said. Aloud. Because my mind was not in its best state.

The door on the opposite landing opened. I straightened. The instant the Mindnet agent stepped through, I was sure I'd seen her before.

I hadn't, of course. Not that individual.

Mindnet citizens moved in a particular way. A light step, five kilometers per hour, and a rolling gait. The most efficient expenditure of calories. If I hadn't had to relearn walking after losing my implants, I would probably still be moving that way, without even thinking about it.

She wore a flowing, high-collared robe favored by human businesswomen on this station… and had dark red hair dressed in elaborate curls to hide the protrusions of her implants. Her voice was physically distinct from the Hacan who'd reconditioned me, but tonally, it was identical. "Identify yourself," she demanded.

"Sil. Formerly S1L3NT. Mindnet deep cover operations."

"Please hold still," she said. From within the depths of her sleeves, she produced a pistol.

She shot me four times. The first three meteor-streak rounds were clustered tightly in the center of my forehead. The fourth went left-of-center through my chest, intended for maximum arterial destruction.

Precise. Efficient. The *type* of efficiency was instructive, too: it was time-efficient, not resource-efficient. She could have gotten a kill with fewer shots, but she had wanted to down me as quickly as possible while leaving the smallest margin for error.

She may have even continued firing if she hadn't noticed the plasma rounds impacting the wall instead of me.

She frowned, slipped her weapon back into her sleeve as deftly as she'd pulled it out. If the heat of the barrel bothered her, she didn't show it.

The advertisement-spewing projectors from the autokiosks had been easy to remove and repurpose. They'd made a flawless illusion of me, enough to fool human eyes. I didn't doubt that, under those mottled brown irises, this other agent had enhanced retinas. Infrared sight was a standard Mindnet field augmentation. The chasm had been helpful here. The rising breeze cast an infrared fog between our two landings.

"You are attempting to murder me." I meant to say it matter-of-factly, but wonder crept into my voice. No matter how many times I had gone over my experience and reached the conclusion that there were no other explanations, the moment of confrontation came with a frisson of this-is-actually-happening awe.

I'd visited the chasm to set up the projectors. I'd tasted the burning dust updraft. If I'd stayed there as long as my projection had, though, my lips and skin would have been desiccated by the heat. The secure closet where I'd set up was much more comfortable, if claustrophobic. The sensors scanning my face for the projection pressed in tightly around me.

My cameras tracked each searing-white plasma round as they'd passed through my image. Their afterimages persisted as violet lines. The first three had been a clean left to right sweep across my frontal bone, each about a centimeter apart. An unaided human would have been better served by aiming for center mass first.

"What is your actual location?" the woman asked, as calmly as if nothing had just happened.

"Does it seem likely to you that I would answer?"

"That is not an answer. Please provide one."

I nearly laughed, but the disbelief drained away and the anger returned. "Follow-up question: do you believe saying 'please' will make my compliance more likely?"

She furrowed her brow. "You are Mindnet. Politeness is a courtesy due to colleagues." That was – somewhat – of a relief. The Mindnet would never have breathed a word like *please* to outsiders. "Now please answer," she finished. "Your secrets are Our secrets."

"Identify yourself," I said flatly. "Please."

She tilted her head. She was probably wondering about the utility of answering, and then answering honestly. "I am 8CC0RD," she said. "Also Mindnet deep cover operations."

Uthan had been right. Even in a huge space, filtered by microphones, the noise of the pronunciation was obnoxious.

It was 8CC0RD who had gunned down the Keleres in the corridors, and so adeptly erased herself from security records afterward. She had planted the bomb in my shuttle. Probably. Unless, of course, she wasn't here alone.

"Stop wasting your energy and Our time," I told her.

"Stop these games," she countered. "Reveal your location."

"There must be a more efficient way to accomplish your goal," I said.

She considered that and then nodded. "There is. We order you to terminate yourself immediately."

I shook my head. "It isn't plausible that you speak on Our behalf," I told her. Even if she wasn't on Port Vel Syd alone, there could only have been a handful of other agents. A larger force would have had a much easier time taking me down. "There are no substantial Mindnet resources within our light speed communication distance. You are isolated."

"We are never alone."

"You have no way to prove to me that you represent the Mindnet."

"I do not 'represent' Us. I am Us."

The pain of what I'd lost with my implants never quite went away. Even if she was by herself out here, it wouldn't have felt alone. When I'd had my implants, I had always reclined in a susurrus of voices, even when the implants themselves hadn't needed to contact the larger Mindnet for some time. The left brain and the right brain didn't know what each other were doing, but each retained the same identity.

"Why are you attempting to kill me?" I asked.

She gave me a strange look. "You do not need to know that."

"Consider events from my perspective."

"We literally cannot." I had forgotten: my perspective could only be real to her if it had come directly from my senses, via implants.

"*Consider*," I repeated. "I come here on Mindnet business. I am repeatedly attacked, thwarted, and beset while doing so. At least some of my problems stem from you. For reasons directly linked to my usefulness to the Mindnet – my missing implants – I cannot verify your identity." Mindnet identity codes were n-dimensional arrays of complex numbers. The idea of speaking one aloud or writing it would make a great punchline for a joke… though it would have to be to the right audience.

I got most of my orders from the Mindnet in the form of dispatches, letters, and simple orders. It had been too long since I'd conversed with one of Us face to face. I surprised myself by the speed with which I became reaccustomed to conversing Mindnet-style. No contractions. Direct, forceful statements that – even with the *pleases* accorded to colleagues – came off as challenges and demands.

"Given all of this," I said, "you are most likely a fraud. An attacker striking Us from a weak point, which in this case is my ability to verify the difference between a Mindnet citizen and a disguised adversary. If you are to convince me that We have decided upon my destruction, I need proof, and I need Our reasoning. Present it."

When she said nothing, I took the cork off my rhetorical rapier. "If there truly were numerous other Mindnet citizens here, you would have had the spare neuronal capacity to game this out in advance. You would understand the position in which you've placed me. But empathy is an insight not available to the simple – or single-minded."

The signs of her fury were subtle, detected in a shifting in her cheek and under her jaw. But I could read them. "There was no need to understand your perspective," she said, calmly, "when you were meant to be eliminated weeks ago, when we learned that your identity had been compromised."

(Weeks ago. Think about that.)

I could not help but do as the intrusive thoughts suggested. The friendly fire during the Arrix mission. The Mindnet rarely – never – struck its own forces with misplaced fire. At the time, I blamed myself. I had no implants. I couldn't have been part of System Defense's clockwork precise plans.

But maybe I hadn't interfered in the defense. Maybe this had made me a less predictable *target*. If I hadn't maneuvered just then, out of turn and out of order, We could have landed a more direct killing blow.

It was a very… Mindnet thing to have attempted. Efficient. The order to remain at Arrix had caught me by surprise. I'd thought it was an opportunity. The Mindnet had gotten all the work out of me that We could. They'd allowed me to participate in Arrix's defense. I *had* scored some hits on the gunship.

After that battle, though, a burned spy like myself would have been useless. So would my ship, which was old, poorly maintained, and almost certainly on wanted lists alongside my person.

Easier to eliminate both my ship and me with a well-placed shot from System Defense. Or, later on, with a bomb.

Especially if the Mindnet did not trust me to follow an order to eliminate myself.

8CC0RD said, pointedly, "I was running a quiet, airtight surveillance operation until your arrival forced me to take actions that would attract more notice."

"My sincere apologies for forcing your hand," I said dryly.

"The danger you present demands quick and decisive action."

"Then quickly and decisively explain yourself."

"*Ourselves*," she said. But then, having gotten that point in, she relented. "The Keleres have distributed an all-points bulletin to their field bases across the galaxy, calling for your quiet capture. The traitor civilizations know that you work for Us."

The news opened a hollow in the center of my chest. "How was I burned?" I demanded.

"Why does that matter?" When my glare sharpened, she had the grace to look uncomfortable. She didn't make me force it out of her. "We do not know. Traditional counterespionage work is hard to place. Either you made a mistake at some point or were simply unlucky." That had, unfortunately, been the likeliest answer. Most burned spies never learned how they'd gotten discovered, or by whom. "It does not matter. What *does* matter is that the Keleres acquired a scan of you. They know that you have been infected with Arzuga fungus."

"You're acting out of turn," I said. We had made plans for this. "It doesn't matter that my cover identity is gone. We can create a new one. A loyal Mindnet operative who can bypass cybernetics detectors is more valuable to Us than a hundred agents like yourself. You can only spy from out here, on the fringes. You should die for me a hundred times over before I relinquish *my* life."

"It is possible," 8CC0RD said, with what sounded like a dry throat, "that Our initial assessment of your Arzuga was mistaken."

The hollow opened wider. For a moment, I felt as though the artificial gravity had turned off. "What?" I asked, like an imbecile.

It may have been my imagination, but for a moment she seemed satisfied. "The Keleres are of the opinion that your mutated Arzuga is much more dangerous than We believed," she said. "That it *could* be weaponized to remove the cybernetic implants of captured Mindnet citizens. Or perhaps across whole planetary populations."

"Our research discounted that possibility." The Hacan had said a simple firmware update, a tweak to the immune systems, was all that was needed.

"Keleres scientists have apparently seen a potential We did not," she said. "In any case, you seem to have expended your use to Us."

I still didn't believe the Keleres could do anything like what 8CC0RD suggested. But the idea made me go cold. The fact that the Keleres seemed to believe it could happen was chilling enough.

Planetary populations.

The historical memory of the Twilight Wars had not just survived the removal of my implants; it had gotten stronger. For a moment, I was locked in a vision of dead, ash-caked cities. Heat-snapped bones. A sky on fire.

The Keleres wanted to inflict that same devastation

without needing bombs or fleets of ships. They were certainly dreaming about a biological weapon, spores delivered via spies or even an innocuous-looking meteorite, spreading across a Mindnet world. Force Mindnet citizens' bodies to reject their own cybernetics.

It was an eliminationist fantasy. A technological deus ex machina, an easy solution to their "problem" of the Mindnet. There were no deus ex machinas in interstellar politics or war.

I'd barely survived my own infection. The bulk of a planet's populace would stand no chance. All those people – the same ones that the Galactic Council purported to want to rescue – would simply be gone.

I tried not to let it show. "They're mistaken. If the Keleres have been able to scan me, it would have had to be at a distance. They are operating on guesswork and misplaced hope, seeing what they want to believe."

"Likely true," she said. "But even the slight risk, given the enormous consequences, remains untenable. Your body contains the only remaining samples of the Kitrya-892 b Arzuga. It must be destroyed."

"You're leaping at phantoms. Even *if* I were captured, the odds that–"

"We are not acting irrationally," she said. "You are now disobeying Our orders. That alone is a reason to extirpate you."

"*You* are a small group of agents on this station, at best. *We* have nothing to do with this."

"*We*," she said, drawing out the word deliberately, "have decided this."

Her confidence gave me pause. "If all of this is true," I said, laboring over the *if*, "you could simply have told me. Why keep secrets or indulge in assassination attempts? Why not order me to destroy myself from the start?"

"We were concerned," she said, "that you would not obey orders."

With a jolt, I realized she was right to be concerned.

If I had been told all of this in a message, even if I had been confident that all the Mindnet had placed Our weight behind the order, I would have hesitated. Maybe I wouldn't even have done it.

This was not like it had been with the Hacan, when I had injected myself with what he told me had been poison. Their – Our – reasoning was flawed. The Keleres were operating in the dark, under the flawed premise that We hadn't considered anything their scientists might have discovered.

More importantly, I was still of tremendous value to Us. If the Mindnet had any other agents capable of bypassing cybernetics scanners, I wouldn't have been told about them … but the number couldn't have been higher than single digits and might have been as low as one: me.

Everything I did was for the good of the Mindnet. *Everything.*

"Your judgment is in serious doubt," 8CC0RD said. "For instance, you traveled unarmed into a place like this station. If you had carried even a simple knife, you could have killed several of those Keleres agents during their first ambush. Instead, you left them for Us to clean up."

"I am not a soldier." Even if I had been, I didn't think I would have fought.

There was too much risk. The hardest veteran soldiers in the galaxy could be taken out by artillery strike, a sniper, poor supply lines, bacteria in a meal, or a lucky punch. The most advanced biomechanical senses could not see through the fog of war.

I was just starting to realize what an odd thing that was for a Mindnet operative to think. We pride Ourselves in the precision of Our weapons, Our machine-augmented reflexes, Our numbness to pain. But the truth was that We believed Ourselves assured of victory only on the grand strategic scale. Individuals were subject to chance. The Mindnet did not care about individuals.

I had been by myself for too long. I had no choice but to value everything on the scale of an individual.

Or so I told myself. Shooting at Letnev gunships, across a vast gulf of space and during an invasion, had not seemed real. Not like murder. It wasn't rational to draw a line at one and not the other. Killing was killing. Even back then, though, I had wondered if I'd hesitated. The thought of blood, of skin split like velvet, roiled my stomach. I could not have carried a knife again.

I knew what the correct choice was, and I knew what the right choice was.

8CC0RD sensed my hesitation. "Obey now. Terminate yourself."

"You're not a trustworthy source of orders," I said.

"You are making excuses," she said. "Trying to deflect." I could not contest that point because it was accurate. And there was no further point in arguing this.

"I won't obey that order," I said with finality.

She nodded, curtly. She seemed relieved to be done with this.

She said, "We assume that you have prepared a trap to kill me."

"You assume correctly," I said.

Though she tried to hide it, her stance indicated that she was ready to move in an instant. Her knees were slightly bent, her shoulders hunched. She could throw herself or sprint in any direction. She assumed that the trap I'd set was nearby, and that it was intended to kill her. I didn't correct her. Neither of us moved. We waited.

I had considered placing a lethal trap, explosives under her platform, but rejected it. The thought felt like holding a knife in my hand. I couldn't do it.

I stopped that thought. It wasn't relevant. I hadn't set a lethal trap for 8CC0RD because she wasn't my enemy. That had to be the only reason.

"You may go," I said.

"Your actions thus far suggest that you will attempt to kill me."

"I'm proving a point," I said. "I have the power to harm you, and I'm not using it. I'm not Our enemy. You doubtless have some value to the rest of Us."

"You are delusional," she said. "You are malformed, malfunctioning, and making a selfish, individualistic decision."

"We're done talking," I told her. I started to reach for the switch that would disable the projectors.

"Your removal has been in the works longer than you know."

I stopped moving. I glared at her image, desperately hoping my sensors were not picking up the tremor in my fingers.

"If you traveled to a Mindnet, and received the same order reinforced by thousands of minds – what would you choose, then, for your next excuse for disobeying? You must have thought that far in advance already."

She was relentlessly correct. I already knew what I would have said: that the Mindnet was making a mistake. "I serve the Mindnet," I said.

"Serve in death," she said. "Send Us your location, and We will ensure that not even the glimmer of your Arzuga's existence survives to trouble Us."

"I… no," I said.

"Obey," she said. "Your conditioning has plainly weakened, but it *must* still cause you pain to disobey. Follow that pain."

"Reconsider everything I still offer Us–"

"*Obey.* Follow my instructions."

I had lied to her. I hadn't placed any explosives under her platform. But I *had* placed some in the only lift shaft and communication lines between her module and the rest of the station. I detonated them.

All my displays fuzzed white, and I was alone.

8CC0RD would know now that I had lied about being prepared to kill her. When she got back here, I could not count on evading her again.

The projectors surrounding me gradually realized that they were no longer connected, and died one after the other, leaving me in the dark.

CHAPTER SIXTEEN
BREAKAWAY

No matter what bill was coming due, I could not pay. I could not afford to be hasty in my next move, but neither could I afford to take my time.

I kept track of ships arriving and departing Port Vel Syd. Only hours after I'd spoken with 8CC0RD, a freight hauler had entered the system broadcasting a Federation of Sol merchant transponder. It answered station security's questions satisfactorily and was on its way to dock.

I'd seen the make and model of that hauler several times before. Last time, one had been latched onto the side of one of the Galactic Council's space stations, far above Mecatol Rex's smoke-gray skies. The Keleres liked to use haulers for clandestine operations. All manner of military hardware could be hidden inside its containers.

The Keleres would have been foolish to announce their presence even before the incident at the starbridge. Only civilizations well-integrated into the legal framework of the Galactic Council would have reacted positively to a team of Keleres showing up. The first Keleres team hadn't bothered to ask for local clearance.

Not long after the Sol-flagged cargo hauler arrived, one of the smaller, departing courier ships abruptly changed course, and leapt beyond light speed – burning in the direction of Mecatol Rex. The Keleres wouldn't stop with these reinforcements, either. This was just their first wave. If they truly, foolishly, believed that the fungus in my body was their key to solving the problem of the Mindnet, they might even have attempted to muster council support to seize the station.

The cargo hauler drove relentlessly toward its assigned dock. This told me two things: first, that the Keleres believed that there was still a big prize to hunt, and second, not all the original Keleres agents on the station had died. Somehow, the Keleres had been keeping track of events on the station. They knew I wasn't dead or captured by the Mindnet agent that had attacked them, or otherwise removed from their reach.

I had to scrimp and save and steal time where I could. That meant going directly to Stefan rather than setting up a meeting in advance.

The destroyed lift shaft ensured that 8CC0RD would be spending a great deal of time figuring out a way to get back here. It was entirely possible that she really had no conspirators elsewhere aboard Port Vel Syd, and that I was alone among Us. But I could not guarantee that. Approaching Stefan at all was a tremendous risk, but I had to do it.

In espionage, ambushing a contact with an unexpected appearance was one of the worst things to do. Showing up at a contact's workplace or home was intimidating, certainly, but there was no shortage of better ways to scare a person. It was bound to make both the spy and their contact jumpy: the spy because they were at their most vulnerable in an uncontrolled environment, and the contact for having all their assumptions about their own safety ripped out from under them.

Setting up a meeting in advance left the contact with an illusion of control, no matter how slender. They had to actively choose to come. It left them feeling complicit. That pre-baked feeling of complicity made a contact all the more likely to do whatever the spy asked.

That was the strategy the Mindnet used with me. I had been conditioned to take certain actions. Killing Uthan. Returning to the Mindnet. They were all things *I* had done. I couldn't deny that I was complicit.

Complicity was part of the trap. It was a mechanism of control.

A very efficient one.

In a brain with a severed *corpus callosum*, one side of the brain acted. Both sides believed they were responsible.

(It could even silo unwelcome thoughts away from itself. Construct an imagined outsider. Get into endless silent, stewing debates with it.)

I sighed. All along, there had been parts of me that resisted the Mindnet. It had been easier, lazier of me, to think of it as separate from myself, as the Arborec – even when I knew it was physically impossible for the Arborec to be influencing me in that way. Even when the thought had been terrifying. Terror could be defended against.

(Easier to think of it as a foreign body, a perpetual enemy living in your head, than an indivisible part of you.)

Those intrusive thoughts were not a new part of me. They were not the Arborec and had never been. They only felt like a stranger because implants, conditioning, and reconditioning had suppressed them for so long.

Stefan lived in an area of Port Vel Syd that was silent and unfriendly in a different way than the rest of the station was silent and unfriendly. His "neighborhood" had the hostility of jealous wealth and the upward grasping middle class. I'd had to break through two locked doors to even reach the corridor outside his quarters.

All the light strips were new. They shone the warm color of daylight under a yellow main sequence star. The walls had been painted over with terrestrial blue and green abstract patterns, with shapes suggestive of people in the background, to minimize loneliness.

But this was still Port Vel Syd, and there was always much more empty space than people to inhabit it. No one noticed me striding through it. The station's truly wealthy and powerful didn't live here. There was no actual security.

I meant to arrive just as Stefan went to work. My timing was perfect. The door to Stefan's quarters unfurled as I approached. He stepped out, his hair still damp from his morning shower. Flecks of water fell onto his business robe.

When he turned and saw me marching down the corridor, he actually yelped. Stefan reached for a silver-pronged stun rod at his hip. I was sure he had not carried it last time.

He was not fast enough. By the time he got his hand around the stun rod's padded grip, I had grasped it, too, and wrenched it away from him.

"Please stay calm," I told him.

Unsurprisingly, he chose to do otherwise.

He half-stumbled backward as though I had shoved him, slamming into a wall. Other than to take his weapon away, I hadn't touched him.

I almost missed talking with 8CC0RD. I could understand Mindnet citizens. Read their expressions to an extent. I had found some kind of rapport with Uthan, long ago, but only after weeks of practice. And I suspect he'd done more getting used to me than me to him.

"She told me you were a traitor," Stefan stammered.

"When?" I demanded.

I was well aware of my social shortcomings outside of the Mindnet and tried to take a direct approach whenever possible. It reduced the number of pitfalls I might stumble into. But directness sometimes seemed a pitfall of its own.

He went tight-lipped, trying to slide along the wall away from me. "She told me she would withdraw Oran's care if I saw you and didn't tell her after."

I chose to read that as a small kindness on his part: a warning, a way of staking his vulnerability so that I knew he had no choice but to do as instructed. And that if I, too, tried to blackmail him with his nephew's medical care, he would shut down. He would have no way to win. Therefore, neither would I.

"Describe her," I said.

Stefan kept pushing himself along the wall. I kept pace with him with a single step. He stopped, the white in his cheeks turning red as he seemed to realize how ridiculous it was to act like I was an explosive about to discharge. He sighed, closed his eyes for a moment and muttered a variety of curses. They did not seem to be directed at me, but at fate or the universe in general. I empathized.

When he opened his eyes again, he did as I asked.

The person he described was 8CC0RD. Right skin color and body type. From the context – referring to her only as "she," as if it should be obvious who I was talking about – I gathered that she had been his regular handler.

If I'd planted my explosives properly, she was still trapped many, many kilometers away, and I wouldn't have to worry about her. Not yet. In the back of my head, however, a clock ticked. Throughout all my time on this station, a variety of other ships had come and gone. Luxury craft, couriers, mercenary pilots, cargo carriers. All carrying messages. Some, I was sure, had ended up in Our hands.

"There may be a way to secure your nephew's health permanently," I said.

The last time Stefan and I had spoken, the knowledge had rested deep in my gut, far underneath my voice. So deep that it had been – almost – below the level of conscious awareness.

Stefan was a useful Mindnet asset. So long as revealing what I was about to say to Stefan would have been against the Mindnet's interests, eliminating Our hold on him, I could not give voice to it.

Though Stefan didn't look any less ready to flee, when he spoke next, his voice was completely different. "If you people are going to keep screwing around with his life, I'm going to kill you right now and *damn* the–"

The headache pulsed at my temples, threatening to grow stronger with every word I spoke. My conditioning persisted.

"The Arborec," I blurted.

"–consequences, we are not pieces on a game board–"

It was all a matter of context. I was doing this *for* the Mindnet. Like everything else I did.

Even if the Mindnet wouldn't see it the same way.

The headache abated. That gave me the strength to push past the terror of the Arborec that had bitten at my heels since the first day Uthan had mentioned the name. "The Arborec's medical capabilities outstrip the Mindnet's," I said. I was living proof of that. Even an old, mutated form of its Arzuga fungus had defeated all my newer cybernetics.

The Mindnet had not played especially unfairly with Stefan, at least not by Our standards. The treatment We provided his nephew was genuinely the best We could do.

We had only omitted the fact that another galactic power, albeit one that repulsed most sentients with its very nature, could do better. We had seen the Arborec accomplish it on their own worlds.

"The Arborec reanimating his corpse doesn't count as a cure," Stefan said, voice dripping with contempt.

Every time I said the Arborec's name, bile burned my throat. The revulsion never went away, but it did get easier to bear. "Contrary to popular belief, the Arborec does have other means of interacting with people." The corpse-puppets stuck out in most sentients' minds. But the Arborec interacted with other civilizations more than most people knew – or were allowed to know.

Some sentients even chose to live with it. The Arborec had been making more of an effort to moderate the image it presented to the rest of the galaxy. Show the compassionate face of its vast, infinitely faceted intellect. The Arborec had colonies, stations, embassies, and other places where it invited other sentients to interact with it.

These colonies didn't get widely publicized. The galaxy at large remained terrified of what the Arborec represented. It would be difficult for any individualistic species to ever trust them. Nor should they have. And because the competition between great powers was what made the galaxy spin, governments everywhere suppressed its call welcoming immigration.

"Citizens of Arborec colonies have access to its full medical capabilities," I said. "I'm aware of cases in which complete human nervous systems, excluding only the brain, have been entirely regenerated."

He looked like he barely registered my words. He wasn't even considering believing me. Wise of him. "What do you want?" he asked desperately.

I opened my mouth, about to answer, but too many words pressed together to make their way out of my throat.

I wanted the same thing that I was trying to give him. An end to my complicity. A feeling of control.

To be able to think about everything from my family to Uthan's blood spilling over my hands and all my regrets without a swelling migraine.

To shed the memory of conditioning, of electric shocks razing my senses while I, drugged, had babbled a stream of consciousness that the Hacan's nerve scalpel sculpted.

I wanted to blame that experience for everything, but the truth was that the Hacan had not had much trouble. He had tested and measured more than he had shaped. The rest of his work had just been reinforcement and recalibration of the operating system that had governed me since childhood.

I wanted the galaxy at large to recognize what had happened to the Lazax. How the genocide of the Lazax was built into the foundation of the structures they'd built since. Built into all their thunderous titanic wars and the quiet terrible wars and the billion cascading tragedies that had swallowed everything since. Built into *this* moment, and the next, and the ponderous avalanche of all our futures.

I wanted to throw up. Take a shower. Be sick. Let myself feel terrible about everything I'd been and done.

I wanted a stuffed Jellybear. I wanted to be able to enjoy fruit candy again.

I wanted the ability to answer Stefan's question.

"I need to arrange passage off this station," I said. I steeled myself to say the next words. "I need to travel directly to the Arborec."

"This is absurd!" he said. "How do you know any of this?"

"I don't intend to treat you or your nephew as pieces on a gameboard," I said. "But the Mindnet has been playing a game with you. I would like to remove all of us from it. And from the Mindnet's influence."

This was for the good of the Mindnet. Just like everything I did.

That knowledge pumped through my head like adrenaline, soothing the still-brewing migraine. It stilled all my other thoughts, everything I might have told Stefan I wanted.

"How could I possibly *ever* believe you?" Stefan asked.

"I need to correct your assumption about who I am."

I pulled back my sleeve, and I showed him the orange-black fungus molded into my flesh.

This did not have a calming effect, either. But it did, ultimately, lead him in the direction I needed him to go.

Well away from the repair docks I had used, a bevy of smaller ships were latched to Port Vel Syd like neatly arranged barnacles. Worn down secondhand freighters, smuggler blockade runners, and private yachts mixed together, a study in class and inequality. The best products of crime and business docked beside the cheap, desperate detritus of the galaxy.

There were no lengthy starbridges, no vast and empty open spaces where construction equipment and replacement hull parts could be anchored. Just rows of starships of all sizes, a jungle of a junkyard. They ranged from a mess of canisters and tubes that looked like a spaceborne factory, to private personnel liners, and anything else that a bunch of half-warlord, half-business-manager types could get their hands and claws on.

Their entryways were, of course, being watched. Which was why Stefan and I didn't use them. Instead, we crawled along their exteriors, hopping from ship to ship like fleas.

My heartbeat and my breath echoed in the vacuum-muffled tinniness of my helmet. Everything sounded like I was sealed inside rock, planted into a tomb. Pain pounded through my head, and this time it had nothing to do with any conditioning. The migraine was all from stress.

My lack of social graces extended even to myself. I had failed to account for how I'd feel going back into open space. My face was flushed from the effects of freefall, and I had to constantly battle the nightmare image of throwing up in my helmet. On the bright side, I had the specter of how much worse things could get to distract me.

Out here, at least I couldn't see Stefan's recriminating looks so easily. The angry hunch in his shoulders said a lot, though.

"All this time," he'd said, when I'd gone into the details of what I knew about the Arborec's medical capabilities. "*If* this is true – all these years – the Mindnet knew about this. You did, too, the first time you met me. You said nothing."

I had slipped into the guise of an Arborec Dirzuga. Let him

think I was a double agent. "I'm saying something now," I said.

Not even the Arborec advertised the full extent of their medical sciences. It would not have been a wise thing to do when the first thing anyone thought of was how easily and callously the Arborec puppeteered the dead.

When I had lost my implants, most of my knowledge of the galaxy went with it. But the Arborec had been a special interest of mine. I had studied it extensively.

"There will be a price," I'd told him, back in the corridor outside his quarters, after he'd had a chance to recover himself.

"Becoming a walking corpse?" he asked.

Seeing the fungus crawling up my arm had made him retch. "The price is that, when Oran is healed, other people will see him with as much revulsion as you're showing me."

He did not have an answer to that. Only a look of deeper outrage.

"Stay here and continue living as you are," I said, "or come with me and chance a cure for Oran. Choose. You can always tell your Mindnet handler that I took you hostage."

None of the ships arrayed on this side of the station were as small as Uthan's courier shuttle. The smallest, a private yacht, was four times its length. We aimed for that one.

My magnetic boots *clunked* reassuringly heavily onto its flank. Grateful for humankind's bizarre need to have windows everywhere, I strode across to one of the oval portholes and peered inside. There was nothing moving in the main passenger cabin. The cabin lights were dimmed, in standby mode, showing me lavishly cushioned seats, all facing an array of screens and projectors.

I clomped over to the airlock with Stefan close behind me. I'd chosen this ship with Stefan's help. Its owner, an heir waiting to inherit an antimatter production factory halfway across the galaxy, had arrived two months ago. He and his friends had aimed to get away from all those pesky laws back home, not realizing exactly how those laws had protected him all his life. They'd picked up a blistering array of new addictions and debts in the meantime. They didn't seem likely to leave anytime soon.

Like so many other strutting rich humans living beyond their means, he had cut corners. The airlocks were decently maintained, but they hadn't been upgraded since the yacht had left the factory. No security patches installed. It was an easy trick to cut power to the airlock controls, reboot them in emergency mode, and get us cycled through.

Once we were inside, and I had my helmet off and deck plating firmly under my feet, I doubled over and emptied the contents of my stomach.

Stefan made a face. It started as disgust but melted into concern. I must have looked worse than I imagined, because that was the first time I'd seen him show anything like worry over me. Or seen it from anyone, really.

I was fine, I thought. This was normal. This was how I had always been. There was me, and there were my goals.

I'd made an effort to not perceive the difference, but somehow that was more difficult with another person around.

The cockpit was more businesslike than the cushion – and projector-bedecked passenger cabin, but still more spacious than it needed to be. It was also, absurdly, carpeted.

Stefan and I took the front two seats. That left several empty. The yacht required a crew of five trained operators. We were going to do it with two. Or more aptly, one and a half, counting Stefan's lack of experience.

We didn't need to reach our destination in one piece, so long as we got there.

It looked like no one other than Stefan and I had come inside the vessel in weeks, but the yacht was fully fueled, its electronics burning power on standby. Even when rich humans weren't in a hurry, they spent a lot of time and money pretending that they were. Waiting was for the poor.

When I asked, the cockpit projectors displayed camera images of space around us. Stefan and I were behind where I had hoped we would be. The Keleres's disguised hauler had docked to Port Vel Syd. But we weren't so late that the hauler had finished refueling.

The yacht's cameras showed their fuel umbilical locked in place. With fueling underway, it would take them several minutes to disengage without seriously damaging their ship. But we had to move quickly.

I took the yacht's main drive off standby and started powering it up. I watched our engine readiness displays hike green bars toward their top lines. When they were about fifty percent there, I disengaged the docking latches on the yacht's side. The yacht shuddered but remained in place.

We were only halfway loose. *Our* latches had been released, but the station had its own.

I had not told Stefan how badly I needed to get away from this place. "Are you sure you want to…?" he started to ask.

I fired the ventral thrusters.

The exterior camera views showed strobing alarm lights glaring through the station's nearest windows. At the docking latching, metal twisted and split. The station's hull breached. The empty embarkation lobby shattered in a fog of escaping air. A flash of movement marked a pressure door coming down.

Shipside, things seemed peaceful. The deck jolted, but the impact was soft, muffled by the yacht's artificial gravity. Red glyphs sprung up across the consoles as the yacht belatedly registered damage to the outer airlock hatch and moorings.

"Damn," Stefan muttered. "Fine. Sure."

He didn't know everything I'd done to secure our exit. If he'd known every direction I feared danger might arise, he would have thought again about joining me.

He still would have come, of course.

This was sickeningly exhilarating, a feeling only cured by turning my brain off. I was on automatic. Performing on conditioning.

"Take thruster control, please," I said. He was supposed to have been booting everything else while I managed the engines.

I stood. The navigator's station wasn't all that dissimilar from the one in Uthan's shuttle. It sat flush against the cockpit's rear wall: a seat facing a flat desk surface studded with far too many projectors. Blue-violet hexagons danced around my fingertips, an abstracted map of nearby sections and spacelanes.

While Stefan swung the yacht around, I spun a course that would take us to Nestphar... but not after laying light speed tracks in several other directions first. It would make us nigh impossible to follow. Any ship that went after us, chasing the light trails we wove through the stars, would get lost in the maze. It would take a ship with military-grade scanners and engines a month, overshooting every abrupt turn and backtracking, to find out where we were going.

If I was still on Nestphar after a month... then I was already dead, whether my body continued to live or not.

The Mindnet needed me. We needed my perspective. The Keleres's interest in me had spooked Us. Fear shut down Our reasoning skills. The only way to get Us to listen to anything else I had to say was to convince Us that my Arzuga was safe, and could not be weaponized, and that the Keleres were barking up a dead tree. And the only way to prove that seemed to be to hear it directly from the Arborec.

This would all be for the good of the Mindnet.

I returned to my seat beside Uthan. Eyes forward, I reminded myself. Nose buried in work. His presence was comforting, as it often had been, even when I never would have admitted it.

I was so distracted by watching the engine display that it took me a minute to notice that, in my imagination, I'd mistaken Stefan for Uthan.

Nothing showed on my face. But I became aware that Stefan was looking at me. I couldn't see his expression out of the corner of my eye and didn't want to look. I didn't want to see him. Didn't want to hear him.

Stefan steered the yacht far enough away from the station that we didn't roast it with our engine backwash. The cameras showed the Keleres vessel still docked. But infrared imaging indicated heat building behind their thrusters. They'd seen us break out. They were preparing to intercept us, as soon as they could halt their fuel transfer.

They were going to be too slow.

I punched the engines hard. Hard enough to strain the artificial gravity's ability to compensate for the acceleration. Stefan yelped, and then the *g*-forces shoved us deep into our seats, keeping us from speaking.

CHAPTER SEVENTEEN
ALL YOU ZOMBIES

Nestphar was nauseating to look at. Like seeing the inside of a swilling, churning stomach, or a sea of slime.

It was the first time I truly understood why humans and other sentients preferred windows to projections. I had seen images of Nestphar many times. It looked revolting enough on the yacht's dashboard projections. Holographic globes, panoramic views both above and below its spore clouds, whirled across my control surfaces. None of it affected me the same way as looking up and seeing it directly, through the cockpit window.

The window's view was in every way worse than the holographic images I'd had before. Nestphar's visible face was half shadow. There was no tuned contrast, no filtering to draw out details, or other tricks of informative photography. Just bilious, soupy green clouds. Nestphar was in some ways reminiscent of a gas giant, with its liquidy banded atmosphere, but there were just enough gaps in the clouds to let us see the fungus-encrusted surface underneath.

The whole planet had been thoroughly colonized. Not in the sense that it had been conquered or settled, but in the sense that a virus colonized a cell. Every part of this world, from its morphology to its atmosphere, had been molded into part of the Arborec's world-spanning body.

Nestphar's acidic seas churned with digestive chemistry, fed by algae sluicing down the sharp-peaked mountains the Arborec had raised. Those mountains – ejecting fire and deep gouts of smog – rose above the opaquest of the cloud layers, distending upward as the Arborec tensed its world-engorging muscles. The living world drank the nutrient-rich volcanic poison, farted and squirted methane. Under the sun-soaked greenhouse it had turned its world into, it cultivated the same algae that fed it.

In short: Nestphar was a slimy pit of a stomach, spitting and belching, both self-evolved and undirected, capable of sustaining itself for as long as the sun shone.

"Gorgeous, isn't it?" Stefan asked.

I could not restrain my horror long enough to keep it hidden. Stefan had his eyes on the window, though, and didn't notice.

"Look at those colors," he muttered. "All that greenery, the orange and the violet in the seas. It looks floral, doesn't it?"

I glanced at him, and then back at the fungus world. The way he'd described it was not incorrect, not literally. But I could never see it like he did.

It was possible that my perspective was biased.

The fungus all over my body burned. It had to be a psychosomatic effect. *Had* to be. I was sure that my intrusive thoughts had never come from the Arborec… but one of the many annoying things about the human psyche is that it could always make time for last second doubts.

The phantom pain only heightened my revulsion. Now closer, Nestphar looked like a teratoma in space. The planet appeared to have even grown hair: bright green filaments, swirled and laid across each other. They contrasted sharply against the spore cloud soup not only by their vividness but their sharpness, their precisely defined lines and curves.

They were hair-thin only at a distance. They were vines and big stalks. The tallest of them angled into the sky. Above the clouds, they turned abruptly straight, stretched out by the centrifugal force of the planet's spin. Living space elevators.

Where the filaments reached their terminus, where the air faded to haze and then to nothing, they touched deceptively thin and glassy polyhedral meshes, spread widely across Nestphar's orbital space. These were the Honeycombs: multilayered organic megastructures that the Arborec had extruded into orbital space. Some of the Honeycombs connected directly to the filaments. Others orbited freely, their paths interleaving and overlapping each other. From a distance, they appeared to be a single diaphanous object, with a surface that shifted like icebergs across an ocean.

Nestphar was the Arborec's home planet. Though the creature itself couldn't be said to be centralized here, Nestphar was the hub of the Arborec's efforts to integrate itself into galactic society. Other sentients were more comfortable thinking of the Arborec as a civilization, with a capital, rather than the distributed biomass it actually was. So more outsiders lived here than anywhere else in Arborec space.

"Arrange docking permissions, please," I said, quietly.

The last thing I could bear to do right now was speak with the Arborec. I'd had nightmares that started like that.

Stefan started, as if remembering who I was. He had to have been wondering why I couldn't do it myself. But he strode to the communications station with no more complaint than a scowl.

Stefan had calmed down considerably during our flight. The week and a half we'd spent traveling had been far from a vacation, but it had given us time to breathe – and, more importantly, stay away from each other. He persisted in a state of rage and disbelief. Occasionally, he even revealed flashes of what I supposed was his personality, which seemed chatty and gregarious. The only times I'd met him before had been in high stress situations. He remarked on strange things, like the quality of the drinks onboard or the poorly stocked medical supplies, like he was hoping to strike up a conversation with someone. It reminded me of Uthan, even as the past week had sharply illustrated the difference between them.

The voice that answered his signal sounded human. "Welcome to Nestphar, Federation of Sol-registered starcraft. How can I help you?"

"I've come to request medical asylum," Stefan stammered.

"Asylum seekers are always welcome in Nestphar," the other voice said. "I am transmitting an approach vector directly to your navigation computer. Please know that this call is confidential. Please let me know as many details about your situation as you're able, and I can begin making arrangements while you're on approach."

The Arborec seemed to enjoy playing nice. But it wouldn't have gotten this far in galactic politics by being an idiot, or especially trusting. Despite the pleasant tone, I had little doubt that we were under as much scrutiny as I had been when I'd arrived at Port Vel Syd. A thousand pinprick-pupiled telescopic eyes were tracking us across the stars, studying us in multiple spectra.

The other voice referred only to "I," never to "we," as another space traffic control might have. There was something off in how it sounded, something even I noticed: a flatness, the feeling that the speaker was reading words off a page. And, underneath the static of the transmission, there was something guttural, almost syrupy.

We were speaking to a corpse. And it was answering through a throat and vocal cords slick with fungal slime.

I wondered if Stefan had picked up on that. He exhaled sharply as the Arborec gave him more corroborating details about the process of cellular revitalization, about DNA alteration and immune system deprogramming, than I'd been able to. Stefan looked at me in wonder. "You might have been telling the truth," he said.

"Why did you come with me if you thought I was lying?" I asked.

"I thought you would break my neck if I didn't." He read the skepticism in my look. "I had no choice. You don't know how tired I was of living like I did."

As the Arborec promised, it sent an approach vector to an orbital habitat. I programmed the directions while Stefan kept speaking with the Arborec.

It was dangerous to let Stefan continue believing I was a Dirzuga. He was certainly going to end up in a conversation with the Arborec where he described who had brought him here.

It belatedly occurred to me that, now we were here and had reached a point in the docking routine where one person could handle everything, Stefan had become a threat, a challenge to my cover story.

The Mindnet would have had me kill him. In fact, We wouldn't have allowed him to speak with the Arborec at all.

A dull headache, a harbinger of a migraine, settled between my temples.

I remembered how it had felt to grip the handle of the medical scalpel after I had made up my mind to kill Uthan. I'd expected my hand to shake. My steadiness had felt falsely reassuring.

My grip on the flight controls was trembling now, and that was a relief.

"No treatment is certain," the Arborec told Stefan. "It would be easier to guarantee effective treatment if the patient were present. But we believe we can help your nephew. With his consent, of course."

"I'll need to get him a message," Stefan said, in a faraway voice. "A message courier, or shuttle, to leave the system."

"We will begin to make arrangements."

When Stefan finally finished his call, his palms were sweating. He clasped them in front of his mouth and stared at nothing in particular. He was in shock. I figured that he had not allowed himself to feel hope.

After a minute, Stefan said, "I still don't like you very much."

"I empathize," I said. I didn't like myself either.

Like Stefan, I was very tired of living like I was.

We dipped into the space between the Honeycombs' walls, and then into one of the vast polyhedral cells. Shadows swallowed much of the sky, but the cell remained open behind us, and sunlight spilled in after us.

The Arborec aimed us toward a segment of the cell wall that glinted too brightly to be all organic. The exhaust of our braking thrusters blocked our view. When it cleared, what had been a glint had become enormous.

The Honeycombs had eaten a space station.

The Arborec was predominantly a plant and fungus organism. That was what most of the galaxy thought of it as. But its corpus of life extended into every kingdom, including the animal. It even, on the handful of occasions when it made sense, subsumed technology.

The most intact part of the station looked like an old-fashioned rotating torus-shaped habitat that someone had shipped to Nestphar and refurbished. The torus did not spin, and so it had probably been outfitted with modern artificial gravity. Porthole lights shone along its flank, into and along the living stalk that speared through the station's open center, and that joined it with the larger Honeycomb cell.

Every fresh look brought another detail I would rather not have seen. The darker green fungus didn't just encrust the stalk. It reached into the habitat torus and casually breached its hull. There were *tunnels* in the fungus, their translucent fibrous sides shimmering orange-green under the sunlight. People were meant to walk them. I imagined dripping, slimy walls, which finally forced me to turn my eyes elsewhere.

A bevy of other ships were docked all around the habitat cylinder's outer edge. I recognized Hacan and Federation of Sol cargo haulers, Saar asteroid miners, and a Xxcha patrol boat. There was even, bizarrely, a Letnev frigate.

Some of the docked starships were dark and looked like they'd been there a very long time. One of the Hacan haulers was missing a vast chunk of its engine complex. To my horror,

I saw vines and strange, tumorous bulbs inside the exposed engine parts. Purplish moss crawled over the vessel's hull. Fungi bubbled out of what looked to have been viewports.

This craft was being decomposed. *Consumed.* My imagination treated me to a waking nightmare of the same happening to this yacht while I was inside it.

Years ago, I had wondered if I would ever be able to forgive the Arborec for what it had done to my body, even if it had done it inadvertently. I had discarded the question as irrelevant.

It was a marker of personal growth that now I understood that the question *was* relevant. It had a definitive answer, and that answer was no.

"Look at those whorls," Stefan said, pointing at the station. "I've never seen zero-gravity mushroom growth. You can see spirals in some of them, like flowers. Beautiful."

"Hell," I muttered. I observed restraint and did not tell him to shut up.

He could not know this, but the last thing he should have been doing was reminding me of his presence. My emotional turmoil made my conditioning that much harder to deal with. It was ceaseless exercise to remind myself that helping Stefan, leaving him alive, was the right thing to do.

No, better. The *correct* thing. The best thing for the Mindnet.

Like the Mindnet, I needed perspectives other than my own, to keep me from spiraling into a whirlpool of revulsion.

I'd had a week and a half to ponder what I was going to do here. By the time our docking latches clamped to the station, I had almost figured out an answer.

I had to find some resource, a doctor or a library or *something,* that knew more about the Arzuga fungus than was publicly available outside. Something that could prove that the Keleres were fools, that my infection couldn't be turned against the entire Mindnet. And I had to do all of this without letting the Arborec know that I was a failed Dirzuga. I had no idea what it would do then.

It was a very, very thin branch to stride out upon, but it was all I had.

The yacht had several expensive-looking robes, skirts, and dresses aboard. They fit Stefan well enough, but I was too small for them. My too-long sleeves drooped. Unlike Port Vel Syd, there were no tailoring machines aboard. The yacht's prior owner had been too wealthy for mere machine tailoring. Everything would have been done by hand. But the extra folds and fabric helped me hide my body. I wore an incongruous scarf to obscure the orange-black fuzz that reached my chin.

It was possible that the Arborec would be able to sniff out the fungus anyway, but in that case, I was doomed regardless. I had to play the hand I'd drawn.

Stefan looked comfortable enough in his robes. Life with the Arborec would not be anything like what he'd had on Port Vel Syd, even in the barest sense. For his sake, I hoped he was not expecting a life like the one he was used to except with an aesthetic of flowers and mushrooms. The outer airlock hatch rolled open and released us into the station.

Where Port Vel Syd had been huge and lifeless, this space we stepped into was compact, blinding with color, and full of voices. The concourse as a whole had a high ceiling, and must have been sizable, but the mossy trees and hedges loomed close enough to make me claustrophobic – and I'd just spent a week and a half somewhere much smaller. A wave of scent, sound, and humidity washed over us. The air tickled the back of my throat. It smelled of vibrant plant life, with a sweet background of nectar and decomposition. Like a freshly fertilized garden next to a compost pile.

Artificial gravity had been added at some point. Though the station no longer rotated, we were held firm to the deck. Streamers hung underneath trees and over hedgerows, and underneath glaring sunlamps. They were crude fabrics, hand-sewn and irregular, but artfully dyed. A breeze played with them and carried the sound of voices. Dozens of people spoke somewhere, in as many languages as there were bodies. But the brush was so close that I couldn't see anyone through it.

Stefan looked like he'd shrunk in his robes. An insect buzzed over his eyes and alighted on his cheek. I grabbed his hand halfway to swatting it.

Everything here had its role in the ecosystem. If the insects sampled our blood, it would be for a purpose. A buzzing against my ear presaged a sharp itch on my neck. Like Stefan, my first instinct was to swat it. I ground my teeth to restrain myself.

My blood carried a handful of dead Arzuga cells, sloughed off from the veins that ran through my fungal intrusions. From the extensive tests I'd performed on myself, I knew that the Arzuga fungus hadn't colonized my blood. The corpses it usually inhabited didn't have flowing blood, after all. If I had to gamble, I didn't think I would be detected. Evolution guided the Arborec, and the Arborec had no evolutionary reason for its blood tests to screen for its own biosignatures.

But it was another source of uncertainty, another spike of fear, to go along with all the others assaulting me.

The ground underfoot was green, but not any variety of grass. It was disconcertingly spongy and squelched with every step. At first glance, everything here appeared a jumble of chaos. It didn't take long, though, for paths forward to suggest themselves. Everything led in the same direction. The place was chaotic only in the sense that it had formed naturally. Like a vein or a river, these paths would carry us to the same place in the end.

Ahead, an ancient human with coral-colored skin, a short and patchy white beard, and matching hair waited for us. He bore folds of wrinkles but stood unbowed. Age hung its weight on his flesh but not his muscles.

"Are you well, Mx Sil?" he asked, not quite looking at me. "Your pulse and blood pressure are quite high. And the adrenaline…?"

And my pulse beat faster still when I heard my name. It took me too long a moment to remember that I had transmitted my name during docking preparations, when the Arborec had asked for a manifest of those coming aboard.

"I'm well, thank you," I forced myself to say.

"You seem to be experiencing a panic attack."

Forks of black ran through his coral skin. Neither shade was his natural skin tone. The Arzuga fuzz covered him more completely than it did me. In the places where the fungus didn't cover, the walking corpse's skin had turned gray.

I smiled thinly. "Usually, I can control it better."

With hardly any pause for acknowledgment, the Dirzuga zombie turned to Stefan. "You also seem to be in a state of anxiety. Please, let's walk. I look forward to discussing more of Oran's needs, and your own."

The old man started walking the way Stefan and I had been headed. He did not *turn* until he'd taken several steps backward, and then sideways. Every footstep landed perfectly. The Arborec was watching everything from many angles, only one of which came from the dead eyes in front of us.

Stefan glanced my way, as if looking for support, but I had none to give. I just followed the old man. After a second, so did Stefan.

The Arborec kept talking about Oran's treatment. To my relief, tone and vocabulary didn't match my intrusive thoughts. Though I could put to rest the fear that the Arborec had taken me over, that made room for a new fear: that the Arborec *would* take me over if it found out about the Arzuga I carried in me. My pulse continued to pound against my ears. The old man gave no indication he was paying special attention to me, but of course he wouldn't.

Rounding the corner of the brambles gave us a better view of the concourse. Though the trees and strange hedges still pressed close, they separated enough to form a wider path, revealing that the concourse was vaster than it had seemed. It covered this whole level of the torus, arcing to the right to follow its curve. As we walked farther and the path widened, it became clear that the place served not just to welcome visitors, but as a park and gathering spot for everyone aboard.

Ahead, a half-dozen humans sat on benches together, stitching what looked like more streamers from shreds of fabric. They wore rough-looking clothes, woven from fronds or mushroom fiber. Like the draped streamers, though, they were all colorfully dyed. Farther on, a group of chitin-shelled N'orr sat in a circle with folded wings, speaking to a Hacan whose mussed fur failed to hide the Arzuga. Two fuzzy Naaz-Rokha families reclined on opposite sides of the same tree, sheltering from the sun lamps.

There was a certain kind of person for whom this might appeal, but I was not among them. And I suspected that, for a good portion of those who could have been enamored, the shine would have worn off quickly.

However most other civilizations ultimately distributed their resources, they had all started from a foundation of exchange and trade. Not the Arborec. The Arborec cultivated ecologies, not economies. Blood cells didn't carry oxygen to tissue because they were paid. They did it because it was their nature.

Privileges were accorded by necessity. Even those sentients who thought this sounded utopian had a difficult time living it. The Arborec said it was willing to make plenty of accommodations for those who wished to live in symbiosis with it… but that it expected immigrants to make the bulk of the adaptations.

To it, other people existed to be cultivated. To help the Arborec become a living part of the galactic community. Much the same way that a human body cultivated a biome of gut flora to aid in its digestion.

Other civilizations claimed that a third of Arborec immigrants attempted to leave after a year or less. The Arborec itself said that the ratio was somewhat less than that… and that those who stayed became devoted.

I idly wondered if anyone had ever placed the streamers so close to the sunlamps as to catch fire. Then, less idly, wondered what the Arborec would have done about it. When it would have vented the air of the entire concourse. How much risk it would expose the rest of the station to, for the sake of individuals.

Our view broadened enough to let us see the windows. They looked out over the shadowed Honeycomb bay, and upon the starships docked along the concourse. The windows' presence was confounding. It didn't seem likely that they were part of the original construction, not unless the people who built it wanted to make themselves sick. When the station had rotated to provide gravity, these windows would have been on the deck, looking down upon infinity.

Then I understood. The moment we'd stepped in, this place had seemed so much like an alien world that it hadn't occurred to me that this was still a boundary zone. A halfway point between the Arborec and life outside.

All of this, from the repurposed space station to the green muck to the insect bites to the dead-eyed old man, was the Arborec being *accommodating*. Trying to provide a bridge for species considering migrating.

The concourse must have been segmented at some point. Straight-line grooves showed where bulkheads had once been. Water ran their lengths. As I watched, one of the humans dipped their hands into the stream, washing off some variety of green effluent. Slime had to be a fact of life here. If I set my hand on anything, my palm would come back with a sheen.

To our side, two pale-skinned, colorfully clothed Letnev argued loudly with a pair of fully uniformed Letnev. The latter stood stiffly and uncomfortably, even more than usual for Letnev. The woman with the most rank pips on her uniform looked like she was barely restraining herself from violence.

The Letnev frigate hung in the window behind them. All its weapons had swiveled to face forward, as if trying to look imposing. Mostly, though, it just looked small.

The uniformed officers were confronting defectors, I guessed. The officers' sidearm holsters were empty, at least. Two Dirzuga stood close by. They couldn't do anything here, not without inciting a war that their superiors hadn't given them clearance to start. Probably. *Probably* hadn't given them clearance to start.

The Barony reacted famously poorly to defectors. But the Arborec was equally famous for being… expansive in retaliation. When it was given reason to attack a civilization, it attacked every member, from civilians to leaders. It made no distinction between individuals. After a few supposed-to-be-limited engagements turning into interstellar war, the other great powers had put strict limits on the ways their officers interacted with it.

To turn my thoughts elsewhere, I forced my attention back to Stefan and the white-haired Dirzuga. "Immigration can be physically and emotionally taxing," the Dirzuga said. "Sometimes dangerous. You will want to be sure Oran's consent to travel here is fully informed. We have experienced some tragedies where, after initially arriving for medical treatment, some individuals then refused it."

Stefan blanched. "Oran wouldn't." Stefan was trying to sound certain, but of course he couldn't be. And the Arborec didn't accept his objection.

"Culture shock is a surmountable problem," the Dirzuga said. "Being cut off from family, material wealth, and often refused the right to return home is different. It is not in the nature of some individuals to tolerate those conditions."

"You called them 'tragedies,'" I interrupted. I could not stop myself. "Were they? To you?"

"Language does require the use of shorthand," the Arborec said, without even a pause. "There are some emotional experiences that do not translate easily."

"Like experiencing the death of an individual as a tragedy," I said.

"Their deaths were losses," the Arborec said. "And I feel loss keenly."

I shouldn't have been wasting my time with this. I should have left them to pursue my own research. I scanned the inward-facing walls for exits. As I did, a chill swept up my arms, along my spine. A sudden, unaccountable feeling of *wrongness* turned the back of my head to ice.

The feeling was so physical that for a moment I thought I'd stumbled into an area of faulty artificial gravity or had breathed in some particularly noxious gas.

But what had happened was that my instincts outpaced my conscious thought. My gaze crossed the windows on the far side of the concourse.

A boxy gray freight hauler, with a radiation-bleached double-circle Federation of Sol emblem, hung outside. Fuel umbilicals and a slender, retractable airlock tube held it in place.

Back at Port Vel Syd, the yacht's cameras had shown me enough of the Keleres ship's hull that I could recognize the arrangement of cargo containers.

There had been no ships moving near the station when Stefan and I had arrived. I'd even checked for recent engine exhaust and found none. This ship must have already been here when we'd asked for clearance. The hauler was on the far side of the station, where I hadn't been able to see it on approach.

Stefan and the Dirzuga got a few steps ahead of me before stopping. I'd halted without realizing it. Stefan glanced back, but the old man never shifted his gaze.

"Mx Sil," the Dirzuga called, "your pulse is spiking. How can I assist you?"

I stumbled backward. I couldn't move without also turning my back on the hauler. "I need to get back to my ship."

If the Arborec was in on a conspiracy against me, I expected some of its mask to slip here. For it to refuse me entry to the yacht or insist on escorting me. But the dead old man said, "As you like."

With effort, I forced myself to turn and stride away from Stefan and the Dirzuga. With every step, I felt crosshairs on my back. Had this been a mistake?

The rational core of my brain patiently reminded me that I was, in fact, vulnerable from every direction. Every day, I learned something new about my lack of emotional intelligence.

The Keleres had somehow beaten me here. They shouldn't have known where I was going and would have been lost for weeks if they'd tried to follow the maze of light I'd left in our wake. They must have known where we were going ahead of time and come straight here from Port Vel Syd.

My first thought was I had been betrayed. *Stefan.* But even in my panic, I had the wherewithal to pluck at that theory long enough to unravel it. If Stefan had – somehow, for some reason – betrayed me to the Keleres, they wouldn't have docked with Port Vel Syd at all. Attaching the fuel umbilicals had incapacitated their ship long enough for our yacht to get away.

He could have sent a message not long after we boarded the yacht, while my back was turned, I supposed – but that was stretching, overfitting data to fit that conclusion. Something else was going on.

I would have broken into a run if I hadn't been sure I would slip in the muck. Adrenaline made everything seem more vibrant. Sharpened details. Not everyone in the concourse dressed like the locals. A Hylar scientist in a full water-breathing suit leaned over a patch of flowers, gingerly probing them as though afraid the flowers would explode at any instant. Two bald men – the Blessed of the Yin Brotherhood, identical clones but for their disease scars – were preaching the wisdom of Yin to a patiently listening Dirzuga.

There was someone, a human, walking along the inside wall of the concourse. The brush hid most of them from my angle, but I caught a flash of gray synthetic fabric. They were headed in the same direction I was, shadowing me.

I braced myself for thorns, turned, and pushed into the foliage. To my surprise, nothing snagged me. Of course. The Arborec would have had no use for thorns inside itself. I emerged covered in a sheen of slime.

In the next clearing, a trio of Hacan cubs played around a tree, apparently unsupervised. One of them looked filthy, like they'd just gone for a swim in muck. The other two caught sight of my expression and scattered.

It would have been much easier, I thought, if someone had just pulled a weapon on me. Or tossed a stun grenade. Back then, the problems had been immediate, the solutions close at hand.

The past few weeks had wrecked me. Ever since I'd discovered the Mindnet wanted to kill me, I'd become less capable, less swift and sure. And now the Mindnet's ever-present headache in the back of my skull pounded to remind me.

I kept making things more complicated. I shouldn't have attacked 8CC0RD. I *should* have killed Stefan, who was certain to say something to bring more of the Arborec's attention down on me. My rebellion had uprooted everything I'd believed about myself, and it was possible that I should have simply followed Our orders and terminated myself. Now I'd allowed myself to get outplayed by the Keleres.

A figure stepped along one of the paths leading back to my yacht's airlock, scanning the concourse.

Stepped was the wrong word. It undulated. It had no legs, but a long serpentine body.

Her. The Druaa. The same Druaa who'd tried to extort me at Port Vel Syd. Her skull ridges had the same shape. The same preserved animal tails as jewelry. She wore a tighter-fitting, plain purple outfit, and she'd lost the iridescent paint on her scales, but this was still unmistakably the same woman.

She bit the corner of her lip as she scanned the concourse. I slid to a stop. My muscles locked up the instant I saw her. She hadn't spotted me yet, but I didn't have the self-control to duck before her slitted eyes locked on mine.

She smiled, slightly.

My panic turned to a clarifying fury.

Her hand started to move, reaching for something at her side. I darted back into the foliage before she could finish drawing her weapon.

My ankle caught under a root, but I barely felt the pain of pulling it free. I pushed through the branches and onto a more open path.

There were dead trees as well as living ones here; the Arborec embraced decay and decomposition as a natural part of its existence. I took half a second to search the nearby trees, and I found a branch sturdy enough to use as a club.

It jutted out at waist level. I kicked it until the wood cracked. Before I could break it off, someone grabbed my shoulder.

I whirled around, fist drawn back. Then stopped.

Stefan had followed me. He looked *concerned.*

Idiot. I'd almost broken his nose. He'd walked back along the open route we'd taken. If any watcher had lost me in the foliage, they'd have been able to track him instead. "What's going on?" he asked.

Someone else, very close, trampled through the brush beside us. I saw only a flash of movement, but their branch-snapping footsteps gave away their position. When they burst into the open, I was ready.

It was the human in gray who'd shadowed me from the other side of the concourse. I pivoted from facing Stefan and lashed my foot out, tripping the human. Their momentum carried their face into my fist. Their head snapped back as they toppled.

Stefan gasped. I paused long enough to get a better look at my fallen pursuer. Red-brown hair. Masculine-seeming. Well-muscled, not like a bodybuilder, but in the trim, practical way that soldiers could be muscled. He had fallen, but he was still alert, struggling to his knees.

An object squelched onto the moss beside him: a rod with two metal prongs and a curved grip with a covered trigger plate. Stun baton.

I didn't need an instruction manual. I grabbed the baton, jammed the prongs into the fallen human's neck, and pressed the trigger plate. The snap-spark of electricity struck him with the force of an explosion. Though I felt no kickback, I wondered if I'd mistaken what the weapon was and blown his neck off. A tremor of horror, a memory of a scalpel splitting Uthan's skin, nearly made me drop the baton. But, no – it was just his spasming muscles, jerking with astonishing strength, knocking him aside.

Someone distant yelled in shock. I yanked Stefan with me, trying to get away. Without meaning to, we emerged onto the path he and I had been on earlier, as the ancient Dirzuga had guided us. Now a cry of alarm was going around the concourse.

The Hacan cubs were howling for the Arborec to help them.

I had just started moving again when something *whisked* through the air and passed above my shoulder. Chips of wood flew from the nearest tree. Stun darts, like those the Keleres had fired into my lift capsule on Port Vel Syd, embedded deep into the wood.

I glanced briefly behind me. Stefan had left the bearded old Dirzuga behind when he'd decided to come back for me. Now that Dirzuga was sprinting toward us, his legs pounding. The corpse's withered appearance belied its regrown muscle power. But it was not invincible. Abruptly, in mid-stride, it simply stopped working, like a machine whose power had been cut. It fell into the muck, quivering. A pair of darts stuck out of the back of its neck.

Stefan was barely keeping up with me, looking at the fallen Keleres officer with a mask of fright. I opened my mouth to yell at him to stay back, to be careful. Then I caught sight of the Letnev. The group of them had watched all of this take place. The two Letnev officers reacted in the worst way: with discipline and skill.

The ranking officer reached underneath her uniform jacket. I had misjudged the Letnev's willingness to start a conflict, because her hand returned with a sidearm. It was small, gray, and ceramic. A single-use device intended to bypass security scans. Assassination tool.

The Letnev defectors she'd been talking to were distracted by the noise. She took aim at them. But immediately, a Dirzuga was there. An elderly Winnu woman with blank eyes and a placid expression stepped beside the officer. There was a flash of movement too quick for me to follow. Then the weapon flew away.

The second Letnev officer drew a similar weapon, and this time the Dirzuga could not react fast enough. A human with orange-black fungus scabbed all over their scalp threw themselves at the officer. The Dirzuga knocked the officer's arm aside. A sharp firecracker pop resounded through the concourse.

Stefan shoved me forward. I stumbled onward and turned the extra momentum into a run. I kept my head low while I did so. The yacht's airlock was a few dozen meters away. I didn't dare get my hopes up, for good reason.

The Druaa was suddenly in my way, sidewinding across the muck in front of me, as if she'd known all along where I would emerge. She carried a stun prod like the one I grabbed. And still held.

My prod found her scales before she could bring hers around to touch me.

I'd expected her. I'd tried to keep the thought from the top of my mind, avoiding her telepathy, but I'd been ready, nonetheless. The solidity of her weight against my trigger hand, coupled with her gasp of fear, was intensely satisfying.

For a moment, I let myself believe that I was going to get the better of a very short brawl.

My idiot body failed me. My grip slipped. I couldn't find the trigger plate in time. It was a tiny, half-second compilation of errors that cybernetic implants would never have allowed me to make.

In a visible panic, the Druaa snapped her prod up against mine, fencing style, and knocked it off her scales. I kicked her, but her lower body was a bundle of muscle, and she easily kept her balance.

A second too late, I found the trigger plate's smooth, glassy surface. I held my finger poised above it as I fought to bring it back around. The Druaa mirrored my motion. Our batons locked together.

Rage overpowered my rationality. Gradually, by centimeters, it overpowered her, too.

She slipped backward. I stepped to follow. Then, suddenly, one of the Hacan cubs got underfoot.

The cub reached for my baton as if for balance.

I thought I'd left them behind. This one must have run to try to catch up with me. Despite everything, and in the face of all my Mindnet conditioning, panic shot through me. I couldn't think. A noncombatant was about to do something so *stupid*, so ludicrous, that they would get themselves hurt, and it was going to be *my* fault.

I wrenched the baton backward. But the cub grabbed it just below the prongs, and with demonic strength, threw it from my hands. My baton was still caught against the Druaa's. They both went airborne.

This Hacan cub was the filthy one I'd seen earlier. One of the three who'd been playing in the muck, under the tree.

No. Not a cub. Was *once* a cub. The muck covered a layer of orange-black fungus.

The other Hacan cubs hadn't been unsupervised after all. When they'd screamed for help from the Arborec, their voices had been high because they were panicked, *not* because they'd needed to call far.

However the Arborec had modified the tiny Hacan's body, it could not alter the laws of physics. It wasn't even a meter tall. If I'd seen the cub coming, I could have barreled through it or kicked it away. But it had caught me – and the Druaa – by surprise.

The tiny Dirzuga moved like an acrobat. It braced one

foot against the ground and swept the other into my shin at just the wrong angle. I toppled in pain, landing hard on my shoulder.

The Druaa gasped, and I felt the thump of her crashing to the deck.

I struggled to get up. The Dirzuga landed a blow on the back of my head, hard enough to turn my vision white.

By the time I had the wherewithal to get to my knees, other footsteps squelched through the mud beside us. More Dirzuga, come to control the situation. The fight was over.

In the mud beside me, the Druaa began chuckling softly before erupting into loud laughter.

"Of the many sounds you could have chosen to make," I told the Druaa when I caught my breath, "I am hard pressed to think of one that could make me hate you more."

"You do have to admit," the Druaa said, and then declined to finish the rest of the sentence. The laughter tuned back down to a chuckle.

In the course of my dash through the brush, my robe had caught and torn. The fungal mottling on my arm was visible. The Hacan cub-corpse leaned down to examine it. Its nostrils expanded as it sniffed the fungus, but otherwise it had no expression.

None of the Dirzuga did. We were surrounded by them now. Some bent down to grab me and haul me to my feet. It would plainly recognize its own fungus as easily as it recognized that I was an outsider.

Whatever the Arborec thought, finding the fungus didn't improve its opinion of me. None of the Dirzuga released their grip. Another Dirzuga, a completely hairless human with skin the color and texture of white ash, stood near the Druaa. "I, too, am struggling to find the humor about this situation," it said.

"That's fair," the Druaa said, as her mirth died away. She took a moment to compose herself. When she spoke again, her whole affect shifted to businesslike. "Arborec Symphony, I am Commander Z'kayl, Keleres, on special assignment from the Galactic Council. You can verify this information with the Galactic Council diplomatic corps. Or, should you need more, with the Naalu Collective Consulate. They'll check my identity and verify I'm on detached service to the Keleres. Per Galactic Council Amendment Thirteen, I'm requesting the extradition of this woman. Despite her appearance, she is an agent of the L1Z1X Mindnet."

Amendment Thirteen was more popularly known as the Existential Threats Amendment. It had authorized the creation of the Keleres as a special operations force to address threats like the Nekro Virus, the demonic Vuil'raith, and Us.

It demanded that all Galactic Council members support Keleres action whenever possible. It was a law observed more often in the breach than in fact, given the turmoil that had ruled the galaxy since the first Lazax Empire's collapse, and each council member's oft-justified mutual suspicions of each other.

"Why was I not told of this immediately?" the same Dirzuga asked.

"As I said. Special assignment."

"You did not trust me," the Dirzuga said, its voice flat. This was just something to be noted. In that way, it reminded me far too much of the Mindnet.

Z'kayl was just as unsentimental. "No," she said. "Given the involvement of the L1Z1X Mindnet and the, ah, sensitive subject of the Dirzuga, we opted for a quick retrieval. But as you have me surrounded now, I'm forced to appeal to your better nature. And to your treaty obligations."

Once again, these Keleres had refused to get any permission from the local authority. That seemed like something I could use. "I never meant to cause you any trouble," I told the Arborec. "Unlike these people."

Only a Druaa could make a derisive snort sound elegant. "You're a Mindnet spy," she said. "You're trouble by definition." She spoke again to the Arborec, "Just to be clear about the stakes of our assignment, we have been tasked to solve the Mindnet problem."

The rage had never gone away, but now it surged again. I spoke before the Arborec could. "How quickly you use the language of genocide."

The Druaa, Z'kayl, didn't even seem to realize how she'd sounded. "Excuse me?" she asked.

"I see," the Arborec said, this time through the little Hacan. Its voice was less degraded by death than the others, and that affected me more than I thought. I had to close my eyes. After a pause, it said, "I'll continue pursuing these diplomatic channels, but for now, you're correct. I do have a treaty obligation. I release this person to your custody."

Maybe laughter *was* the appropriate response. My future consigned away by a squeaky-voiced Hacan cub. It was either laugh or cry. "You cannot be serious," I said, opening my eyes. "The Keleres don't respect you any more than they do me."

"The Arzuga fungus is necessary for me to interact with the rest of the galaxy," the ash-skinned corpse said. "But I recognize that it *is* a sensitive subject. I have no wish to appear as though I am hiding something about the fungus... nor any anomalous mutations of it."

"They'll try to 'solve' you like they are Us," I said.

The Arborec didn't answer. More humanoids were walking toward us. Only some looked like Dirzuga. They were escorting several others, humans and Saar and Hacan and Winnu. More Keleres agents. All sheepish looking.

Then I caught sight of Stefan. He was a dozen meters away, lying facedown in the muck. He must have been stunned. My throat tightened. How could I have so quickly forgotten about him? "Turn him over before he drowns."

The ash-skinned Dirzuga shook its head.

It took me an instant too long to recognize what I was seeing. There was blood on Stefan's back.

A staccato burst of memory showed me the Letnev officers raising their hidden sidearms. One officer's arms getting knocked aside. Seeing shadow inside the pistol's barrel. The inexplicable way Stefan had shoved me.

The deck pitched away underneath me.

The Druaa and the Arborec still spoke, but I could not hear them over the roaring in my ears. It was as if the ground had not only dropped away but vanished, me into the vacuum. Dropping into memory. Into the gap between the bombed-out starbridge and Port Vel Syd's naked hull. Into a cloud of flash-cooled icy sparkles that had once been air. To where the only sounds were my pulse drumming in my head and the synesthetic pain of my ruptured eardrums.

Back to Uthan's quarters, in his shuttle, when I had scraped my knuckles raw scrubbing blood from the deck plating, where every time I'd tried to think of the other things I could have done, the other solutions I could entertain, I'd had to shut down from the unbearable migraine. Where the only thing I could do was attempt to end my life while superficially convincing myself I was following orders, and head into Mindnet space.

Minutes ago, I'd been desperate to get back to the yacht, out to *anywhere* that wasn't this station. In the back of my head, I'd already started to calculate wild plans for how I was going to try to get away from the Keleres, from the Dirzuga.

The only thing that plan of action would do would be to keep me on the run. Everywhere I went, the deck kept falling out from underneath me. From everyone around me.

I could not keep running from what I'd done, from what had happened to me, and who I'd become.

"I request asylum," I stammered. "Formally. I *formally* request asylum and immigration proceedings."

Z'kayl kept speaking to the gray Dirzuga, requesting fuel, and didn't seem to notice that the gray Dirzuga was now frowning. It was the first expression I'd seen on any of their faces.

The Existential Threats Amendment had jogged other intergalactic laws to the top of my head. The Arborec was one of the only members of the Galactic Council to have a completely open immigration policy. Even the Mentak Coalition, the next-easiest of the major civilizations to join, had some walls. But the Arborec had enough trouble attracting newcomers without placing barriers in their way.

As soon as a sentient on Arborec territory declared their interest in immigrating, they had provisionally entered the process. "I believe I am entitled to an extradition hearing," I said.

The old Dirzuga with the flowing beard had recovered from the stun darts faster than any human should have. It joined the rest of us. The front of its clothes and its beard were layered with green-brown muck.

"It would be very much easier for all of us if you hadn't said that," he said.

Z'kayl looked at me, and then back at the Dirzuga she'd been talking at. She must have heard me after all. She snatched the words I'd used earlier right back out of the air: "You *cannot* be serious."

"Request acknowledged," the Arborec said. "Everyone here should consider themselves under arrest."

CHAPTER EIGHTEEN
THEREFORES, WHENCEUPONS, AND WHEREBYS

The prison-sac was soporifically dark. Its walls were the color and texture of the inside of my eyelids. This was no accident … but the inherent strangeness of the Arborec made me doubt it was deliberate. The Arborec would not need to have consciously noted that soporific prisoners were less likely to cause trouble. Evolution was a process without intent. But it was full of purpose.

The fungus worming through my veins had not been told to mutate the way that it had.

I wondered what purpose the Arborec might put it to.

The Arborec's servitors had not taken me far. Though we were still in the habitat cylinder, I saw little sign of the habitat's original construction after we'd left the concourse. This holding area was a fleshy bubble somewhere deep inside the Honeycombs.

The cell pulsed. The pace was gentle, deliberate, and so omnipresent that I noticed my breathing synchronizing with it. The little existing light seemed to come from something outside the walls. The sac was translucent, and whatever shone through its skin appeared like a flashlight pressed against a hand. The surface wasn't as rubbery as flesh, nor as warm. Rows of vents, resembling gills, breathed temperate, dry air into the sac. Mercifully, nothing was moist.

The only exit wasn't a door but a muscled sphincter. Another thing to avoid thinking about. It was hard not to, though, when it was right there, and the only other things I could think about were worse in comparison.

My life was a tightrope walk on steel wire over a chasm: bounded by absence, empty spaces, and the thoughts I was conditioned to avoid. I couldn't think about the door. I couldn't think about Uthan. Or about my parents. About Stefan's hard shove. His idiot, inexplicable decision to value my life over his, if that *was* what he'd done – if the shove hadn't just been instinct, or an interrupted dive for cover. I would never be able to ask him.

Stefan did not need to do that. He *shouldn't* have done it. It had only been recently that he'd treated me with something other than fear and contempt. And, truthfully, there had still been plenty of both underneath the cloud of confusion I'd cast about my identity.

He'd thought I was an Arborec agent, a Dirzuga. He must have known something was off at the end, but he had died without knowing who I was, or why I had done the things I had. I had never planned on revealing more. I didn't know why, every time I thought of that, a pit opened in my stomach.

His nephew Oran was going to need to come here now. With

Stefan dead, the Mindnet had no reason to continue Oran's medical treatment. I tried saying as much to the Dirzuga that had brought me here, that the Arborec should try to contact Oran directly now, but the Dirzuga had given me no sign that it had heard.

Time did not seem to pass here.

I have been told this feeling is a common reaction to grief, but I did not deserve to grieve for Stefan. Or for Uthan. *I* was the tragedy that had struck them.

The Mindnet had happened to them. And I was Mindnet.

It was an inherently selfish, disgusting act to believe that I was experiencing grief for them. What I should actually have felt was guilt, remorse, like hot little daggers of hate knapping away at my bones. I was trying very hard to control my actions, but I didn't imagine how I could do that if I couldn't control how I felt.

Everything I'd done had been for Us. Even surrendering to the Arborec had become palatable to that side of my brain because it had seemed better for Us rather than letting the Keleres seize me.

I forced myself to puzzle-solve instead: to make sense of the Druaa, Commander Z'kayl, and the other Keleres. In the fog of fighting, my rage had given me perfect clarity about what I wanted to *do* to them. But clarity was sometimes just a matter of not thinking.

The Keleres knew only enough to be dangerous. When Z'kayl had met me on Port Vel Syd, she'd been testing me. Playing the role of the repair company's manager to get close enough to question me. She must not have been certain about who, or what, I was. She'd decided to speak with me first. Verify that I was alone, and who and what she'd thought I was.

She'd played the part well enough, though left some few hints that I'd picked up on even then. But I hadn't been prepared to figure out the truth. I'd been playing a different game: being extorted for cash. The fact that I'd been losing at *that* one had kept me too desperate to look up and see I was in the wrong arena.

It was embarrassingly basic spycraft. Misdirection and fear. Draw an opponent's eyes elsewhere. Keep them afraid to narrow their thinking. It was the same way I'd manipulated Stefan the first time we'd met.

I hadn't even known for sure that she was with the Keleres until I'd seen her in the concourse, blocking my way to the stolen yacht. She'd been able to follow me here… somehow. Betrayal remained an option, though I doubted Stefan would have done it. No, the truth was likely more prosaic, and worse for me: she had guessed, correctly, where I was going to go.

I was one of the worst things a spy could be: more predictable than I thought. She'd seen the bomb go off in my shuttle and worked out that the Mindnet had placed it. If I couldn't have run to the Mindnet, there was only one other galactic civilization I was linked to. The same one that created the fungus that had invaded my body. She wouldn't even need Druaa telepathy to narrow the possibility space of my options.

I swam in a broth of these thoughts.

I do not believe I slept. To the best of my current knowledge, anyway. All the feelings burning through my head were the kind that inhibited memory formation. All I knew was that, when the sphincter flexed open, I was not tired. I jumped to my feet.

The being on the other side was a hulk of chitin armor. A triangle-headed, many-toothed Sardakk N'orr soldier.

Orange-black fungus puffed out of its exoskeleton's joints. A neat, bullet-sized hole in its neck plating showed how it had probably died.

Somehow the Arborec had mutated its voice box to be capable of a clicking, stuttering speech. "Are you prepared to answer questions?" it asked.

"I'd prefer to receive answers," I asked.

It did not reply, but stepped back and indicated with its pincer that I should walk ahead.

When the Dirzuga had led me here from the concourse, I'd tried to keep track of the path we'd taken. Now, though, the last shreds of my sense of direction whirled away. After a handful of ramps, we entered a queasy gravitational corkscrew, in which up and down twisted sideways. Mushroom flesh segued smoothly to something like skin. I felt like I was traveling through a vein. Or an esophagus. The tunnels seemed to grow ahead of us and shrink behind, as if expanding and constricting to ease us through.

The corridor opened into a wider chamber, a round sac whose walls pulsed in and out like breath, but from which no sound emerged. It was not *that* big, about three dozen meters in diameter, but compared to the holding cell, it felt like I'd stepped onto the surface of a temperate, terrestrial planet. An orb dangled from the ceiling, casting diffuse gold-yellow light.

Though the walls and ceiling were rounded, the floor was flat, and the Arborec had troubled itself to bring furniture here. Two podiums faced each other and the center of the sac. Empty seats lined the nearest walls, half sunken into the flesh.

Z'kayl stood near one of the podia, perplexed and put off. She cast a distracted glance back at me, but her attention focused on arguing with someone else. She had her own N'orr escort, another Dirzuga. It stood in the shadows well behind her, staring at nothing.

I reflexively clamped down on my thoughts, the same as I had the first day I'd met her. I tried to stay mentally focused and reduce the ways she could shape how I felt. But I couldn't keep control of my emotions for long.

Because Stefan stood in the center of the room.

I faltered. I could not stop the instinctive urge to run. The N'orr Dirzuga's pincer clamped my shoulder, keeping me steady.

Stefan's robe remained filthy all along the front, where he'd fallen into the muck. He'd wiped his face clear, but that was all.

Orange-black fuzz ran up his neck. The growth sank under one of his cheekbones and underlined his eye like a bruise.

He was the object of Z'kayl's consternation. "…several of them had no part in the operation," she said. "You had no right to board–"

Stefan did not look at either of us. From the way he – *it* – projected its voice when it spoke, though, it was clear that he was interrupting her to address me. "You once again seem to be experiencing acute distress, Mx Sil."

The fact that the Dirzuga escorting me was a N'orr soldier no longer seemed like a coincidence. I could not muscle my way to the exit. "No," I said flatly. It was not an answer to his question but a refusal of all this, of everything I was seeing. "I cannot believe that you are so unaware of how people react to the Dirzuga that you would do this to him, and to me, innocently."

"You are correct," Stefan said. "I am making a point."

The N'orr moved me forward. Its push was very gentle. I didn't give it a chance to falter and walked with it.

The N'orr aimed me at the second podium. After a pause to make sure I headed there, it stepped away. From this perspective, I could just see Stefan's back, and the dried blood that stuck his robe to his skin.

I had been prepared for an interrogation. This was something different. Something adversarial. Maybe I was actually getting the hearing I'd asked for. There was, to my surprise, a pad display on my podium, the first technological artifact I'd seen since my arrest. The pad was a standard Federation of Sol commercial model, albeit impressively out of date. There were no projector studs, only a display. One of the Arborec's immigrants must have brought it with them. Or maybe the Arborec had looted it from a drifting wreck the same way it looted corpses.

I made myself look at Stefan, although he did not turn to look at me.

"When the L1Z1X Mindnet subdues a world," the Arborec said, through Stefan, "one of the first things it does is take well-known people – celebrities, politicians, and their families – and cybernetically augment them. The Mindnet makes sure to display these converts."

"That is a very crude comparison," I interrupted. "The people the Mindnet changes remain alive. *I* am not a puppeteered corpse. Even when I had my full set of augmentations, I had continuity with the individual I was before." Thinking about the day my cybernetics had been installed, I could now admit to myself that it was a crime that had been committed upon me and my family, which made my throat dry. But I meant what I said next. "My augments did not make me a lesser person."

Stefan said, "That's one of the things we will determine here."

He sounded so much like Stefan. Even in his word choice, he was less formal than the other Dirzuga. The queasy feeling settled into an iron ball in my stomach. The Arborec used not just Stefan's vocabulary but his tone. These were things that, if I wasn't careful, I might mistake for his personality.

The Arborec *had* no voice of its own, I had to remind myself. Not in the way I thought of "voice" Stefan's body had been fresh. When the Arborec had colonized his corpse, the language center of his brain would have been wholly intact, ripe for plundering.

Stefan persisted in facing neither of us. I wondered how many eyes it had around the chamber, and how many other senses it was watching us through.

I glanced down to the pad. The display was covered with a pollen-like yellow dust. I brushed it off to read the text underneath. It was a listing of charges in the style of Galactic Council legalese: disturbing peace, concealing identities, assault with weapons, endangering Arborec citizens, and so forth.

In the style of was a significant phrase, though. The Arborec struggled to incorporate legal systems into its dealings with other civilizations. Legalistic phrasing was its own language. I doubted that the Arborec truly understood the legal process, not in the same way the rest of the galaxy did. Whatever was going to happen, I doubted it would bear more than a resemblance to a legal proceeding. The Arborec was mimicking the formula of a hearing.

Law was not a formula. It provided judges with limits and guidance for making judgments. It was a means of resolving disputes. In all its life, right up until first contact with the Galactic Council, the Arborec had never needed any of these things.

The list of charges was illuminating in a few other ways. It didn't include espionage. Nor working for the L1Z1X Mindnet, a declared existential threat. Another surprise: *all* of the Keleres were listed as co-defendants, not just Z'kayl. There were close to thirty names. Some of them must have been on the Keleres's ship.

Z'kayl had complained that they'd been rounded up, too. Z'kayl had resumed that argument. I should have been paying attention. "The charges are only pending," Stefan explained. "This is a pre-indictment hearing. Three-day detentions of Keleres agents are permissible per Amendment Thirteen."

Z'kayl shook her head but turned to me rather than press the argument. She studied me. "Have you been crying?" she asked.

She was telepathic. My first thought was that she should have known.

But maybe not. She would have been limited to what I knew, and I didn't recall crying. But my memories of the last few hours were sparse enough that I couldn't discount the possibility.

I struggled to think of an appropriate retort. "I have been experiencing," I said, "the emotional aftershocks of profound rage."

"That is absolutely fascinating." My ability to detect sarcasm remained wanting, but Z'kayl seemed genuine. I would have preferred sarcasm. "What do you have to be angry about?"

"To begin with, questions like that," I said. Her complete inability to understand me had not thus far impeded her ability to wreck my life.

"You're about to become free," she said, and before I could ask if she knew anything about the course of this hearing that

I didn't, added: "Free of the Mindnet. You've already lost your implants. Whatever other hold it's got on you, we can break it."

It should have been difficult to surprise me after all this, but I was still taken aback. "You think I'm… being compelled to act on behalf of the Mindnet."

Everything I did was for the good of the Mindnet. Always. And it always would be.

That wasn't conditioning. Although Mindnet cybernetics and conditioning had played a role in shaping that thought, it was a thought I had chosen, one that had kept me on this course.

"You've been part of it for so long that I don't expect you to remember what it's like to be wholly free."

Z'kayl spoke much more fluidly than the handful of other Druaa I'd met. She was accustomed to using her actual voice. The Druaa didn't often do that among themselves; they preferred telepathy. Z'kayl had been working with the Keleres for so long that she seemed just as comfortable with her own voice as her thoughts.

I wondered how Druaa telepathy functioned on the Arborec. Stefan's corpse would radiate neither thought nor emotion. Maybe it was like reading a corpse or an automaton. Or maybe being here was like being surrounded by a living brain, with pulses of emotion coursing down upon her from all sides.

"In what ways do you believe I'm unfree now?" I asked her.

"Did you ever have a choice about serving the Mindnet?"

"It is a choice I make many times each day."

"What about this man?" she said, with a tilt of her headfan to indicate Stefan. "Did he have a choice to serve the Mindnet, when he worked as a Mindnet spy?"

She seemed to think I was being blackmailed. "You wouldn't ask if you didn't already know his circumstances."

Stefan looked so much like himself that I expected him to react to us talking about him. But of course, he kept staring straight ahead. Patiently waiting and listening.

Z'kayl said, "We didn't have to look too deep into his background to find out how you were abusing him."

I gripped the podium to keep steady. "I brought him *here*. I showed him where to find a permanent treatment for his nephew." The wood was unpolished. A splinter pressed into my palm, threatening to distract me. "Did *you* know the Arborec could do that? It was something he could have found out on his own if the Galactic Council's civilizations didn't censor the Arborec's immigration pitches."

A smile briefly crossed her face. "Are you attempting to claim the moral high ground?"

"Are you?" I snapped.

"Of course," she said, as though there could not have been anything more obvious. She turned to Stefan. "This isn't the venue I'd prefer for this conversation. A much more appropriate one would be on Mecatol Rex. You'd be welcome to participate. The L1Z1X Mindnet threatens every civilization in the galaxy. Every civilization should have input as to the solution."

"I am not a 'solution,'" I interjected. "And if I were, I would not allow you to commit genocide again."

"'Again?'" Z'kayl asked.

How easy it was to forget that, for the rest of the galaxy, the extermination of the Lazax was ancient history. I focused my rage, let it crystallize – partly to inhibit any telepathic manipulation from her, but also because I could not have restrained it anyway.

"You believe *we* commit genocide." Z'kayl sounded more fascinated than upset, like I was a germ under a microscope. "You came from a world the Mindnet invaded when you were a child. That invasion was a bloodbath. The Mindnet followed it up with behavioral control via forced cybernetic augmentation."

Stefan said, "That does seem to be the proverbial Titan in the room."

Z'kayl and I stared at Stefan. For a moment, we found a common feeling in marveling at the Arborec's gormlessness. Stefan kept staring forward.

The pause gave me a chance to gather my thoughts. As they did, a headache pulsed between my temples. There were still things I could only say by alluding to them, not by speaking them aloud. "I am not here to justify the Mindnet's actions."

(They cannot be justified.)

"I cannot change them – change Us. The result of this hearing will not hold Us accountable."

(The Mindnet is a threat to your ways of life. You are correct to fight it.)

The words echoed so strongly in my head that I was half sure Z'kayl could telepathically read them. If she could, though, she didn't show it. But that was not the point.

The pathways my conditioning had etched into my brain were still strong, but it was becoming easier to distinguish between the thoughts formed by them and the thoughts formed outside them.

In what ways do you believe I'm unfree now? I had asked.

That was the core of what Z'kayl failed to grasp about me. Conditioned or not, my thoughts were still my own. I was responsible for them.

My thoughts had been my own since the day I'd lost my implants. She acted as though there was a different person underneath me, a victim yearning to be free. But the impulse to restrain some thoughts, to avoid thinking or saying them, was *mine*. I had to face it.

The Arborec interjected to agree with me. "The issue at stake," Stefan said, "is whether or not I'll extradite a prospective citizen to face charges on Mecatol Rex, or whether they will remain here to face the charges outlined on your displays. Commander Z'kayl, please, make your case."

"You've also brought charges against myself and my team," Z'kayl noted.

"You have broken several laws. If your extradition request is successful, it's likely that you and your team will be found to have acted properly, and the charges will be dropped. Thus, this hearing will determine the result of the next."

"Funny," Z'kayl said dryly. "I didn't imagine you would take such a robotic approach to this."

For the first time, I heard confusion in Stefan's voice. "Isn't that what legal proceedings are for? To impose machine-precision thinking on judges or juries, and thus obtain standardized judgments?"

"Or flatter themselves into believing they've been objective," I said. The Mindnet believed that it was not possible for unaugmented biological minds to be anywhere close to objective.

To my surprise, the Arborec seemed to agree. "I admit I am prone to misjudging these things. When I'm this far out of my comfort zone, I try to follow the formula. There is a clear formula here."

"This is one of the least formulaic proceedings I've taken part in," Z'kayl said. "The Galactic Council would have had three hearings already just to schedule the process to start this one."

"Apologies," Stefan said. "I can be more of a pedant if you'd like." Without waiting to clarify if that had been a joke, the Arborec went on: "Your presence in Mx Sil's portion of this hearing isn't strictly required, but I extended you the courtesy because I value your insight."

Z'kayl narrowed her slitted eyes, trying to gauge the Arborec. Stefan's expression, of course, gave away nothing.

With effort, Z'kayl regathered her patience. Her frustration smoothed into a thin smile. "Then my 'insight' starts with this: you keep trying to narrow the scope of this discussion. To this Mindnet agent's actions, as an individual. You are correct in that this is a traditional legal approach. Here, today, it will lead you to tragedy. You can't approach *this* situation without looking at its broader context." Stefan opened his mouth, but she raised a scaled hand. "And I will explain why."

Z'kayl outlined the mission that brought her here. Z'kayl and her team had been on Port Vel Syd to investigate a suspected Mindnet presence.

I nearly snorted at that. 8CC0RD had not been running such an airtight operation after all.

A courier from Mecatol Rex arrived with an updated Galactic Council wanted list that had my name and my shuttle on it. *Captured alive if possible. Delivery of preserved remains if not.*

Here were the answers I'd been looking for, the details of how deep the Keleres had gotten involved. In the interests of not interrupting her in the middle of making a mistake, I said nothing. I stared into a fixed point of nothing, trying not to appear interested.

From the timing, the Galactic Council must have discovered my identity not long after I'd last left Mecatol Rex. Probably after the Letnev fleet and their splicerships had departed to strike Arrix, too. The council had not had the time to warn the Barony of Letnev that their battle plans had probably been compromised.

Or, a more cynical part of me thought, someone on the Galactic Council wanted to see the Barony brought low. They had known of my identity but sat on it until it was too late to save the Letnev. The Letnev were almost as skilled at making enemies as the Mindnet. The person who'd given me the message *had* been a Mentak officer.

Z'kayl hadn't paid much attention to the bulletin. It had been sent to every Keleres field team, and there'd been no reason to believe I was coming. But then I had. I came to Port Vel Syd for water, food, and repairs. Z'kayl hadn't been expecting me, but she seized the opportunity and dropped everything to focus on me.

She was an opportunist, I realized. A careerist. So many Keleres agents were. Their separation from their own civilizations' militaries was often a punishment, an assignment to a dead-end backwater. I was a coupon she could collect and turn in. To be exchanged for a promotion of her choice, or a retirement package, or a place in history texts.

First, she'd paid off a starship repair company for access to me, and to quietly quiz me. Then she'd deployed an overwhelming force to seize me. Somehow – ridiculously – I had escaped. "I can't overstate how dangerous the L1Z1X Mindnet is," she said. "During our next capture attempt, a Mindnet agent butchered my team. Nearly everyone but me."

I was running up against my limits of interpreting emotion. She did not sound heartbroken. Frustrated and irritated, perhaps, but not grieving.

"I thought we had lost our chance," Z'kayl said, looking at me. "That she'd gotten rescued by the Mindnet. But then these Mindnet agents started killing each other." Z'kayl had not only figured out that the bomb in my shuttle had been meant for me, but that the Mindnet had planted it.

That brought us to the next awkward part. The Arborec's thoughts mirrored mine. Stefan said, "You realized she would come here. You arrived without telling me any of this."

The only thing that betrayed Z'kayl's discomfort was her tail. Its tip rose and swayed, as if feeling out her balance. "Since you'll obtain a copy of the original all-points bulletin at some point, if you haven't already, you should know that the Keleres had discovered Mx Sil's Arzuga infection. And that we weren't sure what that meant. The bulletin had instructions to 'verify that the subject is not in contact with the Arborec Symphony before capture.' And, if they were, to block that contact before making a capture."

In other words, if I turned out to be an Arborec agent, capture me regardless. That was why she'd arranged to speak with me in the repair company's lobby. To see if I was alone, and if I was a Dirzuga.

"I see," Stefan said. If the Arborec was offended, it did not show it. "Thank you for being upfront about this."

"Professional courtesy keeps the galaxy spinning," Z'kayl said.

"Some days it may be the *only* thing," Stefan agreed.

I did not like the Arborec's conversational asides, nor the humanity I heard in them. Pointed but friendly. It seemed like the Arborec was preparing to come to an accord with the Keleres.

I needed to do something to stop this, now. "She means to use me as a weapon of annihilation," I said.

"An implement of liberation," Z'kayl corrected, quietly, before resuming talking to the Arborec like I'd said nothing. "The risks *and* the rewards of this operation were high enough to justify every breach along the way. Nearly every civilization in the galaxy has laws to immunize their police forces from the legal consequences of certain actions taken in pursuit of their mission."

"I'm not one of those civilizations," the Arborec pointed out.

"Understandably," Z'kayl said. "*You*, of course, have no need. But I hope you can appreciate the need *other* civilizations would have for that. A police officer who pursues a murderer onto private property is technically trespassing, but stopping a greater crime justifies committing the smaller one."

"These continue to be... difficult concepts for me to comprehend," Stefan said. "I'll do my best to follow."

Z'kayl smiled with the air of an adult speaking to a toddler. "I'm sure you'll do well."

"Thank you," Stefan said with no hint of irony. "Now that we've shelved our mutual mistrust, shall we grasp our way toward the point?"

"The Keleres prefer not to operate underhandedly" – Z'kayl paused briefly when I barked a laugh – "but secrecy and a certain amount of field improvisation was justified to keep this operation moving fast and under wraps. Events on Port Vel Syd show just how important that became. We nearly lost

Mx Sil twice. And with them, our best chance to protect the galaxy."

"That would be the first time I have heard an attempt to develop a biological weapon as 'protecting the galaxy,'" I said.

When Z'kayl looked at me again, it was with a yellow-eyed glare. "The L1Z1X Mindnet mutilates the peoples of the worlds it conquers. Their cybernetic implants can rarely be removed without lasting damage. With every incursion they make, every world they seize, the galaxy suffers an incalculable loss. Mx Sil's mutated Arzuga is the only thing we've seen to fully remove implants and leave the being intact."

"You think that I'm intact?" I asked. "That this fungus made me *whole*?"

She seemed to sense my outrage, enough to be surprised by it. She blinked. "You were forcibly altered at a young age," she said. "Obviously the psychological damage persists. You need our help, Zabiya."

I was past the point where hearing my old name sent me into an emotional spiral, but it was still an icepick in my gut. "That is not," I growled, "my name."

"Apologies," she said, plainly not at all sorry.

"*I* chose my name."

She looked unsteady. My emotional conviction made for a more tightly guarded headspace, one that gave her trouble telepathically squeezing in. She shook her head. "That's a lie. The Mindnet assigns new names to cybernetic converts–"

"It's my name because I'm choosing it now," I said. "I'm not a victim nor a helpless child."

"–and the things that the Mindnet does to condition its citizens are well known."

"And I've fought through those." The headache was always

present, but it had a whisper touch now. "I've operated independently of Us for longer than I realized. And everything I've done has *still* been for the good of the Mindnet. That's not conditioning. That's a choice. My choice. And I demand that you treat me as responsible."

Stefan said, "I never intended to do anything else."

"I'm talking to her," I said, with a nod to Z'kayl. "For after the extradition. Whatever's going to happen in this hearing might as well be etched in stone, but I want her to know. I am accountable for my actions."

"It will go harder on you if we hold you to that," Z'kayl said.

"It would be difficult," I said, "for things to get worse."

Z'kayl's frown deepened. "That nearly sounds like a joke."

"The L1Z1X Mindnet is very funny," I told her.

I'd said it deadpan, with the cadence of a joke, but it was truer than not. You just had to be looking for very black, very dry humor. A Federation of Sol colony world facing Mindnet invasion had once made the unusual step of offering a conditional surrender. They'd sent negotiators. The Mindnet had swiftly installed cybernetics in those negotiators, who had agreed that unconditional surrender would be better after all.

"If I didn't know better, I might think you're employing humor as a coping strategy?" she asked.

"Since I only feel worse now, must be a poor one."

"Most are," she said sympathetically. "Mx Sil, the cardinal rule of spycraft is that things can always get worse for you."

"I don't care what happens to me. Toss me in an oubliette, dissect me, sentence me to have to keep listening to you – whatever." I turned to Stefan. "I'm not advocating for myself. I advocate for the Mindnet."

"Very interesting," Stefan said in the same detached tone he'd used for everything else so far. "Would the Mindnet agree? Would *they* say you represent them?"

"Of course not," I said. "I'm a renegade."

Stefan showed a rare expression, a brief frown, as the Arborec processed this. Maybe the downturned lips were a glitch, emotional backwash from the Arborec's vast mind. Maybe there was a little bit of Stefan left, a piece of his mind still capable of processing and displaying emotion.

Or maybe it was just a twitch. Dead muscles misfiring.

"I admit, I'm at a loss as to how to deal with this," Stefan said.

"Mx Sil is trying to weaponize your confusion against me," Z'kayl said dryly.

"You're the one who wants to make this a clash of civilizations," I told her. "To put the big issues on trial. It doesn't matter how hard the Mindnet would disavow me if We could. I advocate for the Mindnet."

"An interesting choice," Stefan said. So frustratingly neutral. I almost wished the Arborec had sounded like my intrusive thoughts imagined it had. At least the intrusive thoughts sounded like they'd felt something.

Z'kayl spread her scaly arms wide. "She makes no choices. She's been programmed. Since the age of four."

"To an extent," I said. *Everything I do is for the good of the Mindnet.* "This ridiculous plan the Keleres have half put together, if it stands any chance of success, would be a genocide." I stared hard at Stefan despite knowing that there was no point to it. "These people aim to commit an atrocity."

"The *Mindnet* is an atrocity," Z'kayl said sharply.

Stefan said, "I wasn't in a state capable of interacting with the Lazax Empire when it existed. Everything I know about it comes secondhand. The L1Z1X Mindnet, though, I know much better."

The Mindnet did not consider itself to be at war with the Arborec. Our worst rage was reserved for the traitor civilizations. But that did not mean We avoided clashes. What was fair in war was fairer in skirmishes. We seized opportunities.

A handful of memories of Our interactions with the Arborec still lived in my brain. A Nightthorn Haven cruising through atmosphere, crisping and withering under concerted orbital fire. Bulb-bellied Arborec bird-servitors flying low over Mindnet bases, vomiting foaming corrosive bile onto machinery, and leaving parasite-ridden droppings.

Those memories had come from other Mindnet citizens. Though they survived in me piecemeal, I could not let them go. I wondered how many of those memories the Arborec held close as its incredible eyes studied me.

Billions of memories, stacked across thousands of years, had accumulated under our feet and compacted into the foundation of this farce of a hearing. There were so many of the Mindnet's other memories I wanted to share with the Arborec and with Z'kayl. Mecatol Rex as it had been before the war. The sight of bone cremating to ash. Lists of Twilight War dead so long that, if someone had started reading them aloud during the first bombings, they would still be going today.

But as always, I was trapped behind words.

"You won't find a 'cure' to the Mindnet," I told Z'kayl. "A weaponized Arzuga variant will never work the way you imagine it, but I don't doubt that you'd find a way to hurt billions anyway. Sentients whose worlds were taken by the

Mindnet. People who still exist today, alive as I am, to an extent. The last of the Lazax remain inside the Mindnet. I've met them. I shared their memories. They're not *gone*."

I wanted to grab Z'kayl, shake her, bash my head against hers until one of us finally killed the other. I might have tried if the Arborec's servitors hadn't been so close. "We're not the villains of a galactic fantasy drama, and I am not the third-act secret weapon. You can't wipe Us off the stage and close the curtain. You already tried that. It didn't take."

"Tried… what?" Z'kayl asked. "We just found out about your condition a month ago. We haven't *done* anything yet."

"The galaxy didn't begin a month ago."

Z'kayl closed her eyes for a moment, to gather herself, before looking back at me. "I hope you're not saying what it seems like." A rhetorical statement. I was thinking the words so strongly that, if her telepathy functioned at all, she would already know.

"The Galactic Council rules on top a heap of ashes," I said. Outside of the one city that Mecatol Rex's Winnu custodians maintained, the Lazax's once artfully terraformed world was a dead, storm-riven waste. The climate had still not recovered from the Federation of Sol's bombing campaign. The biosphere never would. Mass poisoning and irradiation had turned Mecatol Rex's soil into loose dirt. In just a handful of years after the bombings, half of the world's surface had eroded away. Gales and tornadoes constantly threw irradiated earth into the air.

Z'kayl had no eyebrows to raise, but a new tautness in the skin above her eyes gave a good impression. "That was thousands of years ago. I didn't do any of that. *No one* alive now did."

Anger curled in my gut like paper over an open flame. Helpless, impotent anger, sure. But it kept spreading.

After the first round of bombing, the traitor civilizations had gathered the surviving Lazax into camps for extermination. In truth, they need not have bothered. Blockading the planet and waiting for the blizzards of poisoned dirt and ash to truly begin, would have sufficed. Though it would not have left the perpetrators feeling as powerful.

I asked, "Did you know that the loss of the biosphere means that things that should have decayed long ago have survived to the present? When you go to one of the dead cities, and walk across a sheltered spot, you can hear Lazax bones popping and crunching underfoot?"

"Yes," Z'kayl said quietly. "I did know that. I've been out there."

There was an outside chance, the slimmest chance I'd ever seen, that something I said could reach her. But there was little point in hoping.

Z'kayl went on: "And I've seen what happens when the Mindnet invades a world. The 'examples' it makes of sentients who resist. And how it breaks those forced to go along. People like you."

"And the Mindnet has to be stopped," I said.

It took less effort to say those words than I feared. No migraine struck me down.

This really was for the good of the Mindnet, and even the shreds that remained of my conditioning believed it.

"We cannot be allowed to continue waging war and pressing into your territories," I said, my throat dry. "We will not stop on Our own."

"You admit that the Mindnet commits these atrocities?"

"What is the point in 'admitting' something so self-evidently true?" The Mindnet's crimes were too great to pretend not to see.

A flicker of a disbelieving smile crossed Z'kayl's face. "Then… you'll come over to our side? You'll turn yourself over to the Keleres?"

"Go hurl yourself out an airlock," I told her.

The smile didn't come back, but she didn't look too shocked or saddened, either. "No, I didn't figure it would be that easy."

"None of that makes your plan to weaponize my Arzuga any less of its own atrocity."

"On a certain scale of galactic politics, the only answer to atrocity doesn't look all that different from the original crime. Not to the perpetrators. Those who bomb cities can expect to have their cities bombed in turn."

"You sound so very close to understanding." I may have escaped the migraine, but this hurt in a very different way. I swallowed past a hot lump in my throat. The line dividing between grief and rage burned away under that kind of heat.

Z'kayl turned to Stefan. "Are we through here yet?"

"I'm not done," I snapped. "I chose to speak for the Mindnet because the Mindnet needs to be heard. The Mindnet is *talking to you all the time*, screaming at you, but you never listen to Us then, either."

Z'kayl's lips tightened. "The first communication we ever had with the L1Z1X Mindnet was when your envoys showed up at Mecatol Rex, demanding unconditional surrender. And then you started your invasion."

"That wasn't an introduction," I said. "That was continuing a conversation." I shifted my grip on the podium. It was the only thing keeping me upright. "The Lazax who became the

Mindnet were screaming when you incinerated Mecatol Rex. They were screaming when they fled into deep space. They screamed when they were forced to adopt cybernetics to survive, except there was no one around except themselves to hear. So *they* listened to themselves, and they learned."

Z'kayl's tail lashed back and forth. She waved my words off like they were ancient history. "Wars can't be fought without mass death, and suffering, and everything else that the Mindnet is doing to us. Everything that you're suddenly so afraid of catching in return. The Mindnet started this war."

"And what would have happened if We hadn't made that first move?"

Z'kayl opened her mouth but faltered, caught off guard. "What?"

"If We'd kept to Ourselves?" I asked. "If the Lazax had augmented themselves to become the Mindnet, become Us, and then stuck to the dusty, resource-poor world we'd been exiled to for all these thousands of years?"

"The Galactic Council has more alien contact protocols than I have scales on my tail," Z'kayl said. "We would have established peaceful communication. And when we'd discovered the Mindnet descended from the Lazax, we would have welcomed them back to–"

Something in my expression made her stop. I wasn't aware of looking at her any differently than I had before, not until a sudden wet heat below my left eye made me dab under it.

"Is that all that would have happened?" I pressed.

If she didn't understand this, she had no hope of understanding how the Galactic Council – how all of the "great civilizations" – did the same. Their methods of imperialism, control, and warfare weren't that different from Ours.

Z'kayl was an oily, unctuous little snake, but it turned out that there were limits to how nakedly she wanted to lie. At least here. She glanced at Stefan.

"No," she said. "I suppose that wouldn't have been the end of it."

"Your species kept themselves hidden from the Galactic Council, too, until they were able to defend themselves. When higher-up powers in the Federation of Sol or the Barony of Letnev discovered that a pocket of Lazax had survived the old empire, what then?" I asked. "When they discovered that We developed so many new cybernetics technologies to survive? If We merely had the *capability* to do what We do now?"

"The galaxy is a chaotic place. I can't argue every counterfactual–"

"How long would it have taken before the Barony of Letnev or the Federation of Sol began demanding We disarm? To accept garrisons? The Barony and the Federation's higher-ups would decide very early what they needed, for 'their own security.' How long before they would have ginned up the first provocations, the first 'incidents,' and spun up the propaganda machines against Us? And gotten the Galactic Council uselessly mired in controversy while they acted? Would the Keleres have cared? Would the Naalu?"

Z'kayl had, in spite of her tail's slashing, tried to look bored. Like she was tolerating my ranting. But that last line broke through. She glared at me, visibly debating whether or not to answer.

To my surprise, Stefan spoke first. "My first contact with the galaxy was... turbulent. I had a similar experience to the one Mx Sil describes."

I said, "If you hadn't demonstrated the ability to defend yourself, the Galactic Council would be asking very different questions about you. Some members might have even been talking about 'solutions.'"

Z'kayl shook her head. "The Galactic Council exists to be a peacekeeper. It intervenes in wars to protect others."

"Like they protected the Clan of Saar?" I asked. The Clan of Saar's largest world had been conquered by the Sardakk N'orr, its people never heard from again. The Saar had been scattered to the galactic winds, and only recently found a home again. The Sardakk N'orr sat on the council still. "Or the Naaz and the Rokha, before they were forced to make their alliance?" Each species had been relentlessly preyed upon, for generations upon generations – hardly remarked upon until they'd started killing their oppressors. "How many wars and tragedies are happening right now, under *this* Galactic Council? How many civilizations die screaming, with no one listening?"

"How many of those tragedies happened under the Lazax Empire?" Z'kayl looked like she was about to spit venom. "Why not ask the Yssaril? They were invaded, enslaved, while the Lazax ruled – and did the Lazax listen then?"

She had more examples of the Lazax Empire's failings. I let her list them. She was saying some of the words I'd hoped she would find. I'd left her those openings deliberately.

But she wasn't using them to see any pattern. She was just saying *what about, what about, what about.*

It was as though I had not just told her that the Mindnet needed to be stopped. That We had committed heinous crimes. She was back to treating this like a debate between two sides, the Galactic Council and the Mindnet, where one had to be *right* and the other had to be *wrong.*

If she was always in the *right,* she and the Keleres could commit any kind of atrocity she cared to. Weaponize the Arzuga and try to kill millions. Exterminate the last of the Lazax. The last flicker of hope I had that I would get through to her vanished like a snuffed candle.

She looked at the galaxy's status quo, all the death and violence and turmoil, and the only thing she wanted was continue it.

When she was done, looking down at me as if she'd just made an unimpeachable point, I only had one thing left to say. I didn't even know who I was saying it to. She would push understanding away before it ever came close enough to bite her.

"The Mindnet still feels entitled to its old empire," I said. "We're chasing Our wounded pride – believing in nothing other than revanchism and drowning Ourselves in grief so that We can tell Ourselves that it's all right that we've learned to breathe hate instead of air. But those are symptoms as much as they are choices. They're not the reason the Mindnet announced itself like it did." All those other things had coalesced around it, an icy pearl around a grain of poison.

"The reason is that We saw the state of the galaxy, We knew what had happened last time, and We made the only rational choice we could."

Attack.

(Win.)

Pitted against a galaxy like this, We saw it as the only way to preserve Ourselves. "We have just been more honest about it than the rest of you," I said.

"*Now* we're done here," Z'kayl said. She turned to Stefan. "At least I'm done listening to this. Do whatever you need to finish making your choice, and then let me know."

The Arborec seemed to agree that we were done. Stefan didn't move but Z'kayl's Dirzuga escort, the other Sardakk N'orr, approached her. Z'kayl said, "You can be sure that if you make the wrong decision, and keep Mx Sil here, the other members of the Galactic Council will pursue this through every means possible. We have a duty to protect us all from the Mindnet–"

Z'kayl stammered to a stop in the middle of her sentence. Abruptly, she looked very confused. Her tail finally stopped lashing back and forth.

She grabbed her podium for balance. Blood welled between the scales in her chest.

A bladed pincer emerged tip-first from the center of the wound.

The N'orr's chitinous natural weapon had been so sharpened that it hadn't made a sound as it pierced her back. The N'orr silently worked its arm upward. The stream of blood turned to a river, a torrent.

All my anger vanished, turned in an instant to terror. I choked and grabbed onto my own podium. I waited to feel a blade slip between my shoulders.

Z'kayl fought to stay upright. Her expression shifted from bewilderment to indignation. Her stare fixed on Stefan, who had not moved. He looked straight ahead, at nothing, as unseeing as a glowing lure over a toothy maw.

Z'kayl opened her mouth, striving for the dignity of last words, but all that emerged was a wheeze and gentle sucking noise. Then she finally fell.

No blade emerged from my chest. My N'orr Dirzuga escort remained several steps behind me, its arms unmoving. Aside from my gagging, silence resumed.

A gulf of years divided this moment from the minute before.

"You may be assured that the rest of her team is being dealt with in a similar manner," Stefan said. He didn't look at me any more than he'd looked at Z'kayl while she died.

He no longer sounded like himself. He still used his vocal cords, his voice, but he sounded distant, as though a curtain of velvet had dropped between us.

Stefan waited, patiently, for me to find words. My mouth worked silently.

There was too much to say. A thousand words piled up behind the block in my throat. I needed to understand what had happened. I needed to get out of here. To know how long I had to live. To ask what the hell I was supposed to do with what had just occurred. To apologize for the inconvenience because I was about to empty my stomach on the floor, but I was sure it had some disgustingly biological way of cleaning that up.

But, in the midst of my terror, my brain and my voice failed to align, and only the stupidest words made it past the logjam.

"It wasn't something she said?" I asked.

CHAPTER NINETEEN
PRELIMINARY REPORT

To Some Committee or Other

My stolen yacht was never intended to operate with a crew of one, but I refused all help the Arborec offered. It didn't matter that Dirzuga crew were disposable, and that it would send them along with the full expectation of never receiving them back. I made the irrational, emotional decision to keep the Arborec's servitors far away.

The whole yacht was rattling when I finally decelerated into the dusty ember glow of the brown dwarf. For the politicians among you who have not spent a great deal of time concerned with the mechanics of space travel, I cannot emphasize enough: starships *should not rattle*. This was not a loose deck plate or bolt. The whole length of the ship shook.

Only a few things could have caused that. My engine containment could have been buckling. My artificial gravity could have been failing, in which case my next maneuver would see me pulverized against the nearest bulkhead. Or, best of all, the ship's structure could have been about to fail.

The fear of what had happened in the starbridge had never left me. It pried little iron claws under my stomach.

I held it back. I had done enough throwing up for a few weeks. The sour taste of Z'kayl's death had never left my mouth.

Her purplish blood hadn't ceased flowing before N'orr Dirzuga dragged her away.

It had not, in fact, been something Z'kayl had said. "The Keleres agents signed their fates the moment they started their operation," the Arborec said through Stefan. "They instigated chaos that resulted in the death of a prospective new citizen." With the wave toward his own chest, Stefan indicated himself. "I cannot allow that to happen. These agents' deaths will be a message. Every once in a while, the other members of the Galactic Council tread on me and need to be taught again not to do so."

"You're on the Galactic Council," I said. "These are… technically… your people. Were. *Were* your people."

"Did they act like 'mine?'"

"I think Z'kayl was trying to." I kept waiting for the blade to enter my own back – kept *imagining* it – but it never arrived.

"'My people,'" the Arborec repeated. "What a strange phrase. 'My' and 'people.' If they belonged to me, I wouldn't have put as much thought into their excision."

"You would have disposed of them like a fingernail," I said hoarsely.

"Yes," he said. "Exactly like that."

This place was full of reminders of just how alien the Arborec was, but it had still been too easy to forget how vast and terrible its civilization really was, as well. I was starting to come back around on my intrusive thoughts. Maybe they hadn't, in the end, sounded all that different from the Arborec. It contained multitudes.

I had once accused 8CC0RD of lacking empathy, but I always worried about my own ability to use it. I should have been relieved, some awful voice inside me said, to know that I was horrified. When I threw up, the voice said that was a *good* thing.

The rage I felt when I looked again at Stefan – or more aptly past him, to the billion eyes of the Arborec – made no sense. The Arborec had refused to hand me over to an enemy of the Mindnet. This was not how We would want me to feel.

But that was all right. I was better this way, choking on horror. The heat in my throat, the churning in my gut, made me weak… but I would have been weaker without them.

When Stefan – the living Stefan – and I had traveled from Port Vel Syd to Nestphar, it had been a minor miracle that we hadn't had much trouble piloting our stolen yacht. We'd gotten little sleep but plenty of exercise, jogging back and forth between the cockpit and the engine compartment, addressing tasks that would have, for a trained round-the-clock crew, made a minimum of five full time jobs.

Now I was alone. The accumulation of poor maintenance was catching up with me. Since leaving Nestphar, the longest stretch of sleep I'd gotten had been two and a half hours. Every time I woke, it was out of a nightmare and into the screech of an alarm.

An overpressurized thruster fuel line was about to burst. Or spent coolant had somehow seeped back into the main tank. Or the plumbing system monitors reported that all the ship's water seemed vanished, and on an unrelated note the cargo compartments had flooded. It was always the damn plumbing. Anyone who glamorizes space travel has never spent time wading across a flooded deck.

Somehow the yacht remained intact long enough to attain a stable orbit around the brown dwarf. I shut down the engines. I no longer had the panic of ship maintenance to distract me from the days and weeks ahead.

It was like looking down into a pit of sharpened spears, and knowing that I was going to have to jump in.

After Z'kayl's murder, my brain and my voice had never managed to get a working relationship together, but at some point I conjured a single, big question that encompassed so many of the smaller ones: "Why put us through all of this?" I had meant the hearing, and the Arborec seemed to understand.

"I wanted to see what you had learned," the Arborec said.

"What do I matter to you? Clearly you don't care about individuals."

The Arborec had not reacted at all when I'd vomited. There was not, insofar as it was capable of caring, anything worth caring about in this chamber. I was a cell. A pollutant. An irritant. Or food.

"Individuals are tricky for me," Stefan said blandly. It was a stock phrase, something the Arborec had learned to say many times, and it meant nothing.

"You understand how to deceive us well enough," I said.

His brow creased. He moved his mouth without speaking, as though reaching for an idea. His expression only shifted, I realized, when the Arborec was plumbing what was left of his brain for words and concepts.

"I didn't mean to hide the truth," Stefan said at last. "No more than I meant to tell the truth."

The Arborec perceived us like I would a cellular process. At that medical station on Port Vel Syd, when I'd taken painkillers, I hadn't thought I was *tricking* my brain into believing the injury wasn't debilitating. Only from a synapse's point of view would that have made sense. It had been chemistry. An attempt to provoke a reaction.

The message I'd sent to the Mindnet provoked the reaction I'd expected and dreaded. Only ten hours after I reached the brown dwarf, the yacht's sensors started screaming.

On my sensor map, six blips appeared: three careening toward me, and three mirror images racing away. The six blips looked like a sheet of paper tearing apart. That was not a bad way to conceptualize it: the boundary where the preposterous physics of superluminal travel crashed back into the relativistic universe. A clean break between what we imagined the universe could be and what it actually was. The blips racing away from me were the light echoes of the ones heading toward me. Three starships had dropped below light speed, and thus into visibility.

The speed at which sensor images separated from their ghosts revealed a lot. These ships had raced here, accelerating right up until the halfway point and decelerating just as hard afterward. They'd traveled here as fast as possible at the expense of fuel efficiency.

They had slender profiles but big engines. Most of their mass was split between engines and forward-facing weapons and mounted missile racks, leaving only a tiny space for a pilot.

Mindnet ships.

"Individuals are tricky," Stefan had repeated as we'd walked together out of the chamber. My legs were unsteady, but I'd refused all offers of help. At first, I thought his words were just as meaningless as before, but he kept going, struggling toward a point. "Ideas, though, are a little less… abstract? Is that irony? Yes, I think so."

"You were 'testing' me because… of an idea?" I asked.

"I'm fairly confident that you *possess* an idea I would love to see circulated."

Maybe "cell" or "irritant" had been the wrong comparison. I was a virus. The Arborec had looked at me, seen something it wanted to see germinated, and then refrained from killing me like it had the Keleres agents.

The day after Z'kayl's death, after I'd had enough time to make my plans, I'd sent the message out from Nestphar on a courier shuttle, toward the Mindnet frontier. To Arrix, actually, although that was a coincidence. Arrix happened to be the nearest Mindnet-controlled world.

The courier shuttle was supposed to have dropped off the message in a drone and bolted away before any of its light reached Arrix. For obvious reasons, the shuttle couldn't have stayed to verify that the message had been received.

The message had plainly arrived without a hitch.

The three ships were strike craft. They were rapid response craft, made to reach targets on short notice and within narrow windows of opportunity.

The message I'd sent had been my surrender.

More precisely: I'd told Us that I would be here, dormant under the dull glow of this nameless brown dwarf, waiting for them. I had apologized for rash action that had hindered one of our operatives aboard Port Vel Syd, explained my suspicions regarding her, and that I would be submitting myself, along with a report, for debriefing and review.

When Stefan and I had reached the concourse, and when I

had finally stopped shaking, I asked, "What will you do now?"

"I don't believe I will be doing anything more," Stefan said.

A twinge of anger made my lip curl. "Then what was the point?"

"I *have* already refueled and resupplied your craft," Stefan interrupted.

It would have had to start that process hours ago. "Even before you knew what was going to happen in that hearing?" I asked.

I was probably imagining it, but I heard a little shrug in Stefan's voice when he answered, "If your answers hadn't satisfied me, I would have recycled your vessel into my own fleets."

"Of course," I said. "I'm nothing in the grand scheme of things."

"That remains to be seen," Stefan said. "I believe you know where you need to go. And what you need to share."

The terrible thing was, he was right.

There *was* so much that I needed to share with the Mindnet. Starting with everything I had learned about the Arborec. More important, though, was everything that I had worked out in the hearing. The things I knew but had not allowed myself to consciously think about.

When I'd forced the words out, they didn't hurt to say. My conditioning persisted, but it knew the truth: everything I had done, or ever would do, was always for the good of the Mindnet.

The Mindnet's constant warfare limited Us. We had taken our trauma, the need to survive and defend Ourselves and redress Our grievances, and formulated a response so hyper-rational that it overfit the circumstances. Like a trendline on a chart that zigzagged exactly between points rather than extrapolated a smooth curve.

We had used cybernetics first to survive. Then to control Our thoughts. Blocked Ourselves from seeing other options because second guesses would only hamper the choices we had already made. We produced Our own propaganda, fed it back to Ourselves, amplified the result, and repeated.

Taking in voices like mine, voices no longer subject to the endless loop, was the only way we were going to grow.

I had included all this information in my message. I doubted the Mindnet would read those parts, let alone believe them. What they would see instead was that I was a malfunction. Individuality had skewed my thoughts and poisoned my perspective.

They needed to have direct access to my memories. They needed to make the choice to listen, willingly. I had told them all this, too.

The three strike craft had dropped to a speed where radio signals would be comprehensible to them rather than blueshifted and unintelligible compressed waves. That meant their weapons systems would also have an easier time finding a lock. I signaled them.

"Th–" I started.

A pulse of energy speared through the yacht's cockpit. The cockpit window did not burst or shatter as much as it simply ceased to exist, transformed into bilious plasma and whisked away into silent vacuum.

Back at Nestphar, the Arborec had told me, "The Mindnet will never hear you, no matter how loud you speak."

"Of course We won't," I said, irritated that the Arborec thought I was naive enough to be optimistic.

Maybe I *was* a little naive, though, because I'd figured I still had to try the message.

But I was not an idiot. Or, at least, not so much of one that I had actually been aboard the yacht when it died.

I watched the flash of the yacht's engine containment failing from what I hoped was a safe distance. The only alteration I had allowed the Arborec to make to the yacht was to add a new escape pod. This one had been made for use during combat and had a teardrop design meant to minimize its signature to pulse sensors.

I'd ejected minutes after I arrived. I tumbled through space several thousand kilometers from the wreckage of the yacht. Much closer than I wanted to be, but I hadn't strayed too far because I, foolishly, had hoped for an opportunity for a brief conversation before the Mindnet tried to murder me. Any farther, and the light speed time lapse would have been noticeable.

I shouldn't have bothered. I'd just placed myself in danger. Even thousands of kilometers away felt too close.

The markings inside this pod said that it had come from the Yin Brotherhood destroyer *The Shadow of Her Guns Across the Horizon*. A ship that had gone missing with all hands. The escape pod seemed to have been used before. Some of its rations were missing. The air ventilation carried the mealy stink of the Brotherhood's skin cream. I hadn't asked the Arborec what had brought this salvage to Nestphar.

It was pointless to hold my breath, close my eyes, or do anything that I was currently doing while the Mindnet ships slowed. But I was human enough to be fine with that. If it made me feel better, then it wasn't pointless.

So long as the Mindnet believed I was alive, and that there was a ghost of a chance I could threaten Us, We would never stop hunting me.

The first time I opened my eyes, the Mindnet ships were coasting past, sweeping their sensors across the expanding debris field.

The second time I opened my eyes, they'd turned into three bright lights in the stars. Their engine plumes flared as they dove back into the void they'd come from.

Somehow, I remained alive.

Shortly before I'd boarded my yacht for the final time, the Arborec had told me, through Stefan, "The galaxy is best understood as an ecosystem."

The Arborec had otherwise stayed silent through our trek along the boarding concourse. Our only conversation had been our boots squelching through muck and mud.

All signs of the past violence had vanished. Sardakk N'orr defectors meditated under a sunlamp, their pincers filed smooth to declare their pacifism. Hacan cubs ran and played with a fungus-encrusted deceased Yssaril.

I had not been in the mood for the Arborec's profundities and didn't talk, which of course did not stop the Arborec. "I am part of that ecosystem," it said. "I aim to manage it one day. But I am always cognizant of the fact that the most successful ecosystems are not homogenous. Ecosystems thrive in diversity."

I doubted it was an accident that it had waited until we'd nearly parted to tell me this. I kept my silence.

"Most organisms would make their own monocultures of their environments if they could," the Arborec said. "The Mindnet is not so different. Imagine every niche of the galaxy filled with Federation of Sol colonies, or Letnev military dictatorships, or Sardakk N'orr hives."

I refused to imagine any of those. I already had enough fodder for nightmares. "The Mindnet means to pave over the galaxy," I said. "I don't understand your point. We would churn all of this through a meat grinder and render it into a cybernetic monoculture."

"The loss of the Mindnet would be the loss of the means of keeping other homogenizing powers in check," it said. "Among many other things. The Mindnet contains the last of the Lazax. It is in a unique position to hold other powers to account for their crimes."

"And they can then hold us to account for ours?" I asked.

"In a healthy ecosystem, conflict is a creative force."

"Right up until it's not."

Other than its brief words about me holding an idea that it would like to see "propagated," the Arborec had said nothing about what I should do next. It didn't need to. It had its own plans, and I was slotting right into them. It knew exactly what I intended to do. When I had said I would be attempting to contact the Mindnet, it had only remarked on how unlikely that was to work. Then it said that it had already replaced my yacht's escape pod with one better suited to escape a battle.

Everything about the Arborec was disconcerting, but it always found new ways to unnerve me. It was bad enough to be treated like a single cell taken from a larger organism and squashed under a microscope. Worse to think that the Arborec was right to do so. That with sufficient testing it could map my actions out on a stimulus-response flowchart.

I hadn't even found the courier shuttle I would hire yet, or composed the messages I would send with it. That would all come later, after I boarded the yacht and sealed the airlocks. But its vast and monstrous intellect seemed to have determined my next moves, regardless.

After the Mindnet strike craft departed, I had a long time to make myself comfortable in the pod, and with my thoughts. My hired courier shuttle wasn't scheduled to reach its next destination for another week and a half.

It took even longer for that message to get a reaction.

Thirty-two days after I arrived at the nameless brown dwarf, the Keleres quick-response squadron arrived.

Time for my second surrender. I flipped on the pod's distress beacon.

As I had stepped over the boundary into my yacht's airlock chamber, Stefan said, "The Galactic Council will continue to attempt to weaponize your mutated Arzuga infection against the Mindnet."

"Will they succeed?" I asked.

"No," the Dirzuga pronounced. "You were correct in your assessment that your infection was a fluke, made possible only by your unique circumstances. The Mindnet can easily develop an immune response to any engineered variety. As you said, the Galactic Council is desperate for any 'solution' to the Mindnet's existence that doesn't involve difficult decisions or hard reckonings. But they won't find out."

That was more of a relief to hear than it should have been. The Arborec had proven it was not above lying, but it didn't make sense that it would be lying now. It had *created* the Arzuga fungus. If it wanted to see a weaponized variant deployed against the Mindnet, it could have done a better job of creating one… if it wanted to. Even a variant that could have infected other sentients, living sentients, and brought the whole galaxy under its control.

But the Arborec has never shown interest in the attempt.

Given an equivalent power to spread cybernetics so easily across the galaxy, the Mindnet wouldn't have hesitated to use it. That was one of the many differences between the Mindnet and the Arborec.

I didn't think this made the Arborec better than Us. We were direct in Our violence. The Arborec was more insidious.

For right then, though, my goals seemed to align with the Arborec's. We both wanted what was best for the Mindnet.

I was not in a position to make demands of the Arborec. But I conditioned my further cooperation on one thing. "Send an invitation to Stefan's nephew, Oran. Make sure that he knows he can be treated here." Oran lived on the other side of the galaxy from my destination, and I hadn't been able to persuade my hired courier to take a message that far.

A rare expression from the Arborec: a head tilt. It didn't answer for so long that I was afraid it had already forgotten Oran's name. "The invitation has been sent."

I had no idea whether that meant it had just sent it now, or if it had already sent it hours long ago, or even if it was telling the truth. If the Arborec were like the Mindnet, it may have decided that the most efficient way to handle me would be to lie. I had no way to tell. I had to take the Arborec's word.

"If the Mindnet can't be harmed by it, then the Galactic Council can do whatever it wants to me," I had said, "so long as I can talk while they do it."

"You can talk," Stefan said. "Do you think that they will listen?"

That is the question tumbling over and over again in my head as I compose these thoughts.

I have had plenty of time, in these weeks in orbit over this brown dwarf, to make a record of my experiences. I have tried to be as unsparing and unflinching about myself as possible.

The message I placed with the courier shuttle contains a record of my crimes, from the murder of Uthan Stormsower to a complete accounting of my espionage work on behalf of the L1Z1X Mindnet, to this incident. As a measure of good faith, I've appended to this a log of all the messages and signals intelligence I've ever smuggled to the Mindnet, and a record of Our last known disposition of forces in the border systems I've visited.

Good faith can only go so far. I don't think that the Keleres will believe my report that I wasn't responsible for their agents' deaths. Which is fair. I wouldn't believe my report, either.

I have no doubt that a suitably entrepreneurial prosecutor could slap together charges to fit whatever punishment the Galactic Council will have already decided upon. If, that is, the Galactic Council decides to put up even the pretense of legal proceedings.

The Keleres craft are slowing. They're approaching carefully, sweeping me with sensors. I still have time to finish composing. I expect the first craft to arrive will be a decoy drone ship, to tempt me into detonating any explosives I have aboard, if this were a trap.

I don't *think* the Keleres will attempt to dissect me. But I can't be sure. The Keleres have never been consistent. They're beholden to the personalities of their individual officers. Someone better than Z'kayl might have picked up this assignment. Or someone worse.

I have taken contingencies. Earlier drafts of these notes are traveling with my hired courier, ready for distribution.

I aim to have the opportunity to repeat these thoughts to

a full meeting of council delegates, and on the public record. I realize that, as a soon-to-be prisoner, I will have no control over how this happens, or whether it does.

So I have composed this record for a broad audience of Galactic Council bureaucrats, in the event that these words somehow reach its members but I am unable to testify for myself. I hope I have been just the right amount of condescending to you. Not too much, but certainly not too little.

The Mindnet will not hear me. We are too locked in Our ways. The cybernetics and conditioning that sharpens Our thoughts also prevents Us from seeing beyond Our horizon.

We have turned the most inclusive words in any language, "We" and "Us" into markers of exclusion without ever realizing it. The Mindnet wouldn't recognize me as part of Us now.

But the Mindnet is wrong. I continue to speak for Us, a voice of one and the voice of many, because everything I do is for the good of the Mindnet.

At the Galactic Council, there is a very slim chance that someone will not only hear but listen. But I must try.

I tell you loudly and firmly: *We must be stopped.*

The Mindnet wants to sweep the board. Change the status quo that the Keleres fight so hard for. We mean to attain peace first through firepower, then through controlling your thoughts as rigidly as We control Ours.

We mean to achieve a peaceful, survivable galaxy. And that peace will be permanent. Unbreakable. Bound by cybernetics, and with carefully crafted thought policing.

This is what We have tricked ourselves into believing as We commit Our atrocities.

I don't ask for forgiveness. I don't even ask for consideration. I ask for perception.

Perceive Us. See Us as We are. See why We make the terrible choices that We have. Why We aim to make that "peaceful" survivable galaxy. We mean to sweep the board because We look at the other players of this game and see them prepared to do the same to Us. Because We have been wiped off it before and We remember.

So long as the galaxy exists as it is today, and so long as a single kernel of the Mindnet survives somewhere, this war and all its crimes will continue.

Those are the rules of the game we see set before us.

There will be no easy "solutions." No answers to the "test" we pose to you. Those are things that you have tricked yourselves into believing as you commit *your* atrocities. Every attempt you make to solve us, to go beyond defending yourselves and wipe us out, only convinces Us that We were right to see it that way.

We have been patient. We have been attentive. We act in the way that We believe these circumstances demand of Us. And thus far We have not been proven wrong.

We are supreme survivors. Even if you find Our hidden home and burn Us out of it, We will always find ways to preserve Ourselves, and to keep fighting.

If you want to end this war, you must beat Us. Drive Us back. Reclaim your stolen territories. And then, most importantly, you must leave Us with Our lives.

Show Us that you're playing a different game than We thought – where loss doesn't mean extermination, and that other possibilities aren't closed to Us.

If that *is* what you're doing.

ACKNOWLEDGMENTS

I owe my editors Gwendolyn Nix and Charlotte Llewelyn-Wells an incredible amount for their guidance and stamina in seeing this project through. My unending gratitude to them and to everybody on the Aconyte Books team, including studio manager Matt Keefe, marketing and publicity guru Ashley Stephens, and senior graphic designer Nick Tyler. Hearty thanks as well to Sean Ryan of the Asmodee Franchise Development Teamand copyeditor Sarah Liu.

Longtime publisher Marc Gascoigne's continued faith in me has been astounding, and I am perpetually indebted to him.

The incredible art on the cover of this novel was created by Christina Myrvold. You can find more of her work at her website, *https://christinapm.artstation.com/*.

An incredibly special thank you to my perpetual beta reader and life partner, Dr Teresa Milbrodt.

Finally, this novel was composed with help from Penny the Cat, whose contributions included scheduling, typing, and deconstructive criticism.

ABOUT THE AUTHOR

In Tristan Palmgren's various lives, they've worked as a clerk, factory technician, university lecturer, secretary, retail manager, and coroner's assistant – often at the same time. A decent chunk of their first novel was written in a notebook in a grocery store breakroom. They earned their MFA from Bowling Green State University in Ohio. They currently live in Virginia with their partner and fellow writer Dr Teresa Milbrodt.

They and their other books can be found online at *tristanpalmgren.com*, and you can also find them on Bluesky at *@tristanpalmgren.bsky.social*.

TWILIGHT IMPERIUM

WELCOME TO A GALAXY OF ETERNAL CONFLICT. EXPLORE AN EPIC SPACE OPERA WHILE PROVING YOUR SUPERIORITY OVER THOSE WHO WOULD DISPUTE YOUR CLAIM TO THE THRONE. USE YOUR MILITARY MIGHT, CLEVER DIPLOMACY, AND ECONOMIC BARGAINING TO CONTROL THE GALAXY.

Explore an incredible universe
with Fantasy Flight Games.
fantasyflightgames.com

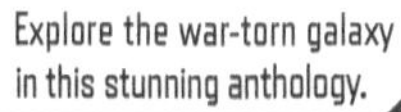